HOW TO CATCH
A GHOST

Ben Cheetham

Copyright © 2025 Ben Cheetham

All rights reserved

The characters and events portrayed in this book are fictitious. Any similarity to real persons, living or dead, is coincidental and not intended by the author.

No part of this book may be reproduced, or stored in a retrieval system, or transmitted in any form or by any means, electronic, mechanical, photocopying, recording, or otherwise, without express written permission of the publisher.

ISBN: 9798313070032

CONTENTS

Title Page
Copyright
Part 1, Chapter 1   1
Part 1, Chapter 2   8
Part 1, Chapter 3   13
Part 1, Chapter 4   20
Part 1, Chapter 5   26
Part 1, Chapter 6   33
Part 2, Chapter 1   39
Part 2, Chapter 2   44
Part 2, Chapter 3   61
Part 2, Chapter 4   64
Part 2, Chapter 5   67
Part 2, Chapter 6   74
Part 2, Chapter 7   83
Part 2, Chapter 8   86
Part 2, Chapter 9   94
Part 2, Chapter 10   103
Part 2, Chapter 11   106
Part 2, Chapter 12   112
Part 2, Chapter 13   116

Part 2, Chapter 14	120
Part 2, Chapter 15	130
Part 2, Chapter 16	134
Part 2, Chapter 17	136
Part 2, Chapter 18	140
Part 2, Chapter 19	143
Part 2, Chapter 20	151
Part 2, Chapter 21	157
Part 2, Chapter 22	166
Part 2, Chapter 23	170
Part 2, Chapter 24	176
Part 2, Chapter 25	185
Part 2, Chapter 26	190
Part 2, Chapter 27	194
Part 2, Chapter 28	202
Part 3, Chapter 1	213
Part 3, Chapter 2	222
Part 3, Chapter 3	228
Part 3, Chapter 4	235
Part 3, Chapter 5	242
Part 3, Chapter 6	256
Part 3, Chapter 7	262
Part 4, Chapter 1	268
Part 4, Chapter 2	273
Part 4, Chapter 3	282
Part 4, Chapter 4	287
Thank You!	293
Free Book	295

Books By This Author	297
About The Author	307

PART 1, CHAPTER 1

*The Most Beautiful Woman
In The World*

August 1999

The tyres sliced through a deep puddle, sending up wings of spray. Latte-coloured water sloshed over the windscreen. The swishing wipers cleared the glass, but grape-sized globs of rain blurred it again an instant later.

"Slow down, Ed!" Josie exclaimed.

The man at the steering-wheel leaned forwards to wipe condensation off the windscreen. He squinted through black-rimmed spectacles into the gathering gloom. "I can't see a bloody thing."

"I told you this was a bad idea. I told you–"

"Please, Josie, will you just let me concentrate on not getting us killed," interrupted Ed, changing gear as the car swung around a sharp bend in the lane.

The road rose between mossy drystone walls. To one side, spindly trees swayed like crazed dancers in the fierce wind. To the other, a steep grassy slope climbed towards a hilltop lost in low-hanging cloud.

Josie eyed the battalions of black clouds overhead. "It'll be dark soon. If you'd listened to me, we'd be home by now."

Ed pursed his lips, holding back a retort. The engine revved as the incline steepened. He kept to the centre of the road, avoiding the water streaming alongside the grass verges. As the clouds closed ranks, a dirty-grey twilight settled over the sodden landscape.

A gust of wind shook the car. Branches lashed the windscreen. Josie flung up her hands, fearing the glass would shatter. A gasp came from the backseat. Braking to a crawl, Ed glanced over his shoulder at the wide-eyed young boy hunkered down on the seat.

Ed raised his voice to make himself heard over the rain drumming on the roof. "You okay back there, Hugh?"

Curls of dark brown hair fell over the boy's forehead as he nodded. "Are we nearly there yet, Dad?"

"No, we're not nearly there yet," Josie put in. Her brusqueness suggested she'd heard the question one too many times.

Smiling, Ed risked reaching back to pat Hugh's knee. "Close your eyes, Hugh. Go to sleep and we'll be back home before you know it."

"Ed! Watch out!"

At Josie's panicked cry, Ed's gaze snapped back to the road ahead. There was a crack like a cannon going off. The next instant, leafy branches enveloped the windows. Ed hit the brakes. The car screeched to a halt, jolting its three occupants forwards.

"Jesus," he gasped. "Is everyone okay?"

Josie nodded, pressing a hand to her heart-shaped lips.

"I banged my head on something," said Hugh, touching a finger to a small cut in the centre of his forehead.

Josie twisted in her seat. "Let me see." She dabbed away a trickle of blood with a tissue, then flashed Ed a look that said,

This is your fault.

"It's nothing," he said. "He'll be fine."

Josie gave Hugh the tissue. "Keep it pressed to the cut."

Eyeing the blanket of leaves covering the windscreen, Hugh stated the obvious, "The wind blew a tree down."

Ed put the car in reverse. Branches scraped across the paintwork, reluctantly relinquishing their hold on the vehicle. The headlights illuminated a big old oak tree lying in the lane amidst countless splinters of bark. Jagged wooden teeth protruded from its fractured trunk.

Josie pointed to a section of drystone wall that had been all but flattened by the falling tree. "A second later and that would have been us."

Ed gave a somewhat unconvincing laugh. "Oh don't be so melodramatic, Josie."

Her lustrous black hair swished across her shoulders as she treated him to a narrow-eyed look. "I don't want to be in this car anymore."

"Neither do I," seconded Hugh.

"Then what do you suggest we do?" asked Ed. "Get out and walk?"

"No, of course not," said Josie. "Now you're just being wilfully stupid."

Ed looked away from his wife and son. Compressing his lips, he drew in a slow breath through his nostrils. With a sudden movement, he plucked a shiny wooden pipe from one of his jacket pockets. As he brought it to his lips, the gold-embossed initials 'E.C.' glinted on the ebony stem. From another pocket, he took out a dented and scratched tobacco tin.

"Is this really the time to be smoking your pipe?" chided Josie.

"It helps me to think."

Ed opened the tin, releasing a slightly sweet aroma. Josie exhaled a breath of annoyance as he began to pack tobacco methodically into the bowl of his pipe. He tamped down the nest of coarse strands and struck a match. Circling the flame over the bowl, he sucked gently on the pipe. The glow illuminated his eyes that matched the dark brown tobacco. He wound his window down a few centimetres, letting out a swirl of smoke and letting in spatters of rain.

Hugh threw nervous glances at the nearby trees as another blast of wind shook them. "Can we please go now, Dad?"

Ed's angular features softened as he smiled at his son. "Yes, Hugh, we can go now. We're going to find a place to stay for the night."

"What place?" Josie asked. She pointed a long pink fingernail at the desolate hillside. "If you hadn't noticed, we're in the middle of nowhere."

Ed smiled thinly at her sardonic tone. "Yes, I'd noticed, but The Lakes is full of hotels. There's bound to be one around here."

Josie replied with a sceptical, "Hmm."

Ed drew deeply on his pipe as if it would grant him the patience to get through this test. Josie made a show of wafting away the smoke. Hugh sniffed the air with the button nose he'd inherited from his mum. The smoke's mellow scent soothed away a cluster of lines from between his eyebrows.

Ed edged the car forwards, angling it around the fallen tree. The vehicle juddered as it mounted the verge. The passenger-side tyres spun, chewing into the sodden turf. Branches clutched at the car as if attempting to deny access to the road beyond. Then the tyres found purchase and the car lurched into the clear.

Ed took a relieved puff on his pipe. "There's bound to be one around here," he repeated, trying to convince himself of his words.

Her arms crossed, Josie glanced at him dubiously.

The car continued its climb, weaving to avoid fallen branches. The wind howled like a wild animal baying for blood. Hugh pressed his hands to his ears, whimpering, "I don't like this. I don't like this…"

"It's okay, darling, your daddy knows what he's doing," said Josie. She tilted a well-plucked eyebrow at Ed. "Don't you?"

He remained silent, chewing on his pipe at her sceptical tone. The road levelled out, passing a ramshackle stone barn with sheep clustered in its gloomy doorway. The wind carried their mournful bleating through the open window.

"They sound miserable," remarked Ed.

"I know how they feel," said Josie.

Ed snatched his pipe out of his mouth. "You know what, Josie, I've had just about enough of your–"

"Dad, look!" Hugh broke in, leaning between the seats to point out of the front windscreen. "There's a sign." A rust-streaked sign was dangling from a pole at the roadside. Its hinges squealed as it flapped in the wind. Hugh read out the sign's spidery lettering, "Coldwell Hall Hotel. One mile."

Flashing Josie a toothy grin, Ed let out a triumphant, "Ha!"

Smiling back, she reached out to stroke his cheek in reward for his victory. "Let's just hope it's open."

"Of course it will be." Ed's voice was brimming with newfound confidence. "You'll see. Ten minutes from now, we'll be sat by a roaring fire sipping brandy."

"Can I have a hot chocolate?" asked Hugh.

"You can have two hot chocolates."

Hugh bounced on his seat with delight. "Yay." Blinking as

blood dribbled into one of his eyes, he pressed the tissue to the cut again. "My head hurts."

"I'm sure they'll have a plaster for that cut at the hotel."

"Roaring fires, brandy, hot chocolate, plasters, it sounds like this place has everything," said Josie.

Ed laughed at her wry remark. "Now, now, don't be a sore loser."

"This isn't a competition, Ed. It's a miracle we're still alive."

He glanced at Hugh, rolling his eyes as if to say, *Here we go again.*

"Ed, keep your eyes on the road."

He saluted Josie. "Yes ma'am."

They passed a small assortment of single-storey stone buildings whose slate roofs glimmered in the gathering dusk. An imposing four-storey building loomed into view. The hotel was a peculiar mishmash of architectural eras as if it had been built by several people with different visions for what it should be. One half had Tudor-style timber beams and wonky leaded windows. The other had a Georgian look, with elegant sash windows set in plain stucco walls. At the building's midpoint was a conical-roofed porch that looked as if it had been added as a random afterthought. A cobblestone path strewn with overturned potted plants led to the porch's double doors. At the front of a gravel carpark, a pole with a sign swinging from it protruded from a low circular wall.

"My, what a delightful place," Josie remarked with more than a hint of sarcasm.

"It looks creepy," said Hugh.

Josie eyed the dark windows. "It looks closed."

Ed squinted at the two of them through curls of smoke. "Would you rather keep going?"

Hugh gave a rapid shake of his head. "Uh-uh."

Josie heaved a sigh. "I suppose anything's better than getting squashed by a tree."

Ed turned onto a short driveway that passed between swamped flower beds. He pulled up alongside a Rolls-Royce that was as big as a small tank. Rain bounced off its pristine silver paintwork. The female figurine on the bonnet was leaning into the wind with her arms flung back as if defying the storm to do its worst.

"Wow, that's some car," said Ed. "I wonder who it belongs to?"

"Maybe the queen got caught out in the storm," Josie suggested dryly.

"Oh isn't your mother just a barrel of laughs tonight?" Ed said to Hugh before leaning across to pepper his wife's silky-smooth cheeks with kisses.

Hugh chuckled as his mum cringed away from his dad. "Ugh, you stink of that filthy pipe," she complained, shoving Ed.

He fell back into his seat, grinning. "You know you love it really." He glanced at Hugh. "Stay here and look after your mother while I find out if this place is open."

PART 1, CHAPTER 2

Ed buttoned up his jacket and pocketed his glasses. As he opened the car door, the wind almost tore it from his grip. Pipe clamped in his teeth, he thrust the door shut behind himself. Feeling like he was pushing against a wall of hands, he battled his way along the cobbles. The rain pelted his face, blurring his vision. He slipped on some soil from the overturned plant pots and was only held upright by the storm's fury. Upon reaching the double doors, he grabbed the brass handles. The doors rattled but refused to open. He hammered on them, shouting, "Hello, is anyone there?"

The wind roared and whipped around him. He gave up on the doors and, shielding his eyes with a forearm, staggered to a window. He rapped on the glass, calling at the top of his lungs, "Hello! Hello!"

A sliver of light appeared between thickly lined curtains. A shadow seemed to pass between Ed and the soft orange glow. He hurried back to the doors. There was the clunk of a lock turning. The doors opened a crack. Eyes so close-spaced there was hardly a cigarette's width between them peered out. A beaky nose poked over a security chain.

"Oh thank god," gasped Ed.

The misty-grey eyes looked him up and down as if to make sure he wasn't armed. "What do you want?" The curt question slid from between thin lips topped by a pencil moustache.

"We need a room for the night."

"Who's we?"

"Myself," Ed pointed towards his car, "my wife and son."

The man squinted past Ed. Hugh and Josie were just barely visible through the deluge. "We don't have any rooms."

Frowning in confusion, Ed glanced at the expanse of dark windows. "Have all your guests gone to bed early?"

"What I mean to say is, we don't have any rooms ready for guests," the man elaborated. "We weren't expecting anyone tonight."

"That's no problem. We just need somewhere to shelter until the storm passes. I'm happy to pay for a room, even if we don't use one."

Ed hunched his shoulders against the lashing rain as he awaited a reply. After what felt like a torturously long moment, the man's dreary voice resumed, "I'm sorry, but we don't have any rooms ready."

Ed's eyebrows knitted together as if he couldn't quite believe his ears. "Please, we really need your help. We were almost hit by a falling tree a couple of miles back."

The man opened his mouth to speak, but a high-pitched, somewhat querulous voice beat him to it. "Arthur, who is it?"

"It's nobody, my love," the man called over his shoulder.

"Well whoever it is, tell them to go away."

Arthur's dour grey eyes returned to Ed. "As I said, we don't have any–"

"Okay, thanks," interrupted Ed. Turning away, he added under his breath, "For bloody nothing."

His eyes were drawn to a nearby window as its curtains twitched apart a finger's width. He heaved a sigh as his gaze shifted to his car. If they got through this night, he would never hear the end of this from Josie. He started towards the car, but the shrill voice piped up, "Arthur, what do you think you're doing?"

"I'm turning them away, as you told me to, my love," Arthur replied.

"I never told you to do any such thing," snapped the voice.

At the rattle of a chain, Ed turned back towards the doors. Light flooded out as one of the doors swung inwards, framing a svelte figure with curves in all the right places. A chic black dress, fishnet tights and red stiletto-heels gave the impression that the woman was on her way to a cocktail party. Golden curls tumbled down the sides of her soft-featured face. Her doe eyes peered at Ed from between long, fluttering eyelashes.

"How could you think I'd turn these poor people away?" she reprimanded Arthur, directing a dollish pout at him. "Only a monster would do such a thing."

"But I… I thought…" he stammered, his baggy jacket sleeves sliding up his arms as he rubbed agitatedly at his bald head. In contrast to the woman's perfectly fitting outfit, a three-piece tweed suit hung awkwardly on his spindly limbs and coat-hanger shoulders. His pinched features drooped into a sort of hangdog grimace. "I'm sorry, Dorothy, I must have misheard you. The storm's so loud."

"More like you're going deaf." Dorothy giggled girlishly as if she'd made a joke. She looked at Ed, clearly expecting him to be amused.

He offered a small smile. "So you can put us up for the night?"

"Of course we can." Dorothy's tone suggested the possibility had never been in question. "Do you have any luggage?"

"Yes, two suitcases."

Dorothy glanced at Arthur. "Go help Mr…"

"Carver. Edmund Carver," Ed told them.

"Go help Mr Carver with his luggage."

Arthur remained where he was, his gaze flicking between Dorothy and the raging storm.

"It's okay, I can carry them myself," said Ed.

As if she hadn't heard him, Dorothy made a shooing motion at Arthur. A flicker of a scowl passed over his skull-like face, but he obediently strode past Ed. Like the figurine on the Rolls Royce's bonnet, he leaned into the wind with his arms outstretched behind him. His long legs quickly covered the distance between the doorway and the car. Ed scurried along after him and ducked into the driver's side door.

"What took you so long?" asked Josie.

Ignoring the spiky question, Ed popped the boot. Smiling at Hugh, he spoke through his long-since extinguished pipe. "We're in luck. They've got room for us." He held up the flat of his palm and Hugh gave him a high-five.

Straightening, Ed saw that Arthur was already striding back to the hotel with the suitcases tucked under his arms. Ed headed around to the other side of the car, opened the rear door and took Hugh's hand. "Hold on tight."

Hugh's eyes narrowed to slits as he exited the car. He winced as the rain battered his forehead, setting off the bleeding again. Josie emerged from the front seat, pressing one hand to her bobbed black hair. Hugh caught hold of her other hand. As fast as the wind would permit, the three of them made for the porch.

Arthur shut and locked the double doors behind them before retrieving their suitcases from the wet flagstone floor. Dorothy was nowhere to be seen. He wordlessly headed for a second set of doors at the rear of the porch.

Josie took a moment to catch her breath and shake the rain off her coat. Hugh's gaze roamed the porch's lofty interior. Prisms of light from a glittering crystal chandelier danced upon the floor. He sniffed the air. "It smells smoky."

"Maybe it's that roaring fire you were on about," Josie remarked dryly, sliding a look at Ed.

"Do I sense some sour grapes?" he teased back, grinning.

Josie's voice sharpened. "I'm glad you find this so amusing."

Ed held up his hands to show that he accepted responsibility for their predicament. "I messed up, but we're safe now. So there's no harm done."

Josie stared narrowly at her husband for a moment more, then pivoted to follow Arthur. Ed gave Hugh a nudge and a wink. Chuckling like naughty schoolboys, they trailed after Josie.

PART 1, CHAPTER 3

Hugh's eyes widened as he entered the lobby, but this time in awe not apprehension. If the hotel's exterior was an unusual fusion of historical eras, then its interior resembled something straight out of a Hollywood movie. One corner of Ed's lips lifted at the sight of a log fire crackling in an enormous marble fireplace.

A portrait of Arthur and Dorothy dominated the chimney breast. Dorothy was elegantly adorned in silk and jewels. Just a hint of a smile teased the corners of her lips. Her eyes shone like the gems on her neck. In contrast, Arthur was attired in a black suit that matched his dour face. His arms dangled rigidly by his sides, like those of a soldier standing to attention.

Hugh's gaze travelled over sumptuous red silk wallpaper and gilded mirrors. More chandeliers dangled from a soaring ceiling, casting their soft glow on an array of indulgently deep velvet sofas and high-backed leather armchairs. A red carpet led across a highly polished mahogany floor to a marble-and-gold reception counter.

"Wow, it's really nice," he said.

"Yes, it is," Josie agreed a touch begrudgingly, wiping a trickle of blood from Hugh's forehead. Scrutinising herself in a mirror, she dabbed smudges of mascara from under her eyes. "God, I look ghastly."

Ed leaned in to kiss her cheek. "You look gorgeous, as always."

She drew away from him with a look that said, *You're not getting off the hook that easily.*

Thunder rumbled outside the windows. The chandeliers flickered, throwing a thousand shadows in every direction. Hugh sidled closer to his dad.

There was a soft thud as Arthur set a large leather-bound book down on the countertop. Ed took a comb from his pocket and swept back his wet hair before approaching the counter. Disapprovingly eyeing the trail of drips left in Ed's wake, Arthur proffered a gold fountain pen.

Ed accepted it with a somewhat apologetic smile. He put on his glasses and signed the guest book. "You have a beautiful place here."

"My wife," Arthur stated in a flat tone that implied no further explanation was needed. He made a sweeping motion with hands that were massive out of all proportion to his thin wrists. It was as if a giant's hands had been grafted onto him by some insane surgeon.

Ed's gaze followed the gesture to a staircase that curved gracefully towards the lofty ceiling. Dorothy was descending the stairs, chin thrown high like a movie star entering a scene. Her skin glowed like alabaster. Her sensuously full lips were as red as the carpet. Not one of the shining hairs that cascaded over her shoulders was out of place. A trio of cats were slinking around her stiletto heels. She moved with the same grace as her feline companions. As she caught sight of Josie, her step faltered, only for a heartbeat, but long enough to suggest some displeasure.

An intoxicatingly sweet scent preceded Dorothy. Ed couldn't resist the temptation to inhale deeply, feeling like he'd plunged his nose into a bouquet of roses. God, this woman was beautiful, and she clearly knew it. The way she carried herself screamed, *Look at me!*

He glanced wonderingly at Arthur's sallow, hollowed-out face. How on Earth had this man, who looked as if he'd just crawled out of a coffin, ended up with Dorothy for a wife? Money. It had to be money.

"Welcome to Coldwell Hall," Dorothy said with a flourish of her hands that were as delicate as her husband's were huge. "I'm Dorothy Dankworth."

"This is my wife, Josie, and our son, Hugh," Ed said, motioning to each of them in turn.

A smile graced Dorothy's ruby lips as she looked at Hugh. "Well aren't you a handsome chap. How old are you?"

"I'm ten," he answered.

Dorothy pushed her lips out into a theatrical O at the cut on Hugh's forehead. "That looks painful. How did that happen?"

"My dad crashed into a tree."

"No, the tree crashed into us," corrected Ed.

"Oh you poor darling," Dorothy said to Hugh. She glanced at her husband. "Arthur, get the first-aid kit. Quickly now!"

Arthur obediently stooped to rummage beneath the counter.

The three cats – a stocky ginger tom, a little black panther and a flat-faced white fluffball – nosed Hugh's ankles. "Can I stroke them?"

"Go ahead," said Dorothy. "They love attention."

The cats purred as Hugh ran his fingers through their velvety fur. "What are their names?"

Dorothy pointed to the ginger, then the white, and finally the black cat. "Sy, Yo-yo and Bel." As if trying to take Ed by surprise, she suddenly focused her sapphire eyes on him. "You wear glasses." She was smiling, but there was a definite hint of disappointment in her statement of the obvious.

"Erm... yes, I do," he replied, a touch taken aback.

Josie smiled, displaying her own flawlessly straight teeth. "Thanks ever so much for this. You've quite literally saved our lives."

Dorothy took in Josie's face like she was studying a painting by a rival artist. Josie found herself blinking under the intent gaze. Dorothy's impeccably sculpted makeup betrayed her, revealing fine lines at the outer corners of her eyes as she scrutinised Josie's high cheekbones. She wafted a hand as if dismissing Josie from her presence. "Oh think nothing of it."

Josie's smile faltered at Dorothy's aloof tone. Ed looked at Dorothy's telltale crow's feet. How old was she? Mid-thirties? No, he decided, she was a good few years older than Josie. Probably more like forty. Christ, imagine what she looked like in her prime. She must have had men falling at her feet.

"How long have you been here, Dorothy?" he felt compelled to ask.

"You mean how long have Arthur and I been running the hotel?" When Ed nodded, Dorothy pouted in thought. "I'm not sure exactly how many years, but... well, it seems like forever."

A peculiar melancholy tugged at Ed's heart. It seemed almost criminal that this exquisite creature had been hidden away in this isolated place 'forever'.

"Twenty years," Arthur put in, rising from beneath the counter with a first-aid box in his hands. His monotone voice echoed in the expansive room. "My parents bought this land in 1950. Back then, there was a brewery here that made–"

"Arthur." Dorothy's voice was condescendingly soft. "Our guests don't want to be bored with a history lesson." She motioned to Josie. "Look at the state of the poor things. Give them their key, so they can go to their room and tidy themselves up."

A slightly strained smile touched Josie's lips as if she suspected the kind words were an insult in disguise. With a self-conscious movement, she smoothed down her wind-ruffled hair. "Yes, we are exhausted. It's been a long day."

"We're on our way home from holiday," Ed explained. "We just spent a lovely week on Saint Bees Head. The weather's been wonderful until today."

"The weather can change fast around here," stated Arthur, proffering a plaster and a tube of antiseptic cream to Josie.

She thanked him with a smile. Hugh winced away from his mum's hand as she rubbed the cream into his cut. "Hold still," she remonstrated gently. He remained motionless, his teeth gritted, as she applied the plaster.

"There," said Josie. "Good as new."

Dorothy smiled down at Hugh. "What a brave little soldier. I bet the storm doesn't scare you."

"It doesn't scare me one bit," he said. As his mum arched an eyebrow, he admitted, "Maybe it scares me a little bit."

"It's my fault we got caught out in the storm." said Ed, glancing contritely at Josie. "I should have taken the weather warning seriously."

"Oh well, we live and learn," Dorothy said with a vaguely disinterested waft of her hand.

As if that was the signal to bring the proceedings to a close, Arthur plucked a key from the board behind him and gave it to Ed. "You're in 'Helen'."

"Our rooms are named after some of the most beautiful women who ever lived," explained Dorothy. She asked Hugh, "Have you heard of Helen of Troy?"

"No."

"Well Helen of Troy was so beautiful that two countries went to war over her. They call her 'The face that launched a thousand ships'. Can you imagine that?"

A distant look came into Dorothy's eyes as if she was fantasising about just such a thing. She blinked out of her daydream as Arthur informed their guests, "First floor, follow the righthand hallway."

"It's one of our best rooms," Dorothy told them with an unmistakable ring of pride in her voice. Once again, she looked at Ed so suddenly that he blinked. "Will you be requiring a meal tonight, Ed?" His name slid off her tongue with such silky familiarity that it made his scalp tingle. He tried to remember if Josie had used his shortened name in front of Dorothy.

"No thank you," Josie chimed in, her tone polite but not overly friendly.

"Actually, I could do with a bite to eat," said Ed, drawing an irritated look from his wife.

"The kitchen is closed," Arthur said firmly.

"But you'll open it up for our guests," said Dorothy. "Won't you, Arthur?"

She didn't bother to afford him a glance, obviously expecting him to do her bidding without question. He pressed his lips into an almost invisible line.

"If it's too much bother–" Ed began.

"It's no bother," said Dorothy. This time, her gaze glided towards Arthur. "Is it?" His lips held firm for a few seconds, then parted.

"No." There was a sort of infinite weariness in his voice. His drab grey eyes travelled slowly over the three guests. "Food will be served in the dining room in half-an-hour."

Without another word, he turned and strode through a door behind the counter. Ed's scalp tingled again as Dorothy let out a laugh as irresistible as her perfume. "My husband is such a grump," she told Hugh.

Wide-eyed and open-mouthed, he looked up at her as if

entranced. A touch more forcefully than was necessary, Josie caught hold of his arm and pulled him to her side. "Hugh will catch his death in these wet clothes," she pointedly said to Ed.

He didn't respond for a few seconds, then his eyes blinked away from Dorothy to Josie. Upon meeting his wife's glacial gaze, he quickly picked up the suitcases. Flashing a somewhat sheepish smile of gratitude at Dorothy, he headed for the staircase.

PART 1, CHAPTER 4

Hugh glanced back wistfully at the trio of cats as his mum drew him up the creaking mahogany staircase. The cats arrayed themselves around Dorothy's ankles, their inscrutable emerald eyes staring after the guests.

"Did you see Mr Dankworth's hands?" said Hugh. "They were the biggest hands I've ever seen."

"Murderer's hands," Josie replied. "That's what they looked like to me."

"Murderer's hands," Hugh parroted uneasily, picturing himself being torn limb-from limb like a daddy longlegs by Arthur.

Ed lugged the suitcases up the curving staircase to a hallway lined by doors and portraits. Hugh's gaze moved over oil-paintings of men of all ages, shapes and looks – old, young, fat, thin, handsome, ugly. The only commonality was the look in their eyes – a haunted glimmer that seemed to hint at a yearning for some impossible thing.

"I wonder who they are?" said Josie.

"Maybe they're VIP guests," suggested Ed.

"*VIP guests.*" The wry amusement in Josie's voice made her words sound like a euphemism for something inappropriate.

"Their eyes are following me," said Hugh.

"It's an optical illusion," said Ed. "It has something to do with two-dimensional things looking the same no matter what angle you see them from."

"Yes, it's an illusion of depth," Josie added dryly. "Something your father knows all about."

Ed puffed his cheeks at the caustic remark, knowing there would be plenty more to come before the night was through.

A plush burgundy carpet deadened their footfalls as they made their way along the dimly lit corridor. The upper panel of each door had a name engraved into it in gold letters. Hugh read out the names, "Cleopatra, Guinevere..."

The portraits clustered to either side of the doors, like suitors vying for the attention of the legendary beauties the rooms were named after.

Ed stopped to sniff at a bouquet of red roses in an urn-shaped vase. He plucked out a stem and proffered it to Josie. "Your name should be on one of these doors."

Arching a knowing eyebrow at his flattery, she took the flower and returned it to the vase. She winced as a thorn pricked her thumb. A dot of blood welled up. "Now look what you've made me–"

She fell silent as an eerie wailing drifted along the corridor.

"What's that?" asked Hugh.

Ed waggled his eyebrows. "Maybe it's the ghost of Coldwell Hall."

Letting out a little whimper, Hugh moved closer to his mum.

"Ed, why would you say such a thing?" snapped Josie. "If Hugh wakes up with nightmares, you can deal with him."

"Oh come on, Josie, I'm only having a bit of fun."

"Well it's not funny, so pack it in."

Detaching herself from Hugh, Josie resumed walking. She eyed a narrower corridor that branched off from the main one. The portraits on its walls and the names on its doors told the same age-old tale of men chasing beautiful, unattainable women. More vases of red roses occupied arched recesses, perfuming the air with their sweet scent. "Where the hell is this room?"

"This place is a lot bigger than it looks from the outside," said Ed.

As the moaning flared up again, Hugh pointed along the side corridor. "It's coming from there."

"It must be the wind," said Josie.

"It can't be much further to our room," said Ed. He walked on a few paces before halting at a door. "Ah-ha. Here it is."

Hugh eyed the name on the door. "Did Helen's face really launch a thousand ships?"

Josie gave a soft snort. "Countries don't go to war over that sort of thing." She glanced meaningfully back the way they'd come. "Although some women clearly think they're so beautiful entire armies would die for them."

"Let's see what the room's like," said Ed, moving the conversation swiftly on. He reached for a brass doorhandle. The door swung soundlessly inwards. He flicked a light switch.

Hugh let out an impressed, "Ooh," as light cascaded from a small chandelier, sparkling upon an array of antique furnishings and golden embellishments. A four-poster bed draped in shimmering silk occupied the centre of the room. A fold-down bed had been setup by the rattling sash-window.

"Not bad, eh?" said Ed, putting down the suitcases and moving to close the velvet curtains. With the darkness shut out, the room had an opulent yet cosy feel.

Hugh plonked himself down on a black-leather chaise longue at the foot of the four-poster bed. He perused a portrait hanging from a chain above a marble fireplace. A pale woman with braided blonde hair and enigmatic blue eyes stared back at him. He rose to examine a brass plaque attached to the painting's gilded frame.

"Sweet Helen, make me immortal with a kiss," he said, reading out the passage etched into the plaque. "Her lips suck forth my soul, see where it flies. Come Helen, come, give me my soul again. Here will I dwell, for heaven be in these lips. And all is dross that is not Helena." He turned to his dad. "What does that mean?"

"It means beautiful women can get you into a lot of trouble," said Ed.

Josie arched an eyebrow. "Men don't need women to get them in trouble. They excel at doing that all by themselves."

She poked her head into a bathroom whose marble floor, walls and sink gleamed in polished perfection. A plethora of bath oils invited her to take a long soak in the deep bath.

Hugh's gaze descended to an ornate dressing table. He grabbed a packet of biscuits from beside an out-of-place looking electric kettle. "Can I have these?"

"No," said Josie. "Have a piece of fruit."

Hugh frowned at a silver bowl of apples and oranges. He sulkily picked up an ivory-handled paring knife and stabbed it into an apple.

"Don't do that, unless you're going to eat it," reprimanded Josie, taking the knife off him.

"You can have one biscuit," Ed told Hugh. "I don't want you ruining your appetite."

Grinning, Hugh tore open the packet of biscuits. Josie expelled a sharp breath through her nostrils, irritated at having her authority overridden. "I'm going to have a bath."

"You'll have to wait until after we've eaten," said Ed.

"I'm not hungry."

A frown creased Ed's brow as he watched Josie turn the taps on and pour bubble-bath into the steaming water. She stared at the gathering bubbles, biting her upper lip. He knew that look only too well. She was brooding over something, working herself up to speak. It didn't take a genius to guess what that 'something' was. He decided to make a pre-emptive move.

He came up behind her, slid his arms around her slim waist and murmured into her ear, "You know I'm crazy about you."

Josie tried to wriggle free, but Ed tightened his grip. "It's true. I've always been mad about you. You're the most beautiful woman I've ever met."

With a doubtful, "Ha!" Josie prised Ed's hands off her waist and went into the bedroom.

He followed her. "I'm serious." He nudged Hugh playfully. "Tell your mother it's true that she's the most beautiful woman in the world."

Hugh paused with a biscuit halfway in his mouth. His puppyish face scrunched with uncertainty as he eyed his mum.

Ed nudged him again a little less playfully.

Frowning, Hugh elbowed him back. "Sure Mum's beautiful, but Mrs Dankworth is really, really beautiful."

Ed rolled his eyes. Josie directed a tellingly small smile at her son. "You're right, Hugh, Mrs Dankworth is really beautiful." With that, she turned to stalk back into the bathroom. She slammed the door hard enough to rattle the walls. There was a click as the lock slid into place.

Hugh looked at his dad as if to ask, *What did I do?*

Sighing, Ed ruffled his son's damp hair. "Come on, let's get out of these wet clothes."

Ed unzipped a suitcase and picked out his favourite plaid shirt and charcoal grey blazer. As he buttoned up the shirt, he examined himself in a tall mirror. He wasn't in bad shape, although he was starting to develop a pot belly. Tucking his shirt into his trousers, he turned side on and sucked in his belly. He released his breath and felt his belly pushing against his belt. Puffing his cheeks, he made a mental note to go on a diet as soon as they got home. He scrutinised his glasses for a moment before reaching up to take them off. Maybe he should look into getting contact lenses. In fact, maybe it was time for a whole new image. One that didn't scream sensible middle-aged dad.

He turned to Hugh. "Ready?"

"Yes, Dad."

Ed smiled approvingly at his son's choice of chinos and a short-sleeved shirt. "Good boy." His smile faded as his gaze shifted to the bathroom door. The taps had stopped running. What felt like a pointed silence was emanating from the bathroom. He knocked tentatively on the door. "We're going down now, Josie. Do you want me to bring you back something to eat?"

The silence persisted. A sigh escaped Ed as, motioning for Hugh to follow, he turned to leave the room.

PART 1, CHAPTER 5

As Ed stepped into the hallway, he stumbled and thrust out a hand to steady himself. The black cat skittered away from his feet. He frowned down at it. "The bloody thing almost had me over."

The cat returned his stare, slowly slitting its eyes. It began to purr as Hugh stooped to stroke its head. "Hello Bel." He giggled as the cat nosed his hand. "Her whiskers tickle."

Bel turned and padded away along the side corridor. She glanced back as if she wanted Hugh to follow her.

"I'm not going that way," he said.

Bel swished her tail, seemingly annoyed. Head held high, she continued on her way. A wry smile tugged at Ed's lips. "That cat reminds me of your mum."

Hugh gave him a puzzled look. "What do you mean?"

"Nothing." Resting a hand on his son's shoulder, Ed ushered him onwards.

Watched by a host of tortured eyes, they made their way to the landing. The storm-wracked building creaked and quivered like a ship in heavy seas. Ed and Hugh paused at the head of the grand staircase to once again admire the sheer lavishness of the lobby. A tangy aroma wafted up the stairs.

"It smells like tomato soup," said Hugh.

As they descended the staircase, the chandeliers flickered on and off. Hugh reached for his dad's hand. Upon seeing the ginger tom, though, he let go and hurried down the remaining stairs. Sy purred as Hugh tickled him behind the ears.

A sign engraved with 'Dining Room' directed Ed to a set of double doors. Beyond them, a sprawling room dotted with circular tables continued the luxurious décor. White tablecloths, silver cutlery and crystal glasses adorned the tables. Music tinkled from a gleaming ebony grand piano. A fresco of a lush garden brought the ceiling to life. The Dankworths were nowhere to be seen.

As Hugh followed his dad, Sy slunk alongside him. "How does that work?" asked Hugh, pointing to the piano whose ivory keys were moving as if being played by a ghostly pianist.

"It must be mechanical." Ed spotted a table set for three in the middle of the room. Steam curled from a silver tureen beside a wicker basket full of bread rolls.

Hugh ran to the table and rose onto tiptoes to peer into the tureen. "It is tomato soup!" he exclaimed delightedly.

They took their seats and Ed ladled the ruby-coloured soup into their bowls. He sipped a spoonful and made an approving, "Mmm." The rich, creamy soup obviously hadn't come from a tin.

Hugh dipped bread into his soup and wolfed it down. Ed poured himself a glass of wine from a decanter. The burgundy liquid slid smoothly down his throat. His palette tingled with pleasure at a hint of oak and spices. Hugh filled a tumbler with milk and gave it the same treatment as his soup.

"Where's Dorothy?" wondered Hugh, looking all around.

Ed couldn't help but smile at the hopeful note in his son's voice. Hugh was clearly smitten by Dorothy. A touch of melancholy crept over Ed as he reflected that it wouldn't be long before Hugh started noticing girls. It only seemed like the blink of an eye since he'd been crawling around in nappies.

As if in response to Hugh's question, a door at the far side of the room swung open. Dorothy glided into view. She'd changed into a flowing regal red dress embroidered with gossamer gold thread. Her hair was piled up on her head like a crown. With balletic grace, she weaved between the tables. A sudden impulse to gulp down his entire glassful of wine overcame Ed. Hugh and he watched Dorothy with matching puppy-dog eyes. As she drew near, she openly looked Ed up and down. Unused to being eyed up like a cut of meat, he resisted an urge to squirm.

As if he'd met her approval, Dorothy flashed him a dazzling smile. "Well hello again. How was your meal?"

Ed smiled back, revealing wine-stained teeth. "It was delicious, thanks."

"Tomato soup is my favourite," announced Hugh.

Dorothy let out a laugh as musical as the *plink-plonk* of the piano. "Mine too. All the best people love tomato soup."

"Not my mum. She says she's sick of the sight of it."

Prompted by Hugh's words, Dorothy eyed the unused place setting. "Where is your wife?"

"She was too tired to come down," Ed answered as she lifted her gaze to his.

"Oh dear, what a shame."

Ed's lips curved into a lopsided smile. Was that a hint of sarcasm he detected? "Where's your husband?"

Dorothy made a vague gesture. "He's tired too. May I join you?"

"Please do."

Dorothy looked at Ed expectantly. He returned her gaze uncertainly for a brief moment before giving a little start of comprehension. "Oh right, sorry." He rose to pull a chair out for her.

She sat down, smiling thanks and smoothing her dress underneath herself. She reached for the wine bottle, refilled Ed's glass, then filled her own. She raised her glass. "A mighty pain to love it is, and 'tis a pain that pain to miss; but, of all pains, the greatest pain is to love, but love in vain."

Ed clinked his glass against Dorothy's. "That's very true. Who said that?"

"Some poet or other." Her gaze slid across to Hugh. "So, Hugh, what do you think of my little hotel?"

"It's more like a palace than a hotel," he said.

Dorothy laughed. "Then that must make me a queen."

"You look like a queen."

Dorothy's eyes sparkled like diamonds. "Not only handsome, but charming to boot. All the girls are going to be fighting over you."

Blushing as red as the soup at the compliment, Hugh shyly lowered his eyes.

Ed gestured to their surroundings. "So did you design all of this?"

"Yes. Who else?" A slight edge to Dorothy's voice hinted that she took offense at the mere suggestion of others being involved. "You should have seen the place when Arthur and I took over. It was just like everywhere else around here – so dull and dreary. I wanted to bring some glamour to the area." The faintest network of lines imprinted themselves onto her forehead. "Although I sometimes wonder why I bother."

Her sour tone made Ed wonder whether the business was struggling. It would hardly have been a surprise if it was. How could anyone hope to recoup what it must have cost to do this place up so lavishly, especially out here in the back of beyond?

As if sensing it was needed, the white cat emerged from under a nearby table and rubbed itself against Dorothy's legs.

Her smile returned. She purred at Yo-yo and the cat responded in kind. Hugh got off his seat and knelt down by Yo-yo. The cat rolled onto her back, exposing her downy underbelly. She playfully pawed at Hugh's hand as he stroked her silky fur.

"She likes you," said Dorothy. "Cats are excellent judges of character."

"I think cats are way smarter than dogs."

A chuckle slipped between Dorothy's plump lips. "Dogs are like men. They need to know who's boss."

"Hmm, well we certainly know who's the boss in our household, don't we, Hugh?" said Ed.

"Mum, of course," Hugh answered as if it was the easiest question ever.

"But your dad doesn't always do as he's told, does he?" Dorothy glanced at Ed as she spoke.

The desire to take a big gulp of wine washed over him once again.

"No he doesn't," said Hugh. "That's why he keeps getting in trouble. Mum says he knows just enough to think he knows it all."

Dorothy kept her almond-shaped eyes on Ed. "Your mother's a wise woman."

Much to Ed's horror, it was now his turn to feel himself blushing like a teenager. As he habitually did when he was nervous, he reached for his pipe. "Do you mind if I smoke?"

"Not at all. I've always liked the smell of pipe smoke."

"Me too," said Hugh. "Mum hates it. She says smoking is a filthy habit."

"Well I think a pipe makes a man look distinguished."

"What does 'distinguished' mean?"

"It means you should respect me and do as I say," Ed told

Hugh in a jokey-serious tone. Dorothy laughed as Hugh poked his tongue out at his dad.

Ed filled his pipe with tobacco and tamped it down. Dorothy watched the methodical process intently. "There's something so relaxing about watching someone doing something they're really good at. Don't you think?"

Ed settled back in his chair, puffing contemplatively on his pipe. "I've never really thought about it before, but I suppose it's true."

Dorothy picked up the open tobacco tin and put it to her nose. Her nostrils pinched as she inhaled. "It smells like..." she searched for the right word, "autumn."

"Autumn Evening." Ed sounded impressed. "That's the name of the blend."

Dorothy closed her eyes. Her bosom expanded as she drew in another deep breath. A slight shudder of pleasure passed through her slender frame. "It makes me think of burning maple leaves."

Ed stared at her like someone spellbound by a masterpiece. She opened her eyes abruptly. He redirected his gaze just as swiftly. Something overhead caught his eye – an apple dangling from a tree at the centre of the fresco. The oversized apple looked ripe enough to drop on his head.

"It looks delicious, doesn't it?" said Dorothy. "Looking at it always makes me hungry." She lifted a hand. Her long fingers curled as if plucking the apple from the tree.

She met Ed's gaze again. A silent moment passed between them. He cleared his throat loudly enough to draw a glance from Hugh. "Thanks again for the meal, Dorothy."

"You're not going, are you?" she asked with a hint of dismay as Ed pushed back his chair.

"I'd love to stay and chat, but... well..." *If I sit around drinking wine with you for much longer, I'll be in for an almighty tongue-lashing from Josie*. That would have been the truth, but instead he said somewhat lamely, "I'm tired out."

Dorothy smiled as if she saw straight through him. Fluttering her eyelashes, she tapped Ed's half-full glass with a gold-painted nail. "At least finish your drink."

"You're right. This is far too good to waste." He picked up the glass, swallowed its contents in one, then motioned to Hugh. "Come on you, it's bedtime."

"But I'm not tired," protested Hugh. "Can't we stay a bit longer?"

Ed's voice became firm. "What did I just say about doing as you're told?"

Hugh's hand rested on Yo-yo for a moment more, then he sighed and stood up.

"Say goodnight to Mrs Dankworth," said Ed.

"Goodnight, Mrs Dankworth." There was a sulky lack of enthusiasm in Hugh's voice. Head hanging low, he trudged towards the lobby.

Ed smiled at Dorothy. "Goodnight."

She replied with the slightest of nods. A glaze of disinterest covering her eyes, she wafted a hand lethargically as if to say, *Run along now.*

Ed looked at her like a confused schoolboy. With an awkward little shuffle, he turned to follow Hugh.

PART 1, CHAPTER 6

As Ed stepped out of the dining room, he became aware that the storm was still battering the hotel. A vague feeling of disorientation tugged at his brain, as if he'd just emerged from a dream.

The storm seemed to be reaching a crescendo. It sounded like two armies were battling it out. Hugh stared at his shoes, sulkily scuffing them across the carpet.

"Come on, I'll race you up the stairs," said Ed, breaking into a run.

"Hey, that's not fair!" exclaimed Hugh, instantly forgetting his displeasure at being parted from Dorothy and Yo-yo. He sprinted after his dad, his face a picture of determination.

Ed slowed down just enough to let Hugh beat him to the first floor landing. Grinning, Hugh thrust his hands triumphantly in the air. "I'm the winner!"

His smile vanished as a banging reverberated along the corridor. "What's that noise?"

"Perhaps another tree was blown over."

Hugh shook his head. "It's coming from inside the hotel."

Wrapping an arm around his son's shoulders, Ed shepherded him onwards.

Bang!

Hugh put a hand to the plaster on his forehead. "It's making my head hurt."

Bang! Bang!

With every step, the noise grew louder. *What the hell's making that racket?* wondered Ed. Had the storm smashed its way into one of the rooms? Was Arthur nailing a board over a broken window? A grimly amusing image came to mind of the hotelier hammering nails in with his breeze-block fists.

Ed's footsteps quickened as his thoughts turned to Josie being alone in this unfamiliar place. Hugh gave a start as an eerie wail cut through the air. The cry seemed to speak of an almost otherworldly suffering. It was as if the portraits were coming to life and lamenting their unrequited love.

"Dad," whimpered Hugh.

"It's okay, Hugh. It's only the wind."

"No it isn't."

Ed didn't dispute the assertion. On some instinctive level, he knew Hugh was right. As the banging continued, Hugh flinched repeatedly.

"Where in God's name is this room?" Ed muttered. The hallway seemed longer than ever, like an elastic band being stretched out as far as it could go.

He pulled up abruptly as something caught his eye. The black cat stared back at him from the lefthand corridor, its eyes shining like green lamps. A sudden thought occurred to Ed. "That's what's making that horrible wailing. It's these bloody cats."

"I don't think I like Bel anymore," said Hugh. "She's creepy."

Ed ushered Hugh to their bedroom door. He inserted the key in the lock and tried the handle. The door wouldn't open. He knocked. There came the clunk of a deadbolt being unlocked. Josie opened the door, wearing a fluffy white dressing-gown with 'Coldwell Hall' embroidered on its chest pocket. Shorn of makeup, she had a washed-out pallor. She peered past Ed and

Hugh as if making sure they hadn't been followed.

"Why did you double-lock the door?" asked Ed, squinting as he stepped past her. Every light in the room was on.

"There were some strange noises out there," said Josie.

"It's the cats," said Hugh.

Josie closed the door and threw the deadbolt. "What about all that banging?"

"Maybe Mr Dankworth's doing some emergency repairs," said Ed, removing his pipe from between his lips and sidling up to Josie. As he tilted his head to kiss her neck, a fresh floral scent tickled his nostrils. "Mmm, you smell good."

Wrinkling her nose, Josie nudged him away. "You smell like cheap wine."

"Actually, it's a very good Burgundy."

"And very good tomato soup," piped up Hugh.

"Go brush your teeth," Josie said a touch sharply.

Pouting, Hugh turned to do as he was told.

As Hugh went into the bathroom, Josie eyed Ed intently. Her dark eyes seemed to be searching for something. "So did you have a nice evening?"

He let the loaded question hang in the air for a moment before answering diplomatically, "Yes, but we missed you."

"Did you now?" Josie's voice was laced with doubt. "And was the most beautiful woman in the world there?"

Ed moved closer to her again. He stroked her cheek with the back of his fingers. "Josie, you know there's no one more beautiful than you to me."

She stared into his eyes as if trying to gauge his sincerity, then turned her face away from his hand and looked in the mirror.

Resisting the temptation to tease, *Mirror, mirror on the wall*, Ed put his pipe back in his mouth and puffed on it.

Josie let out a conspicuously loud cough. "God, why do you have to smoke that disgusting thing around me? Not only does it stink, but it makes you look like a ridiculous old man."

"Dorothy says it makes me look distinguished." The words were out before Ed could stop them. A sharp prod of regret followed hot on their heels.

Anger and amusement flashed in Josie's eyes. "Oh she does, does she? And what else did she say? Did she tell you how devastatingly handsome you are? I'll bet she was delighted I didn't come down for–"

"Shh, keep it down," cut in Ed, glancing meaningfully at the open bathroom door. "Hugh's upset enough without having to hear us at each other's throat."

Leaning in close to Ed, Josie whispered with a sort of spiteful relish, "I hope you've stored away a mental image of Dorothy to fantasise over, because you're going to have to make do with fantasies for the foreseeable future."

He drew away from her, chewing on his pipe. "You know, Josie, I love you, but sometimes I wonder–" He broke off, thinking better of speaking his mind.

"You wonder what? Why you married me?" Josie thrust her chin towards him like a prodding finger. "Well ditto."

Ed dropped onto the chaise longue so heavily that it seemed like his legs had given out. "Jesus, Josie, you really know how to stick the knife in. What I was about to say is, I love you, but sometimes I wonder if you feel the same way about me."

Josie stared at Ed as if musing over how she really felt about him. She drew in a deep, controlled breath. "I'll tell you how you make me feel – you make me want to scream."

Ed gave a dry chuckle. "I suppose that's better than making

you feel nothing at all."

Josie opened her mouth to say something else, but closed it as Hugh entered the room. Whilst he undressed, she fetched his pyjamas from a suitcase. He put them on and clambered into bed.

"Sleep tight, matey," said Ed as Hugh's mouth gaped in a yawn.

Hugh's eyes drifted shut, but snapped open again as the wind howled and a loud bang came from somewhere nearby. He pressed his hands to the sides of his head. "I've got the worst headache ever."

Stroking Hugh's wavy brown hair, Josie sang softly, "Howling winds tearing through the land, but Mum's love, like a shield, takes my hand. Through the storm, she always protects me. Staying by my side until…" She paused to find the right words, then resumed somewhat matter-of-factly, "Until her lullaby carries me away and we both get some much-needed sleep."

As he listened to his mum's lilting voice, Hugh's eyelids slid down. The song soothed the tension from Ed's face too. Humming along to himself, he tapped the ash from his pipe into a cut-glass ashtray. His brow creased as he put a hand into his jacket pocket. "Damn it."

Josie shushed him, rising to slink away from Hugh. "What's the matter?" she whispered as Ed searched his other pockets.

"I can't find my tobacco tin. I must have left it downstairs."

"Well it can stay there."

Ed's frown deepened. "You know I like a smoke first thing. It sets me up for the day."

Josie's eyes narrowed as if she suspected the tin's misplacement wasn't quite as accidental as it seemed. "I'd rather you left it where it is until the morning."

Her tone made the suggestion sound more like a warning. With a little wrench, Ed freed himself from her gaze and turned towards the door. "I won't be long."

Josie's eyes followed him. They remained on the door, even after he'd closed it behind himself.

"Mum."

Upon hearing Hugh's sleepy voice, she returned to his bedside. His eyes were open a crack. "Where's Dad going?"

Josie found a smile for him. "Nowhere. Go to sleep."

She stayed by Hugh's side until his soft, steady breathing signalled that he'd fallen asleep. Approaching the four-poster bed, she took off the dressing-gown but didn't get under the sheets. She sat perched on the edge of the mattress in her lace-trimmed pink chemise, her gaze alternating between the door and a carriage clock on the mantlepiece. Five minutes crawled by. She unconsciously bit a perfectly curved fingernail and swore as it broke between her teeth. More minutes passed like hours.

Hugh moaned in his sleep, flinging out an arm as if he was fighting someone. His knuckles thudded into the wall. Josie rose to put his arm under the sheets and tuck them tightly around him.

Her eyes returned to the door, then the clock, then the door, then the clock…

PART 2, CHAPTER 1

Time Is A Cruel Lover

Twenty-five years later

As Hugh entered the room, he resisted an impulse to pinch his nose. The combination of smells hit him like a physical assault. Uppermost was the bitter medicinal aroma of antiseptic. Then came the nauseatingly sweet scent of industrial cleaner. Under that lurked a fetid mixture of sweat, urine and other bodily fluids. And at the bottom of it all was something that defied description, something that no amount of scrubbing could wash away.

The suffocating perfume intensified with every step Hugh took towards the bedbound figure. He could almost feel it squirming up his nostrils and gnawing at his insides like some parasitic worm, sapping his strength, weakening his limbs.

He squinted as he passed beneath a harsh fluorescent strip-light. An array of heart monitors, CPAP machines and movement sensors emitted a dissonant symphony of beeps and whirrs. Someone in a neighbouring room had a TV turned up too loud, possibly in an attempt to drown out the voice that kept wailing over and over, "I want to go home. I want to go home…"

"You and me both," murmured Hugh, lifting a hand to his forehead. A headache was thumping behind his eyes. Like always, it had been triggered by the hospital's relentless soundtrack of metal doors slamming shut and heavy-duty locks clunking into place. God, he hated that sound more than any other in the world.

He came to a stop at the foot of a metal-framed bed. Its occupant was propped up on a mound of pillows, head lolling awkwardly to one side, mouth hanging open. Gunmetal-grey hair curtained a gaunt, deeply wrinkled face. Dark chocolate-coloured eyes stared out of hollows overhung by caterpillar eyebrows. Misty, unfocused pupils seemed to stare into another world. They gave no hint as to what thoughts or emotions lay within. Was there anything going on in there? Or was it simply a blackhole?

"Hello Mum," said Hugh.

There was a choked edge to his voice. Her condition had visibly deteriorated since his last visit. It twisted him up inside to look at her sunken cheeks, pale lips and sallow complexion. Her legs were swathed in bandages. IV lines in her forearm fed her antibiotics to combat the bedsores that the bandages covered. A catheter snaked under the bedsheets from a bag of urine hooked on the bedframe. A sense of dread stole over Hugh at the liquid's rusty red colour.

Not for the first time, he found himself wondering, *What's the point?* How long had it been since she last uttered a word? Eight years? Nine? Why keep her alive like this? Why not just let her fade away? Or better still, inject her with enough painkillers to end it quickly? Wouldn't that be the most merciful thing to do?

Uncertainty swirled in Hugh's sad brown eyes. What if she didn't want to die? What if she'd stubbornly clung on all these years, trapped in this hideous place and in her own mind, for a reason?

He skirted around the bed to her side. Slowly, almost fearfully, he laid his hand on hers. Her skin was as cold as a fish. He glanced at a camera embedded in a corner of the ceiling. Strictly speaking, it was forbidden for visitors to touch inmates, but at this point, what did it matter?

As Hugh brushed a few strands of hair out of his mother's eyes, a faint gurgling issued from her throat. He plucked a tissue from a box on the bedside table and wiped a snail-trail of saliva off her chin.

He forced himself to stare into the black wells of her pupils. "The doctor says the antibiotics aren't working. He's going to try you on a different type."

Hugh was momentarily silent, as if hoping for a reply, then he continued, "Apart from that, he says you're doing quite well..." He trailed off with a shake of his head. No, there was no time left for lies. "That's not true. What he actually said was that you're dying. It's not just the infection. It's everything. Your body's had enough. It's shutting down. The doctor doesn't know how long you've got left. It could be months. It might only be weeks."

Hugh's voice wobbled. He swallowed and brought it back under control. "I've never doubted you, Mum." He leant in closer, so close that he could smell her skin – it exuded a strangely synthetic odour that reminded him of his wife's nail polish remover. "And I'm going to prove you were telling the truth. I'm going to clear your name."

Another faint gurgle passed between Josie's cracked lips. Hugh reached for a little sponge, dipped it in a bowl of water and tenderly moistened her lips. "I'm going back to Coldwell Hall."

He looked at her with a sort of desperate hope. Nothing. Not even the faintest flicker of a spark of consciousness showed in her eyes. "I'm going to catch the thing that did this to us."

Thing. The way he said it suggested he was going after some entity that defied description.

"I should have done this years ago, but..." A lump of shame

formed in Hugh's throat, threatening to choke off his voice. "I couldn't face going back there. I was so scared." Determination hardened his tone. "I'm not scared anymore." He repeated the words under his breath as if he needed to convince himself they were true.

"I want to go home! I want to go home!" rang through the walls again.

As if the desperate voice was a projection from the depths of his mother's mind, Hugh said, "I'm not going to let you die in here, Mum." He gave her frail hand a gentle squeeze. "I promise you that."

He looked at her in silence for a while, occasionally dabbing her lips with the sponge. He turned at the clomp of boots on the rubberised floor. A po-faced female officer in a white shirt with black shoulder epaulettes entered the room. Voices crackled through a walkie-talkie attached to her utility belt.

"Time's up, Mr Carver," she informed Hugh.

He nodded, then bent towards his mother's face. The synthetic smell wafted from her mouth so strongly that he almost retched. Fighting back the nausea, he kissed her cold cheek. "I love you, Mum."

Hugh followed the officer from the room. A buzzer sounded and another female officer opened the door out of the ward. To the accompaniment of slamming doors, he navigated a series of long, starkly lit corridors.

Bang! Bang!

His shoulders twitched at every echoing impact. Fresh air flowed through an open sash-window shadowed by iron bars. Taking a deep breath, he cleared the ward's sickening cocktail of odours from his nostrils.

At the waiting area, he retrieved his mobile phone, wallet and keys from a locker. Then he took off a plastic wristband and returned it, along with the locker token, to the reception desk.

His footsteps quickened as he headed for the outer doors. He hurried across the carpark to his car. Turning to eye the institutional redbrick building he'd just left, he wondered how many more times he would have to come to this place.

"Just one more time," he told himself.

A long, straight driveway led to a pair of finial-capped brick posts. As he passed between them, he put his foot down, accelerating sharply away from a sign bearing the name 'Rampton Hospital'.

PART 2, CHAPTER 2

The sight of the house at the end of the leafy cul-de-sac smoothed the tension from Hugh's forehead. From its modest proportions to its traditional suburban architecture, the property was perfectly average in every way. Just how he liked it.

A few furrows returned to his brow as he saw the black Transit van in the driveway. He glanced at the dashboard clock. They were early. He'd intended to talk to Louise before they arrived, let her know about his plan, give her a little time to come to terms with it. But now the cat was undoubtedly out of the bag. He heaved a sigh. He could just imagine Louise's reaction.

Hugh pulled up alongside the van. He got out of the car, eyeing the mud-spattered, dented Transit. His gaze dwelled briefly on a cartoon-style ghost air-freshener dangling in the windscreen.

A flagstone path led between neat lawns adorned with a modest sprinkling of flowers to the front door. Hugh stepped through the door and closed it quietly behind himself. He was greeted by a palette of cream carpets and beige walls bathed in sunlight. He stood there for a moment, soaking in the soothingly bland tapestry of colours.

A murmur of conversation from beyond a door drew his attention. He slid off his shoes and started to tiptoe upstairs. He stiffened at the sound of a door handle turning.

"You're back." The soft, accentless voice was perfectly in tune with its surroundings.

Hugh responded with his own statement of the obvious. "Yes, I'm back." He turned to meet the hazel eyes of a petite woman about his age. Despite the lingering sadness of seeing his mother, he couldn't help but smile at Louise's shoulder-length mousy hair, freckled cheeks and muted makeup.

"Ava and Graham are here to see you." There was a hint of something in her voice – not anger, but concern and possibly hurt.

Hugh gave an apologetic little nod. "I'm just going to get changed. You know how it is, the smell of that place gets into your clothes."

"How is she?"

"She's not good," was all Hugh could bring himself to say.

With that, he turned away from Louise and continued up the stairs to a comfortably furnished bedroom. After practically tearing off his clothes, he stuffed them into a dirty-washing basket as if they were contaminated.

A little girl with black hair trailing down her back and chocolate button-eyes entered the room. "Hello, Daddy."

His smile returning, Hugh stooped to kiss the girl's glossy hair. "Hello you."

"Have you been to see Grandma?"

Hugh's smile twitched, but didn't slip. "Yes."

The girl pushed her heart-shaped lips into a pout. "I wanted to go with you."

Hugh was struck by how much she looked like the childhood photos he'd seen of his mum. The resemblance was almost uncanny. "I know, Isabelle, but Grandma's only allowed one visitor at a time. And besides, the place she's in… well, it isn't a place for children."

"Then it isn't a place for grandmas either."

The words brought a sad glimmer to Hugh's eyes. "You're right, it isn't. And I'm going to do my best to get your grandma out of there."

Isabelle nodded firmly as if to say, *Good*.

His heart lifting at how much she cared for her grandma, whom she'd never met, Hugh kissed her head again. "Go play in your room."

Pride pushed aside the sadness in his eyes as he watched her leave the bedroom. He put on clean clothes and returned downstairs. The aroma of fresh coffee and cigarette smoke wafted from the living room. He paused in the doorway, taking in the scene. Louise was in one of the three-piece suite's armchairs. A bear of a man with a beard that would have put a Viking to shame filled the other chair. In contrast, a woman who made Louise look well-built was blowing a plume of cigarette smoke out of the front window.

Ava's narrow, small-featured face turned towards Hugh. From under hooded eyelids, she took in his polo-shirt, chinos and tartan slippers. The next instant, like a child mightily pleased with itself, she broke into a broad grin. "You're exactly as I pictured you."

"Am I?" he asked, trying to figure out whether or not she was complementing him.

Ava's gaze travelled the room. "I really like your house. It has a good energy. Very calming."

"Thank you. My wife's the decorator."

"I know." Ava's tone suggested nothing could be more obvious. "One look at her aura tells me that." She followed her cryptic comment with a cheeky wink at Louise.

There was a moment of silence, disturbed by Graham munching on a biscuit and slurping coffee. A faint frown creased Hugh's forehead as Ava took a final drag on her cigarette and flicked it carelessly out of the window.

"Ava and Graham have been telling me how they met at a paranormal conference," Louise said, treating Hugh to a pointed look.

Ava let out a raucous laugh that sounded like it came from someone twice her size. "You make it sound like we're a couple." She jerked a thumb at the hulking, bearded man. "Can you imagine me and him rolling around on a bed together? I'd be turned into a pancake."

Graham showed no offence at the remark. Shoulder length, thinning ginger hair curtained his big round face as he reached for another biscuit. "Actually, it was an EVP conference," he corrected in a precise, pedantic tone.

"EVP?" echoed Louise.

"Electronic Voice Phenomena."

"Ghost voice recordings," elaborated Ava. "Basically, it's a bunch of geeks getting together to show off their ghost hunting tech. I only went along to see if there was anyone worth hooking up with for a bit of no-strings-attached." She puffed her cheeks. "I should have known better. Those guys are more afraid of girls than ghosts."

Another gust of laughter burst from Ava at her own quip. Graham unconcernedly dunked his biscuit in his coffee and popped it whole into his beard-fringed mouth. Unsure what to make of their visitors, Hugh and Louise exchanged a glance.

"I didn't expect you until this evening," Hugh said to Ava.

She spread her hands as if to say, *Well here we are.* A spicy perfume wafted through the air as she moved to plop down onto the sofa. Her sleeve rode up as she put an arm behind her head. A tattoo of a voluptuous woman wearing a turban with a feather sticking out of it decorated her inner bicep. A crystal ball was balanced in the woman's palm. Her other hand was beckoning, enticing punters to come and see what the ball foretold.

"So come on then, Hugh," said Ava. "Let's hear it."

"Yes, Hugh, 'let's hear it'," said Louise, crossing her arms and eyeing him intently.

He avoided her gaze. "You know the basic story, right?"

With plodding exactitude, Graham began to recite from memory, "On Saturday the seventh of August, 1999, you and your parents, Edmund and Josie Carver, were returning home from a week's holiday on St Bees Head. Gale force winds forced you to seek refuge in Coldwell Hall Hotel in Eskdale. The hotel was, and still is, owned by Arthur and Dorothy Dankworth. You stayed in a room on the hotel's first floor. On the morning of Sunday the eighth of August, you awoke to find your father deceased from a single stab wound. He'd been stabbed through the left eye into the brain."

As Graham reeled off the grim details, Hugh's gaze drifted towards the window. Little tremors ran through him as if he was watching horrific images play out on a far-off screen.

"Your mother was holding a bloodstained knife," continued Graham. "Post-mortem analysis showed it was the knife that had inflicted the wound. She told the police, and I quote, 'I pulled the knife out of my husband, but I didn't see who put it in him.'. Neither the police nor the courts believed her. The door to the room had been double-locked from the inside. There were no signs of forced entry. On the first of December, 1999, Josie Carver was convicted of murder and sentenced to life in prison. She was sent to HMP New Hall. In 2010, after suffering a psychotic episode, she was transferred to Rampton high-security psychiatric hospital, where she remains to this day."

As Graham fell silent, Hugh came back to himself with a slight start. Louise's concerned eyes caught her husband's gaze.

He summoned up a small smile for her.

"You've obviously done your homework," Hugh said to Graham.

"When Graham was in school, he thought being called teacher's pet was a compliment," teased Ava.

"An insult from a moron is a compliment," Graham said matter-of-factly.

More loud laughter from Ava jarred on the sombre atmosphere. "Spoken like a true nerd." Her bright little eyes zeroed in on Hugh suddenly as if she hoped to catch him off guard. "What makes you think your mum was telling the truth?"

"Because..." He searched for an answer and found one that might have come from his ten-year-old self. "Because my mum isn't a liar."

Ava smiled at his childish logic. "Apart from the obvious, what stuck in your head most about your stay at Coldwell Hall?"

Hugh thought for a moment. "I remember there were lots of strange banging and moaning noises."

"Banging and moaning." A lewd grin split Ava's thin lips. "Sounds like my kind of hotel."

Hugh frowned. "Perhaps this was a bad idea. Perhaps you're not the right people for this job. I was led to believe you're the best clairvoyant around–"

"She is the best," Graham interrupted flatly, as if stating an irrefutable fact. "She's annoying, loud and rude, but there's no one better at what she does."

Ava placed a hand over her heart. "Aww, thanks Graham, that means a lot." There was no hint of sarcasm in her reply. She made a circular motion for Hugh to go on.

Hugh's eyes alternated uncertainly between the waifish

clairvoyant and her pro-wrestler-sized sidekick before he continued, "I also remember that Mrs Dankworth was nice." He lifted a hand, feeling for an almost imperceptible scar near his hairline. "She gave me a plaster for a cut on my forehead… Or at least I think she did. Maybe it was her husband." His voice became more certain. "I do remember that Mum was annoyed with Dad for ignoring the weather forecast and for smoking his pipe in the bedroom."

"Did they argue?" asked Ava.

"Yes, but don't ask me what was said." Hugh's gaze grew distant as he delved deeper into his memory. "When I fell asleep, I had nightmares. I couldn't tell you what they were about, but I remember feeling like someone was holding me down. Smothering me." His breath caught in his throat as he relived the sensation.

"Sounds like you had a visit from a sleep demon," said Ava.

"It sounds like sleep paralysis to me," countered Louise.

"That's what they call it these days. Maybe they're right. Maybe not." Ava gave a noncommittal shrug.

"No one knows exactly what causes it," chimed in Graham. A frown disturbed his forehead at his inability to provide an explanation.

"I'll tell you what I *do* know," said Louise. "Demons don't exist." She glanced meaningfully at Hugh. "Neither do ghosts."

"Are you saying my mother's a liar?" he demanded to know.

"What? No… I…" stammered Louise, taken aback by his vehemence.

"The door was double-locked. It was impossible for anyone else to get into the room. So if it wasn't something supernatural, how else can you explain what happened to my father?" Slamming his fist into his palm, Hugh reiterated, "How?"

"Calm down, Hugh."

"To hell with being calm! I've kept my calm for twenty-five years and what has it achieved? Where has it got me?"

With a wounded look in her eyes, Louise motioned to the room. "It got you here."

Her words extinguished Hugh's anger. "You know that's not what I mean, Louise. I…" He hesitated self-consciously before going on, "I love you and Isabelle. I love our life. But I have to find out the truth. I *have* to." The way he said it suggested he didn't have a choice in the matter.

Louise's lips lifted into a sympathetic smile. "So much time has passed since your dad died. How can there possibly be any trace left of what happened?"

"Time means nothing to ghosts," said Ava. "Most of them aren't even aware they're dead. They're stuck in a loop, reliving some moment from their life over and over. But a few – maybe one in a hundred – are fully conscious and seriously pissed off. Those are the dangerous ones."

Graham scratched his beard. "It's debatable whether they're conscious in the way you and I are. Can the mind truly exist separate from the brain?"

Ava laughed. "Oh no. No way am I getting into this with you again."

"Is this all just a joke to you?" Louise asked with a tremor in her voice.

In an instant, Ava's expression became serious. "I wouldn't be here if it was." Her eyes slid back and forth between Louise and Hugh. "I'm well aware of what's at stake."

"Are you? Because…" Louise swallowed, visibly uncomfortable at confronting Ava. "Because it seems to me that you're only here to exploit my husband's grief."

Graham's broad chest emitted a rumble of disapproval.

"With the greatest of respect, Mrs Carver, you're talking absolute–"

"Ah-ah," interrupted Ava, raising a hand to signal that she didn't need anyone to fight her battles for her. There was something oddly sensuous about the way her eyelids drooped even lower as she looked at Louise. "You're not the first person to say that to me, and you won't be the last."

Louise's forehead creased in confusion. "Is that it? Aren't you going to try to convince me I'm wrong?"

"What would be the point? If you think I'm a scammer, nothing I say will change your mind." Ava turned to Hugh. "Shall we get on with it? Or do you want us to leave?"

"I told you, I want to find out the truth," he replied without hesitation. He treated Louise to a resolute stare. "I don't care what it takes."

She opened her mouth but said nothing, seemingly at a loss for words. Silence momentarily held sway over the room. There was a creak of springs as Graham reached for yet another biscuit. He drew back empty-handed at a sharp glance from Ava.

"Finish your story," she prompted Hugh. "What happened next?"

"What happened next?" he murmured, his eyes glazing over as the question transported him back to that terrible moment. "Whatever it was that had held me down, lifted me up and threw me out of bed."

"You felt it pick you up?" asked Graham.

"No, but I felt myself hit the floor as if I'd been body-slammed."

"Could have been a poltergeist," mused Ava. "They love to bang around and cause trouble like naughty children. They can be really dangerous. Especially if you feed them."

"What do they feed on?" asked Hugh.

"Negative energy – anger, fear, jealousy. That type of thing."

Hugh pursed his lips in thought. "Mum used to get jealous of other women. I don't know why. She was a beautiful woman herself." He brought up a photo on his phone of his mother set against the backdrop of what looked to be a church's interior. She was cradling a baby swaddled in a white blanket. Despite her tired eyes and the shapeless dress obscuring her figure, she possessed a striking beauty.

"Wow, she was a real stunner," said Ava. She pointed at the baby. "Aww, look at those chubby cheeks. Is that you?"

"Yes. That was taken at my christening."

"Do you believe in God?"

"I… err…" Hugh hesitated, thrown by the question. "I suppose I must do if I believe in the supernatural."

"It's not necessarily a logical contradiction to believe in one but not the other," pointed out Graham. "Naturally, most atheists are sceptical about supernatural phenomena. However–"

He broke off as Ava cleared her throat pointedly. She gave him a quick pat on the knee as if to say, *Good boy*.

"What about you, Ava? Are you religious?" asked Louise.

Ava responded with a dismissive flick of her wrist. "Religion is about control. No one controls me."

"So you don't believe in God?"

"Did I say that? Anyway, this isn't about what I believe." Ava's gaze slid across to Hugh. "It's about what you husband believes."

"All I can tell you is there was something other than my parents and me in that hotel room. I felt its…" Hugh searched for the right word, "hate."

"Coldwell Hall has no history of paranormal activity," said Graham. "No one in my network had even heard of it. The building itself isn't all that old. It was built in two phases. The mock-Tudor part was erected by Gerald Dankworth in 1951. An extension was added by his son Arthur in 1980. Of course, we also have to take into consideration the history of the land the hotel was built on. In this case, the site was originally occupied by a brewery that went out of business in 1950."

Ava chuckled. "Perhaps the ghost was drunk and that's why it started a fight with your dad."

"Perhaps," Hugh replied in a distinctly unamused tone. "And perhaps Louise is right and you're as fake as Coldwell Hall's Tudor beams."

Ava's laughter swelled to fill the entire house. "Oh I can see you're going to be fun to work with." She twirled a finger in the air. "Come on, let's hear the rest of your story."

Hugh's gaze dropped away from hers. He fixated somewhat sullenly on his feet as if channelling his ten-year-old self. "When I opened my eyes, the first thing I saw was blood on the floor. My nose was bleeding. The next thing I saw was my dad. I didn't even recognise him at first. There was so much blood on his face. It was all over the bedsheets, too, and..." he faltered briefly before resuming, "and my mum's hands. Mum was staring at me. I've never seen anyone look so scared. That's always stayed with me. 'It wasn't me. It wasn't me.' I remember she said that twice. Her voice was emotionless."

"Shock," said Graham.

Submerged in his memories, Hugh went on, "I remember screaming and running out of the room." His eyes narrowed like he was trying to see through mist. "I have a vague memory of running along a corridor, then..."

He trailed off, seemingly unable to recall what happened next. He met Ava's gaze. A nervous gleam in his eyes suggested he was afraid she would laugh at him. She lifted a hand to the crown of her boyishly short black hair, like she was putting on her thinking cap. Louise joined her husband in staring expectantly at Ava. Graham eyed the biscuits as if wondering whether he could get away with snaffling another one.

Ava began slowly, weighing up each word, "First, Hugh, you have to accept that your father's death might have nothing to do with the supernatural."

The muscles of his cheeks pulsed as if he was chewing on some tough morsel of meat. After an extended moment, he replied with a reluctant little nod.

"Now let's assume it does have a supernatural cause," continued Ava. "The question is – what are we dealing with here? A ghost? A poltergeist?"

"What's the difference?" asked Hugh.

"There's a lot of disagreement about that amongst the paranormal community," said Graham. "Some believe poltergeists are a manifestation of RSPK – recurrent spontaneous psychokinesis. Most psychics are unaware of their innate abilities. When such people suffer pain, anxiety or whatever, they unconsciously build up psychokinetic energy. Once the pressure becomes too great, it's released in a burst of paranormal activity – objects moving on their own, lights turning themselves on and off, that sort of thing."

"Are you suggesting my mother might be a psychic?"

"Not just your mother," Ava said, looking at Hugh meaningfully. "Do you often experience déjà vu?"

"No."

"Do you dream of things that come to pass?"

"No." Hugh spread his hands to indicate his almost wilfully unremarkable surroundings. "Besides the obvious, I'm just an ordinary bloke."

"Another theory suggests poltergeists are powerful spirits that are drawn to trauma," said Graham.

With a nod, Ava indicated that she favoured this explanation. "You were scared by the storm," she said to Hugh. "Your mum was angry with your dad. Bringing those emotions into a place with high paranormal activity is like pouring blood into shark-infested waters. What you have to understand about poltergeists is they've inhabited the spirit world for too long. They've forgotten what it is to be alive. And they hate the living with an almost demonic intensity. But..." she held up an index finger to illustrate her point, "they're not demonic. If we're dealing with a poltergeist, that's bad enough. But if it's a demon..." She left her words ominously suspended in the air.

"What if it is a demon?" asked Hugh, his voice betraying a trace of apprehension.

"Let's just say it would make things difficult for us."

"Difficult is an understatement," said Graham. "Demons don't just want to kill us – although they take great pleasure in doing so – they want us to destroy ourselves."

Ava puckered her lips as if something had occurred to her. "Have you considered that the real target of the attack might not have been your dad?"

Furrows gathered on Hugh's forehead. "I'm not sure I understand. What are you saying?"

"I'm saying that by returning to Coldwell Hall you might be playing into the hands of your dad's killer."

"Whoa, hang on a moment," interjected Louise, her voice rising in alarm. "Surely you're not thinking about going back to that place?"

Gently but unwaveringly, Hugh said, "There's no other way."

Louise shook her head. "No, no. no. This is crazy. It's crazy!"

"My mum needs me."

Louise pressed a hand to her chest. "I need you." She gestured upwards. "Isabelle needs you. Why do you have to go back there?" She swept a hand towards Ava and Graham. "They're the so-called experts. Send them to the hotel."

"We could go alone," said Ava, "But our chances of success would be far higher with Hugh. Like Graham said, paranormal activity is often triggered by certain people. Someone could live in a house their whole life without experiencing anything unusual. Then someone else moves in and suddenly things start going bump in the night."

"So you're going to use Hugh as bait?" said Louise.

"I'm going to use myself as bait," corrected Hugh.

Louise stared at him as if wondering whether he'd taken leave of his senses.

His eyes pleaded for understanding. "I'm sorry, Louise, but this isn't up for debate. I'm going to Coldwell Hall tomorrow. The rooms are already booked."

Her shoulders sagged under the weight of his words, but she quickly straightened back up. She nodded gravely, like someone accepting an unpleasant but inevitable task. "You're obviously going to do this no matter what, so tell me what I can do to help."

Hugh gave her a smile in which relief mingled with gratitude. "Just support me. That's all."

Ava's gaze traced his outline. "Aww, his aura's gone all fuzzy and pink," she said to Graham. "Isn't love grand?" She laughed as he arched a less than convinced eyebrow.

"Actually, it would be better if Hugh was in a negative emotional state," he pointed out.

"Oh I'm sure he'll be emotional enough to catch the attention of any spirits hanging around the hotel." Ava's heavy-lidded eyes returned to Hugh. "So what's the plan?"

"I've booked us into three rooms. I'm in 'Helen'. You're in 'Nefertiti' and 'Roxelana'."

"Interesting room names," said Graham.

"They were–"

"I know who they are," interrupted Graham, sounding mildly affronted that Hugh might think otherwise.

"Well I haven't got a bloody clue who they are," Ava admitted.

Graham grunted, signalling his lack of surprise. "They were queens renowned for their beauty." His deadpan gaze bored into Hugh. "I take it you're in the room where your father died?"

Hugh nodded. "I've paid for two nights, but we'll stay as long as needs be."

"As long as needs be," Louise echoed, her eyebrows bunching together. "And what if you don't find what you're looking for? What then?"

"Don't worry, we shouldn't need more than a few days," Ava assured her. "And if there's nothing to find, I'll personally give your husband a kick up the arse and send him running back to you."

Louise gave Ava an appraising look, then smiled and nodded as if to say, *Okay, I'll trust you.*

"But we *will* find something," Hugh said determinedly. "And when we do, I'm going to catch it."

"Do you mean catch evidence of it on a recording device?" asked Graham.

"I mean I'm going to expose this thing and clear my mother's name."

Ava's voice softened as if she was talking to a delusional child. "The police wouldn't believe you, no matter how much evidence you had."

Irritated more by her sympathy than her pessimism, Hugh said with a touch of sharpness, "They'll believe me. I'll make them."

Ava directed a look at Graham that asked, *What do you think?*

He tugged at his long beard, seemingly reluctant to commit to an answer.

Ava clapped her hands to dispel any misgivings either of them might have. "Right then, it's all set." She sprang to her feet like a young girl embarking on an adventure. "We'll see you tomorrow at Coldwell Hall."

"Do I need to bring anything in particular with me?"

"No, just yourself." With a wink, Ava added, "And your wallet."

Graham's belly overlapped his belt as he heaved himself out of the armchair. He nodded solemnly at Louise and Hugh before lumbering after Ava towards the hallway. Hugh followed them to the front door. He watched them get into the battered Transit van.

As Graham started up the engine and pulled away, Hugh commented, "What a pair of characters."

"They make me nervous," said Louise, coming up alongside him. She took his hand. "Promise me you'll come back safe."

Looking into her gentle hazel eyes, Hugh lifted his free hand to stroke her hair. "I promise you I'll come back safe."

Louise glanced towards the receding van. "Do you think Ava really has psychic powers?"

"I guess we'll find out soon enough." Hugh leaned in to kiss her lightly on the lips. "I'm going out."

"Where to?"

Hugh's hand dropped to his trouser pocket as if to check

something was there. "To see my dad."

PART 2, CHAPTER 3

The setting sun cast long shadows across the headstones. Hugh's shoes rustled through dry grass as he made his way along a row of graves. Some of the stone slabs were as weathered as the church they surrounded. Others were shiny new and adorned with bouquets of fresh flowers. The rumble of passing traffic dwindled to a murmur as he approached a grey marble headstone whose shape mimicked the church windows. Needles from an overhanging yew tree speckled the headstone. He swept them off with his hands. His gaze descended the inscription.

'In

Loving Memory Of

EDMUND CARVER.

Died 8th August, 1999

Aged 39 Years

A loving Father

Who will be sadly missed

Rest In Peace'

"Rest in peace," Hugh murmured. He heaved a sigh. How was his father supposed to rest in peace when justice hadn't been done? Something Ava had said played through his mind – *Time means nothing to ghosts. They're stuck in a loop, reliving some moment from their life over and over.*

What if his father was stuck in a loop? What if his soul was trapped in Coldwell Hall, re-experiencing the moment the knife plunged into him over and over again?

Shuddering at the thought, Hugh squatted down and rested a hand on the gravestone. "Hello Dad. I'm sorry I haven't been to see you in a while."

Time means nothing to ghosts, Ava's voice reminded him.

"I visited Mum today. She's…" Hugh faltered, unable to bring himself to describe her condition. "She's still not given up. And neither have I."

A murmur of voices drew his attention. An elderly couple were laying flowers on a nearby grave. Hugh closed his eyes, his thoughts travelling back to his dad's funeral. Two things had stayed with him from that day – his mum's absence and his grandparents relentlessly sobbing over their dead son. He remembered desperately wanting to see his mum and tell her, *I believe you*. He'd been denied the chance to do so, at least until he was old enough to visit her. But she'd been denied the chance to ever say her final goodbyes to her husband. So now she, too, was stuck in a loop. Trapped in some timeless zone between life and death.

Hugh's eyes popped open as if he was afraid he might get ensnared in that same space. "I'm going to set you and Mum free," he told the gravestone. "I'm going to give you both peace."

He took a dented tin out of his pocket. A faded picture of a high-backed armchair facing a moonlit window decorated its lid. White lettering outlined with gold read 'Autumn Evening'.

He opened the tin and put it to his nose. A faint maple syrup aroma lingered, although it had been years since the tin contained tobacco. The scent summoned an image of his father with a pipe clasped between his lips.

Hugh smiled, recalling how he'd loved to sit and watch his dad puffing contentedly on a pipeful of Autumn Evening. A spasm of anger wiped the smile off his face. Something had stolen those moments from him.

"I'm going to catch it, Dad." The words hissed through his teeth. "And I'm going to bring it to you."

Hugh dug his fingers into the turf at the base of the gravestone. He pulled up a clump of grass, scooped a handful of soil into the tobacco tin and put the lid back on.

He laid his hand on the cool marble again. "I'll see you soon, Dad."

He lingered a moment as if waiting for a reply. A breeze whispered through the yew. The church bell tolled six times.

With that, Hugh rose and retraced his path through the graves.

PART 2, CHAPTER 4

Louise scrutinised the contents of Hugh's suitcase. "Have you packed socks?"

"I've packed more than enough of everything," he replied a touch testily. From the moment he'd got out of bed, Louise had been fussing around him like an anxious mother hen.

Isabelle skipped into the bedroom, singing tunelessly, "Cats are cool. Cats are great. Cats smell like tuna on toast."

Hugh's face softened into a smile. "What's that you're singing?"

"It's just a silly song I made up." Isabelle gave him a drawing of a black cat with her name written above it. "I made this for you to take with you."

"Thanks, sweetie. I love it." Hugh stooped to kiss Isabelle's head.

She watched him packing clothes into the suitcase. "Where are you going, Daddy?"

"I told you, I have to go away."

"Yes, but where to? How long will you be gone?"

"I haven't got time for this now, Isabelle." Hugh rubbed his bleary eyes. He'd barely slept a wink. All night, his stomach had churned with apprehension and anticipation. Seeing a flicker of hurt cross Isabelle's cherubic face, he added tenderly, "I'm not sure how long I'll be gone, sweetie. Hopefully, it'll only be for a few days."

Pouting at the vague response, Isabelle stood up and dragged her feet from the bedroom.

"She's worried about you," said Louise.

"I know, but there's no need for her to be."

"Isn't there?" Louise reached to feather a fingertip along the worry lines on Hugh's forehead.

"I'm fine," he lied, drawing her hand to his mouth and kissing her knuckles.

"I could come with you," Louise suggested. "My mum can look after Isabelle."

Hugh gave a hard shake of his head. "I don't want you anywhere near that place."

Before Louise could say anything else, he turned to enter their ensuite bathroom. Feeling her gaze on his back, he began putting toiletries into a washbag. He avoided eye contact as he returned to the bedroom, not wanting to waste time on something that wasn't open to discussion.

As he picked up the suitcase, Louise said, "Don't forget this."

She handed him Isabelle's drawing. He smiled. "I'd be in big trouble if I forgot that."

He headed for the stairs, hesitating as he noticed Isabelle peering around her bedroom door. In an attempt to lighten the mood, he stuck his tongue out at her. She returned the favour.

"Be good for your mum," he told her. "I love you. I'll be back soon. I promise."

Without replying, Isabelle slid sulkily out of sight. Heaving a sigh, Hugh descended the stairs. Louise followed him to the front door. He turned to kiss her. Clasping her hands to either side of his face, she held him against her lips. When she drew away, her eyes were shimmering with tears. "I hope you find what you're looking for, Hugh."

Her voice had a cryptic edge that made him wonder what exactly she meant. "All I'm looking for is the truth. I just want to make things right."

Louise pursed her lips as if she doubted that was possible.

Hugh put his suitcase in the boot of his car, then got behind the steering wheel. He briefly looked at the drawing of the cat before folding it up and putting it in the glove compartment. He didn't want to keep seeing it and being reminded of Isabelle. She was the present. He needed to focus on the past.

He reversed out of the driveway and paused to wave.

Smiling, Louise waved back. The instant the car pulled away, though, her smile disappeared.

PART 2, CHAPTER 5

As Hugh travelled north, cotton-ball clouds lazily traversed the sky. Hills rose into view, green and rolling at first, but gradually getting higher and more rugged. Sheep grazed on their slopes. Picture-postcard stone cottages peeked out of wooded valleys.

Everything outside of Hugh was calm, but inside him a storm was raging.

He pulled over and took out a pouch of tobacco and a pipe. After pressing loose tobacco into the pipe's bowl, he put the stem in his mouth. As he held a lighter to the tobacco, its flame licked his fingers. He flinched, then tried again. This time, the tobacco crackled and glowed.

Hugh coughed as the smoke hit the back of his throat. A bitter taste stung his tongue. *Mum's right*, he reflected with a wry smile, *it is a disgusting habit.*

He knew exactly what his dad would have said in response to that – *It takes time to learn how to enjoy a pipe properly, just like with a fine cigar or a good whisky.*

Still puffing away, he resumed driving. The bitterness gradually mellowed to a mild, woody flavour.

The road climbed a range of hills blanketed with purple heather and crowned by rocky outcrops. The clouds darkened and closed ranks, blotting out the sun. Rain pattered on the windscreen. The mere sound of it was enough to flood Hugh's mind with images – water gushing along a road, trees swaying wildly, his mum's frightened eyes…

His own eyes mirroring hers, he sucked on the pipe as if hoping the hot smoke would burn away his nerves.

No, don't fight it, he told himself, recalling what Ava had said about poltergeists being drawn to negative energy. He clenched and unclenched his fingers on the steering wheel, kneading his fear, leavening it with anger.

The road narrowed to a single lane flanked by drystone walls so caked in moss that they looked like natural formations. A stream bubbled alongside the road. Trees trailed their branches in its reddish-tinged water.

Hugh took the pipe out of his mouth. His dad used to say smoking helped him focus, but it was having the opposite effect. He was starting to feel a little faint. He lowered his window, letting out the smoke. As he inhaled the cool, damp air, the light-headedness receded.

The road curved around a sharp bend. As Coldwell Hall came into view, his ten-year-old self piped up from some usually unreachable part of his mind, *It looks creepy.*

Would you rather keep going? he heard his father reply.

Yes! Hugh wanted to shout at the top of his lungs.

The hotel looked as if it had been frozen in time. The amalgamation of Tudor and Georgian architectural styles was even more jarring to Hugh's adult eyes. There was something not simply eccentric, but schizophrenic about the fusion of asymmetrical beams and symmetrical stone blocks. It was like looking at the physical manifestation of a split personality.

His gaze swept over the ivy-clad walls, steeply pitched roof and intricate timber frames, drinking in every detail. As he drew closer, he saw that the passage of time had indeed left its mark. Several top-floor windows were boarded up. The paintwork was cracked and peeling. Weeds speckled the cobblestone path leading to the porch.

For an instant, an image of his dad scuttling along the rain-lashed path overwhelmed Hugh's consciousness. Back then, the hotel's double doors had promised salvation. Now they gave him a shrinking feeling as if he was staring into a pit of unknown depth.

Graham's van was parked in front of the hotel next to a Rolls Royce. The sight of the big silver car tickled Hugh's memory again. Was it the same car as twenty-five years ago? The patchwork of rust eating at the paintwork suggested so. The rain considerately stopped as he pulled up alongside the van. Ava waved at him from its passenger seat. He waved back and noticed his hand was trembling.

As he got out of the car, Ava clambered down from the van. Her knobbly-kneed legs protruded from a revealingly short, off-the-shoulder, pink summer dress. High heels only elevated her to Hugh's chest height.

"Lovely day, isn't it?" she said breezily as the sun poked its face from behind a cloud.

Hugh didn't reply. His throat was so tight he doubted whether he could have got a word out.

Ava's eyes twinkled knowingly. She reached into a crocheted handbag that was slung across her chest and took out a hipflask. She unscrewed its top and put the flask to her bright pink lips. With a slight grimace, she swallowed. "I always work better with a nip of brandy inside me."

You'll see. Ten minutes from now, we'll be sat by a roaring fire sipping brandy.

Hugh almost flinched as, with startling clarity, his dad's voice resurfaced once more. Ava offered him the hipflask. With a grateful smile, he accepted it and threw back a mouthful. He heaved a sigh as the bittersweet brandy burned its way down his throat.

Ava glanced at the pipe smouldering in Hugh's hand. "I

didn't take you for a pipe smoker?"

"I'm not." Hugh lowered his voice, wary of being overheard. "My dad loved his pipe. I thought if I smoked one it would…" He gave an awkward shrug. "I don't know, help me to connect with his spirit."

"Was that his pipe?"

"No. I don't know what happened to his pipe. It wasn't with his belongings that the police returned to us."

"Oh well, it would have been ideal if it was his pipe, but yours could help to attract his spirit." Ava's gaze moved over the hotel's windows as if she was looking for someone. "That is, if his spirit's still here."

"I'd say there's a good chance of that." Graham's deadpan voice came from behind the van. Ill-oiled hinges creaked as he opened its rear doors. "There are countless case studies of murder victims haunting the places where they died and the people that killed them."

"The places yes, but not the people," disputed Ava. "That's mostly just manifestations of guilt."

Graham stepped into view carrying a big rucksack. As he hoisted it onto his shoulders, his belly pushed against what looked to be the same faded black t-shirt and baggy blue jeans he'd worn the previous day. "Mostly," he agreed. "Near Death Experience Research indicates that the majority of disembodied souls don't remember who they were."

"Life is but a dream," Ava said with a chuckle. "Why should we remember it after passing on?"

Graham retrieved a couple of large holdalls from the van. He unzipped one, exposing a jumble of wires and video cameras. He took out a mini voice recorder, pressed a button and spoke into it in his usual monotone. "Coldwell Hall. Day one. August 5th, 2024, 2:15 PM. Equipment check. SLS camera one. Check. SLS camera two. Check…"

Ava rolled her eyes at Hugh. She took another swig from her hipflask and headed for the rear of the van. Hugh tapped the tobacco out of the pipe before pulling the boot lever and retrieving his suitcase.

Ava's miniskirt rode dangerously high up her scrawny thighs as she leaned forwards to grab a small cloth bag from the van.

Taking in her androgynous short hair and flat-chest, Hugh wondered how old she was. She could have been anything between late teens and early thirties. She exuded a sort of naïve sensuality that threatened to bring out the father in him. He resisted an impulse to tell her to change into something less revealing.

"I like to travel light," she said, noticing him looking at her.

"Don't you have any…" Hugh paused for the right words, "clairvoyant equipment?"

Ava's oversized husky laugh burst from her. "You mean like a crystal ball and tarot cards? That stuff's mostly just theatre. Makes the punters feel like they're getting their money's worth." She took a bottle of brandy and a packet of cigarettes from her bag. "These are the only 'equipment' I need."

"EMF recorder. Check. Digital thermometer. Check…" droned on Graham.

Ava let out an impatient groan. "Give it a rest, will you, Graham? I bet you've already checked that junk three times today."

Stonewalling her, he moved on to the other holdall. He took out a black baseball cap and pulled it down over his carrot-orange hair. He looked at his phone. Its screen displayed an image of itself. "SLS camera baseball cap. Check."

"What does SLS stand for?" asked Hugh.

"Structured Light Sensor. It projects thousands of infrared dots that generate 3d images of phenomena invisible to the naked eye."

"I thought infrared only worked in the dark."

Graham exhaled heavily through his nose as if he was dealing with an inept co-worker. "You're thinking of night vision. As I said, infrared measures light that isn't visible."

"Basically, it's an expensive gadget for nerds who get their kicks out of confusing people with big words," put in Ava, drawing a po-faced glance from Graham.

Hugh pointed to the holdalls. "Do you want a hand with those?"

Graham slid him a sidelong look that said, *Don't even think about it.*

Ava chuckled. "Graham's very precious about his toys."

"These 'toys' are highly sensitive."

A *pfft* escaped Ava's lips. "That stuff's about as sensitive as roadkill. It's good for one thing – spying on people."

"I'm not a voyeur." Graham's voice betrayed a trace of indignation.

Grinning at having got under his thick skin, Ava patted his broad back. "I'm only winding you up, Graham. You know I couldn't do this without your technical expertise."

He eyed her as if he suspected she was still having him on. As the clouds began to spit again, he swiftly bent to zip up the holdalls. "I'll finish my equipment check inside."

"You're booked in under your own names," said Hugh. "I'm booked in as Hugh Smith."

Ava laughed. "'Smith'. How original."

Hugh's gaze returned to the hotel. Drawing in a steadying breath, he looked at his hands. With a small measure of satisfaction, he noted that they'd stopped trembling. He extended his suitcase's handle. The wheels juddered over the cobblestones as he started towards the front doors.

Heels clacking like castanets, Ava tottered after him. She eyed the porch's conical roof, which was drooping like a wizard's old hat. "This place could do with a bit of TLC."

"Just a bit," Hugh agreed with dry understatement. Pausing at the double doors, he ran a finger along their chipped paint and weathered wood. "It wasn't like this last time I was here. Back then, it was like the owners had more money than sense."

"Things have obviously changed."

"Maybe no one wanted to stop here after what happened."

"Are you kidding me? Murder hotels are big business." Ava chuckled at the look of distaste on Hugh's face. "It's messed up, I know, but people can't get enough of death, just so long as they're not the ones doing the dying."

The van doors clanged shut. Graham plodded towards the porch, lugging what looked to be about a ton of baggage. He detoured to peer into the circle of stones from which the hotel's faded sign protruded.

"Is it a well?" asked Ava.

"It's a fake well."

Ava turned to the front doors. She closed her eyes, moving her head from side to side and sniffing the air like a bloodhound searching for a scent.

"Do you... sense anything?" Hugh asked.

"No." Ava motioned to the doors. "Shall we?"

PART 2, CHAPTER 6

Sweat seeping out of his palms, Hugh reached slowly for the brass handles. With a sudden movement, he pushed the doors wide open. A faint sooty aroma wafted out of the porch.

"Smells smoky," said Ava.

Hugh shot her a look as her words triggered yet another memory. "That's what my dad said as we went into the hotel." He rubbed his forehead. "Things keep coming back to me that I'd forgotten. I feel like I'm undergoing some kind of regression therapy."

"That's good. Let the memories come. Just don't let them take control."

"It smells like creosote to me," said Graham, his size twelve boots clomping on the flagstone floor as he passed Hugh. "Probably a dirty chimney."

Ava followed Graham, glancing up at a cobwebby chandelier, then over her shoulder at Hugh. Seeing his knotted brows, she offered him a smile. "Do you want another nip of brandy?"

He shook his head and entered the porch. His eyes darted around as if he expected to be assaulted at any moment by an invisible force.

"There's nothing here," Ava assured him. "If I feel anything unusual, you'll be the first to know."

Hugh mustered up a grateful smile. Wide-eyed, he pulled his suitcase into the lobby. Despite the warm weather, a log fire crackled in the marble fireplace. It was just about the only thing that exactly matched the mental image he'd retained of the lobby.

The march of time had stomped as mercilessly over the interior as it had the exterior. Along with the smoky scent, a musty odour of age and damp permeated the air. The once sumptuous furniture was now shabby and threadbare. Dust particles danced in the sunlight seeping between the faded curtains. Above the windows, green-black mould speckled the red silk wallpaper and ornate cornices.

"I bet this place was something to see back in the day," said Ava, her high heels clicking on the scuffed mahogany floor.

Hugh gave a distracted, "Mm," of agreement. More memories were rushing at him. He pointed at the floor. "There was a red carpet here."

"Like for movie stars?"

"Uh-huh."

Ava pouted at Graham like an actress about to step in front of the cameras. "How do I look, darling?"

He exhaled a breath of infinite patience. Ava responded with a laugh that echoed around the high-ceilinged room. Her gaze landed on the portrait that covered most of the chimney breast. "Beauty and the beast."

"Dorothy and Arthur," said Hugh, eyeing the drastically mismatched couple.

As Graham turned in a circle, directing the peak of his hat at every corner of the lobby, Hugh cautioned, "The receptionist's looking at us."

A sleepy-eyed twenty-something with shaggy blonde hair and scruffy stubble was slouched against the countertop, looking as out of place as an old man in a nightclub.

"I shouldn't worry," said Ava. "He looks like he's away with the fairies."

"He's probably stoned," said Graham, sniffing the air. "I smell weed."

As they neared the gold-trimmed counter, the receptionist lethargically drew himself up straight. A badge on his crumpled white shirt identified him as 'Leo'. "Welcome to Coldwell Hall," he said in a thick-tongued drawl that seemed to confirm Graham's suspicion.

Ava flashed him a toothy grin, her chin barely clearing the countertop. "Hi, Leo."

Without returning her smile, Leo gave the guests a bleary-eyed once over. "Do you have a booking?"

"Yes, it's booked under Smith," said Hugh.

"Smith, Smith…" echoed the receptionist, flipping open a dog-eared reservation book. "Oh yeah, here's your booking. Have you been to the hotel before?"

Hugh answered quickly, "No."

"Well it's a bit of a wacky place. The rooms don't have numbers, they have names." Leo turned to retrieve three keys from hooks on the wall and placed them on the countertop. "You're in Helen, Roxelana and Nefertitty."

"You mean Nefertiti," corrected Graham.

Leo shrugged. "Whatever."

"You haven't worked here long, have you, Leo?" Ava said with a giggle.

"A few months."

"And do you like working here?"

"It's alright." Leo pointed to the curved staircase, which had what looked like a mini monorail track attached to one side of it. "You're on the first floor. Turn right at the landing. Oh and a bit of advice. This place is way bigger than it looks from the outside. It's easy to get lost if you go wandering about."

"Don't worry," said Ava. "If I go wandering, I'll leave a trail of breadcrumbs."

Confusion creased Leo's unshaven face. "I wouldn't go making a mess. You'll get in trouble with the owners."

Ava rolled her eyes at her companions as if to say, *Not too bright, this one.* She gave a little start as something brushed against her ankles. Her nose wrinkled as she looked down at a solidly built ginger cat. "And who's this?"

"That's Sy."

Hugh eyed the cat's striped auburn head and white underbelly. Surely this couldn't be the same Sy. Could it? "How old is he?"

"How should I know?" From Leo's terse response, it was evident he was getting irritated at all the questions.

Taking the hint, Hugh picked up the room keys. "Thanks. We'll find our own way to our rooms."

Placing a finger under her nose as if to stop herself from sneezing, Ava retreated from Sy and turned to totter after Hugh and Graham.

"Oh, will you guys be eating with us this evening?" Leo remembered to ask as they started to climb the staircase.

"Yes," replied Hugh.

"What time shall I book you in for?"

"As early as possible," said Graham.

"Is seven-thirty alright?"

Graham gave a nod of confirmation. The stairs creaked like old bones as he lumbered up them.

"That smell's not weed," Ava whispered to him. "It's cat pee."

Sy slunk alongside the barley twist spindles and pushed his

head against Hugh's calves.

Can I stroke him?

The words vibrated through Hugh's mind. He nudged Sy away with a foot. Flicking his tail, the ginger tom turned to go back downstairs.

Slowly, as if weighed down by lead boots, Hugh ascended to the first floor landing. The portraits lining the walls met his gaze with eyes full of longing. Unlike the air of neglect that hung heavy over everything else, the paintings seemed more vibrant than he remembered, as if the undying devotion captured by the artist had somehow staved off time's hand.

Their eyes are following me, a little voice piped up in his head.

Ava glanced at a stairlift chair at the summit of the monorail track. "That looks like fun."

"They must get a lot of old people staying here," remarked Graham.

Ava's gaze shifted to a portrait of a sunken-eyed man. "I think that's what they call a thousand yard stare." She wiped her watering eyes with the back of her hand. "I'm not crying at his sad face. I'm allergic to cats."

"There used to be three of them," said Hugh. "Sy…" he searched his memory and dug up the other two names, "Bel and Yo-yo."

Graham tapped at his phone. "The typical lifespan of a domestic cat ranges from twelve to eighteen years."

"So it's not the same Sy?"

"'A twenty-seven-year-old feline from London has become the world's oldest cat.'," Graham read out.

"Sy would have to be at least twenty-five."

"Maybe he's the oldest cat in the world," said Ava, taking out her hipflask. She knocked back a tot of brandy and let out a loud, *Ahh*. "Best medicine for allergies that there is."

"Has–" Hugh fell silent as a maid who looked even older than the hotel emerged from a room. Carrying a bundle of bedding, she doddered to a trolley loaded with clean sheets. He waited for her to pass, then leaned towards Graham, his voice dropping conspiratorially. "Has your camera picked up anything?"

"Not that I'm aware of, although I can't be certain without properly analysing the footage."

Hugh's questioning gaze shifted to Ava.

"Nothing to report here either," she said, pre-empting him. "Come on, let's get to our rooms. I'm gasping for a cig."

The thin burgundy carpet rustled like dry grass as they progressed along the corridor. As he had done twenty-five years ago, Hugh read out the names engraved on the doors, "Cleopatra, Guinevere, Eve…"

"Antony and Cleopatra. Arthur and Guinevere, Adam and Eve. They're all love stories," said Graham.

"Love stories that don't end well," added Ava. She chuckled. "Mind you, I can't think of many that *do* end well."

"I've never understood the fascination with tragic love stories."

Ava snorted. "That's because you've never been in love. And don't give me any crap about love just being a chemical reaction."

"Well what else is it?"

Ava frowned uncertainly, then jerked her chin at Hugh. "Ask him. He's the one who's married."

Guilt tugged at Hugh as he pictured Louise, her supportive smile juxtaposed with the worry in her eyes. His thoughts turned to his parents, the way they'd used to bicker yet always seemed to end up laughing and embracing. Two more faces came to mind – one as gaunt as a skull, the other as exquisite as a porcelain doll. Arthur and Dorothy Dankworth. "Love is…" he faltered for a heartbeat before adding with a slight shrug, "strange."

Ava smiled crookedly. "Well I could do with a bit of 'strange'." She puffed her cheeks, eyeing the corridor. "Leo wasn't lying. This corridor goes on forever."

"It's the paintings," said Graham. "Judging by the hotel's external dimensions, this corridor's not actually all that long. The paintings make it seem bigger than it is. It's an old trick."

"It's an illusion of depth." Hugh said, recalling his mother's words.

He paused at an arched recess in the wall. A bouquet of wilted flowers was dangling over the edge of a vase. Brown petals littered the sill of the recess. His mum's face materialised in his mind, untouched by the ravages of grief and prison – her eyes like pools of chocolate, her nose a perfect button, high cheekbones curving towards her delicate lips.

"Your name should be on one of these doors," he murmured.

"What did you say?" asked Ava.

"It was just something my dad–" Hugh's voice froze in his throat as a high-pitched wail oscillated along the corridor. "That's it!" he exclaimed. "That's the noise I heard!" He darted forwards, his suitcase bobbing along behind.

The side corridor came into view. He dashed around the corner, fist clenched as if he expected to come face-to-face with his father's killer. Two cats – one midnight-black, the other snow-white – were hunkered down in the middle of the carpet, eyeballing each other from a few metres apart.

The sight of them brought more of his father's words rushing back – *That's what's making that horrible wailing. It's these bloody cats.*

As Hugh came to a sudden stop, the white cat sprang up and shot off like a bullet. The black cat melted away into the gloom of the corridor, moving like a wind-up toy.

Ava wobbled after Hugh, as unsteady as a little girl trying out her mother's high heels. "What was it?"

"Two more cats. They were yowling at each other."

"Was it Bel and Yo-yo?"

"It looked like them. I remember now, Bel was yowling in the same spot last time I was here."

Ava doubled over as a sneeze racked her skinny frame. Pinching her nostrils, she said with a nasal twang, "This isn't a hotel. It's a care home for old cats."

"It's an odd coincidence," observed Graham. "Possibly the same cat, in the same spot, doing the same thing as all those years ago."

"Cats are creatures of habit."

"Yes, but still…"

Ava closed her eyes. She turned her face from side-to-side, tongue poking out like a child concentrating intensely. Hugh watched with a hopeful gleam that faded as she said, "Still nothing." She gave him a vaguely apologetic look. "This place has a funky energy for sure. But I get the sense it has more to do with the owners than any spooky goings on."

"The Dankworths must be well into their sixties by now," said Hugh. "They might not have much to do with the day-to-day running of the hotel."

"Maybe the stairlift is for them."

"Sixty's not that old."

"They might be in poor health." Ava gestured at the worn-out luxury of their surroundings. "Buildings tend to reflect their owners."

"Nefertiti, Roxelana," said Graham, reading the gold lettering on two doors facing each other across the side corridor.

Hugh's face turned several shades paler as, looking at a door on the main corridor, he read out, "Helen." Clutching the room key, he advanced slowly. It rattled against the brass casing as he inserted it into the lock. He grasped the doorhandle. A shiver coursing through him, he pulled back his hand. "It's freezing."

Graham touched the doorhandle. "No it's not."

Ava did likewise. "It's cold, but not unusually so."

Hugh rubbed his clammy hands together in an attempt to warm them up. "Sorry. I'm so bloody jumpy. My nerves are all over the place."

A trace of softness found its way into Ava's husky voice. "Do you want us to come into the room with you?"

Hugh began to nod, but switched to shaking his head. "I think it would be best if I go in on my own." A shudder lifted his shoulders at the prospect.

Ava proffered the hipflask. "Here, this'll warm you up."

Hugh smiled thinly. "I'd love to down the whole lot, but I need to keep a clear head."

He took hold of the doorhandle again. The soft click as he turned it was enough to make him flinch. The door swung open, revealing a silent gloom. As he stepped into the room, though, he seemed to hear a distant echo of his mother's oddly emotionless voice.

It wasn't me. It wasn't me.

PART 2, CHAPTER 7

Hugh closed the door. He stood in semi-darkness, his heartbeat pulsing in his ears. After a moment, as if startled into action, he flung open the curtains. He blinked as sunlight streamed across a dead fly-speckled windowsill. Fidgeting at something in his pocket, he stared at the outside world with eyes like a trapped animal.

He took out the tobacco tin. With a care verging on reverence, he opened it and lifted it to his nose. The maple scent was barely detectable alongside the musty, slightly sour aroma of the soil. Closing his eyes, he inhaled deeply as if trying to draw in the soil's essence.

His eyes snapped open at the sound of an engine sputtering into life. The Rolls Royce reversed away from the hotel. As the car pulled out of the carpark, he glimpsed a cadaverous face behind the steering-wheel.

"Arthur," he murmured. So at least one of the Dankworths was in good enough health to get out and about.

Hugh swept aside the dead flies and placed the open tin on the windowsill. He wandered around the room, absorbing every little detail. As far as he could tell, it was the same furniture – chaise longue, wardrobe, dressing table, armchair – just older and shabbier.

As his gaze came to rest on the four-poster bed, he was transported back in time. His mother's horror-stricken eyes stared at him. Blood was dripping from the blade of the ivory-handled paring knife in her hand. A crimson rose was blooming on the bedsheets. His dad's face was nothing but blood.

Hugh blinked back to the present. He kept his gaze fixed on the bed, like someone forcing themself to look at something unspeakably horrible. After a minute, his gaze fell to the duck egg-blue rug in front of the chaise longue. Was that the same rug he'd bled on after being lifted out of bed and body-slammed by the killer?

His brow wrinkled as a glistening red spot appeared on the rug. It was joined by another and another. He touched a finger to his nostrils. It came away with blood on it.

He sat down on the chaise longue, tilting his head back and pinching the bridge of his nose. A salty taste flooded the back of his mouth. His gaze followed the same route as on the night of the murder, taking in Helen of Troy's portrait, then dropping to the dressing table. There was no fruit, no paring knife, no biscuits, not even a kettle.

The brandy was wearing off, leaving behind a thumping headache. He rose and entered the bathroom. A faint whiff of urine tainted the air. At the chipped and stained marble sink, he washed the blood off his nostrils.

Tell your mother it's true that she's the most beautiful woman in the world.

Hugh glanced over his shoulder at the disembodied whisper of his father's voice. He frowned as his subconscious spat out the reply, *Sure Mum's beautiful, but Mrs Dankworth's really, really beautiful.*

Why had he said that? Why couldn't he have just told his mum what she needed to hear? Would it have made a difference if he had done?

A heavy sigh escaped him as the questions circled his mind. What did the answers matter? They wouldn't bring back his dad. Nothing would. His shoulders sagged, a sense of futility pressing down upon them.

"What the hell am I doing here?"

Hugh frowned at himself in the mirror for asking the question out loud. If anything was listening, he didn't want to give it the satisfaction of knowing he was plagued by such doubts.

Drawing himself up to his full height, he strode back into the bedroom. His eyes sweeping the room, he demanded to know, "Are you here?" He held his breath, waiting for a response. When none came, he continued, "You know who I am, don't you? I'm Hugh Carver. You murdered my father. I don't care what you are – ghost, poltergeist, demon – I'm going to make you pay for what you did. Do you hear me?"

Hugh spread his arms like a boxer trying to taunt an opponent into a reckless attack. "Well? Here I am. Do something." After another brief silence, his lips twisted into an ugly smile. "What's wrong? Why don't you do something? Is it because I'm not afraid of you?"

A slight tremor in Hugh's voice revealed that his claim wasn't entirely true. As too did the way he gave a start at a knock on the door. He squinted through the spyhole before opening the door.

PART 2, CHAPTER 8

Ava greeted Hugh with her usual toothy grin. A fresh coat of pink gloss glistened on her lips. Her eyes were red and puffy as if she'd been crying. Graham loomed over her from behind, baseball cap on head, holdall in hand, po-faced as ever.

Her eyes narrowed as she scrutinised Hugh's pale, tense face. "You tried to call it out, didn't you?"

"I don't know what you mean."

Ava chuckled. "You can't bullshit a bullshitter, Hugh."

He stood aside for her and Graham to enter the room, closed the door behind them, then admitted, "Okay, I called it out."

"And what happened?"

"Nothing."

Ava gave an unsurprised nod. "This thing could be older than this hotel. Hell, it could be thousands of years old. If it's conscious, it's not going to be goaded into revealing itself."

Graham opened his bag and fished out a cylindrical black object about as big as the end of his thumb. "Mini Wi-Fi camera," he informed Hugh. "Night vision. Motion detection. 160-degree audio recording. 300 DPI. That's 100 DPI more than most comparable cameras on the market."

Hugh's face relaxed into a smile. "It sounds like you're talking about your children."

"You need a woman to have children," Ava teased.

"I'm setting up a couple of cameras in all our rooms," said Graham, ignoring her.

Ava gave Hugh a wink. "He's kinky like that."

Graham gazed around the room, homing in on the four-poster bed's sagging silk canopy. The mattress springs squeaked as he stepped onto the bed. He lodged the camera between the canopy and a post, angling it to take in the bathroom and hallway door. The floor trembled as he jumped off the bed and bent to take out another camera.

Ava took off her high-heels. She strolled around so lightly her feet hardly seemed to touch the floor. Her gaze landed on the cluster of vivid crimson specks at the centre of the rug. "They look like fresh bloodstains."

"I had a nosebleed," said Hugh.

"Another odd coincidence," said Graham, exchanging a glance with Ava.

"Did your nosebleed begin before or after you tried to start a fight with thin air?" she asked Hugh.

"Before," he answered.

"Then I'd say it's unlikely you've been punched in the face by an angry ghost." Ava chuckled, clearly amused by the thought of that actually happening.

"It was probably a stress nosebleed," said Graham.

Ava squatted down to lay her palm on the rug. "Is this where you hit the floor?" When Hugh nodded, she pointed to the lefthand side of the bed. "And your dad was lying there?"

Hugh's eyebrows lifted. "How did you know he was on that side of the bed?"

"Men usually sleep closer to the door to protect their partner," said Graham. "It's basic caveman psychology."

"Oh, right."

A smirk played on Ava's lips at Hugh's disappointed tone. "You might want to adjust your expectations, Hugh. Retrocognition isn't one of my talents. I can't magically see into the past or, for that matter, the future."

She turned to meet the blue-eyed gaze of the portrait's subject. "My, my, aren't you a beautiful creature." She rose to look at the brass plaque. "'Her lips suck forth my soul, see where it flies. Come Helen, come, give me my soul again. Here will I dwell, for heaven be in these lips–"

"'And all is dross that is not Helena,'" Graham finished off for her. "It's from Marlow's *Doctor Faustus*."

"Faust? Didn't he sell his soul to the Devil?"

"He made a bargain with Mephistopheles, a demon."

Ava shrugged as if to say, *Same difference*. "All demons serve the Devil."

"What did he get for his soul?" asked Hugh.

"Twenty-four years of unlimited power," said Graham. "He conjures Helen to distract himself from thinking about what will happen when those years are up."

"And what will happen?"

"He'll be dragged to Hell," Ava stated simply. "Same as everyone who makes those kinds of bargains. Once you've signed the contract, there's no going back."

"Do you know anyone who's made a deal with the Devil?"

"No, but I've known people who'd do anything to get what they want. It doesn't matter whether it's knowledge, power, wealth, fame..." Ava paused before adding meaningfully, "or revenge, the Devil will use your desire against you."

Hugh blinked away from her penetrating gaze. He watched Graham balance a second camera on the frame of the hallway door.

Graham glanced at the CCTV image on his phone, checking that the wide-angle lens captured the entire room. He turned his attention to the door itself, opening it and twisting a rectangular brass knob. A metal cylinder slid into view. "It's a heavy-duty tubular, single-sided deadbolt."

"Can it be picked?" asked Ava.

"Not from the hallway. You'd have to saw through the bolt or use a screwdriver to pry it open. There's no way anyone's getting in here without leaving some visible damage." Graham ran his meaty fingers up and down the doorframe. "Not unless there's some secret way of opening the door. A hidden latch or button."

"Are you certain the door was double-locked?" Ava asked Hugh.

He nodded. "I had to unlock both locks to get out of the room." His voice grew distant. "I remember it seemed to take forever." He lifted tormented eyes to Ava. "It was me that told the police the door was double-locked. They used my words to put my mum in prison. I spent a lot of years hating myself for that."

"Good." Seeing Hugh frown, Ava elaborated, "If there's anything around here, it'll definitely pick up on those vibes." She turned to the sash window. "Could someone have got in through the window?" She fiddled with a brass lock fitted just above the lower sash.

Graham moved to her side. "It's a stop lock. You need a key to open it." Noticing the soil-filled tobacco tin, he shared a silent look with Ava.

"Maybe there's a secret passage," she suggested, grinning. "Wouldn't that be exciting?"

Graham made his way around the room, rapping his knuckles on the walls, producing a series of dull thuds. "The walls sound solid."

"I think if there was a secret passage, the police would have found it," said Hugh, his voice tinged with impatience.

Ava bent to sniff the tobacco tin's contents. She peered at him from under overly long fake eyelashes. "Do you know what necroleachate is?"

"No."

"When a body decomposes, it turns into a nasty, gooey mess. It doesn't matter how well made a coffin is, the goo eventually leaks into the soil. It has a sort of salty smell that makes my nose tingle."

"That soil's from my dad's grave."

"And you think it will lure in his spirit?"

"I was thinking more about the ghost that murdered him. Do you think it could work?"

Ava gave a noncommittal shrug. She frowned at Graham as he said, "It's worth a try. People all over the world use Spirit Traps to get rid of unwanted spirits. In Thailand, they trap them in clay pots and throw them into–" Noticing Ava's disapproving stare, he fell silent.

Her gaze returned to Hugh. "What if you do capture your dad's killer? How do you think your prisoner's going to feel?"

Anger seeped into his voice. "I hope it feels how my mum felt when she was arrested." His eyes darting around the room, he spoke to the empty air. "That's right, I'm going to imprison you and make you suffer like my mum's suffered."

Ava shook her head, clearly not convinced that was a good idea. "You're playing with fire, Hugh."

"Don't waste your time pretending to care about me, Ava. Just do what I'm paying you for. That's all I want from you."

"Okay." There was no trace of offence in her tone. "But don't say I didn't warn you."

After a brief silence, Hugh asked, "So what's next?"

"I suppose I'd better find out if there's anyone other than us three in the room." Ava approached the chaise longue. She reached into her shallow cleavage and withdrew a bronze medallion.

"What's that?"

"It's a Saint Benedict Medal." Ava showed Hugh the medallion. On one side was a cross. On the other, a bearded figure in flowing robes was carrying a crucifix and an open book. 'V R S N S M V - S M Q L I V B' was inscribed into the medal's rim.

"Catholics call it the devil-chasing medal," said Graham.

Ava's voice filled the room as she proclaimed dramatically, "Vade retro Satana! Numquam suade mihi vana! Sunt mala quae libas. Ipse venena bibas!"

"Begone Satan," Graham translated. "Never tempt me with your vanities. What you offer me is evil. Drink the poison yourself."

"I thought you weren't religious," Hugh said to Ava.

"Better safe than sorry," she replied with a grin and a wink. She lay down on the chaise longue, folding her arms across her chest.

Graham beckoned Hugh over and whispered, "Whatever happens, don't disturb her."

Slowly, ever so slowly, Ava's eyelids drooped so low that she looked like she was about to snooze off. Her belly rose and fell. Up, down, up, down. As steady as a sleeping baby's.

The air seemed to thicken. Hugh could almost feel it pressing against him. Was it simply anticipation? Or was something else at work?

Graham's gaze shifted between Ava and the camera images being fed to his phone. Multiple white dots connected by green lines mapped out a 3D stick-figure image of her. Satisfied the camera was working properly, he took out what looked like a handheld radio, plugged in a set of headphones, put them on and pressed a button marked 'REC'.

"Coldwell Hall, Day one, 3:32 PM, first attempt at contact," he murmured into the device.

A shudder passed through Hugh. "Is it getting colder in here?"

"Not that I've noticed," said Graham. "You're probably just nervous. Anxiety causes your blood flow to become irregular and gives you the chills."

"I don't think it's me this time. The air feels strange–"

"Shh," cut in Graham, pointing to Ava.

Her breathing was quickening. Her fingers were twitching against the Saint Benedict Medal. "545854585458..."

The jumble of numbers streamed from her lips so quickly and quietly that Hugh moved closer to catch what she was saying.

Graham put a hand on Hugh's shoulder and drew him backwards.

"5458," Ava whispered one last time before lapsing into silence. Her breathing returned to normal. Her eyelids flickered apart. Like someone waking from a deep sleep, she sat up yawning and blinking.

"What does it mean?" Hugh asked eagerly.

Ava shrugged. "It was just gobbledygook coming out of the ether. I didn't feel a presence." She looked enquiringly at Graham.

"The cameras didn't pick anything up," he told her.

Hugh pointed to the handheld recording device. "Play it back."

Graham scrolled through timestamps of sounds on the device's screen, then pressed 'PLAY'. Ava's voice emerged through a faint hiss of static. He wrote the string of numbers on a notepad, tore out the page and gave it to Hugh.

"5458," read out Hugh, his eyebrows pinching together. "Five thousand four hundred and fifty eight."

"That's about how much I owe on my credit cards," said Ava. She stood up, stretching and arching her back like a cat.

"Where are you going?" Hugh asked as she headed for the hallway door.

"I'm going for a lie down."

"But we've only just started. Aren't you going to try again?"

Ava spoke through a yawn. "Later." As she opened the door, she rubbed irritably at her nose. "This place is playing hell with my sinuses."

"Expending even a small amount of psychic energy is extremely tiring," Graham explained to Hugh as Ava turned from view. "Some mediums will sleep for days after a seance."

Hugh threw up his hands in exasperation. "I haven't got days."

As Graham set about packing away his gear and lugging it from the room, Hugh's gaze returned to the numbers. He murmured them to himself over and over, as if he was trying to solve a mathematical problem.

PART 2, CHAPTER 9

Hugh lay down on the bed. As his head touched the pillow, his mind conjured up an image of a knife plunging towards his face. With a flinch, he swiftly rose and moved to the chaise longue. He stared at the sequence of numbers again. Counting through the alphabet, he replaced the numbers with their corresponding letters. "E D E H."

"Ed, Ed, Ed," he murmured as if gently summoning his father.

Grief pricked at him. With a shake of his head, he pushed the feeling deep down into himself. Anger, hate – those were the emotions he needed to fuel his determination.

"Dad," he said, tentatively probing the air with his voice. "Are you there?"

He held his breath for a few heartbeats, then tried again. "Dad, speak to me. Say my name. Or just knock on something."

More breathless seconds passed. Nothing. The room seemed almost obstinately silent. Hugh opened his eyes, scrutinised the numbers for a moment more, then put the page in his pocket and rose to head for the hallway.

After closing the door behind himself, he glanced from side to side, unsure which way to go. His gaze came to rest on the side corridor where the cats had been yowling at each other. He set off in that direction, his footfalls resonating like a pulse on the threadbare carpet.

He passed 'Nefertiti' and 'Roxelana'. Heavy metal music

thumped faintly behind one door. A whiff of cigarette smoke emanated from the other.

The corridor continued past several more doors. Silence was the only thing that seemed to occupy the rooms they led to. Hugh wondered whether there were any other guests. A few strides further on, his question was answered. A smartly dressed old lady emerged from a room. She smiled at Hugh, leaning on a walking stick as she hobbled by.

He smiled back and watched her shuffling off the way he'd come.

At the end of the corridor, a heavy 'Fire Escape' door opened onto a narrow staircase. A grimy window overlooked overgrown lawns crisscrossed by weed-ridden footpaths. The flowerbeds were a rainbow of ragged old rosebushes.

Hugh cocked his head at the sound of singing from above. The warbling voice was too muffled to decipher. He ascended the stairs towards it.

The echoing wooden staircase led to another fire door. Beyond it was a door-lined hallway – 'Marilyn', 'Lucrezia', 'Nzinga'... Some of the names on the doors were familiar to Hugh, others not. Yet more men stared desperately out of oil paintings, like souls imprisoned in eternal longing.

The shrill singing started up again, closer now, yet still too distant to make out all but the occasional word. "Memory... Fade..."

A door opened. Another well-dressed lady with permed grey hair and a deeply wrinkled face stepped into view. As if summoned by the singing, she turned her back to Hugh and set off at a sprightly pace. He followed her, keeping a polite distance. The hallway intersected with a broader corridor, forming a T-junction. The second floor's layout appeared to mirror that of the floor below. The old lady turned right towards the main staircase.

"Desire turned to…"

The snatches of song drew Hugh rightwards too. The voice was becoming fainter. Its owner seemed to be on the move. He quickened his footsteps, head twisting from side to side as he took in the names on the doors – 'Sappho', 'Grace, 'Diana'…

"Poison… My veins… All alone…"

Alone, alone… The word echoed away into silence.

Yet another elderly woman came out of a room. Was she the singer? The wheezing that emanated from her as she set off towards the staircase suggested not.

Hugh trailed after her, wondering if the hotel was running some sort of special offer for OAPs. Every twenty or so metres, she paused to catch her breath. It seemed to take an age to reach the staircase. A couple of well-to-do looking old ladies emerged from the mock-Tudor side of the building.

A stairlift chair glided into view from above, its motor whirring gently. The plum-pudding-shaped lady strapped into it was grinning like a child on a fairground ride. "Hello, Barbara," she called to one of the other women.

"Hello Ellie."

"I see her majesty's up and about."

A murmur of voices drifted up from below. Eyes to the steps, taking care with their footing, the ladies descended the staircase. Wondering who 'her majesty' was, Hugh followed them to the first floor landing, where they were joined by yet more of their ilk. The scent of perfume and rouge hung heavy in the air, masking the sour odour Ava had blamed on the cats.

Perhaps it wasn't the cats, reflected Hugh. Perhaps it was the smell of old people. His Adam's apple bobbed as he thought about the greasy, weirdly fruity aroma that had seemed to seep out of his mother's pores.

A steady stream of slow-moving figures were making their

way down to the lobby and filing into the dining room. The shaggy-haired receptionist was leaning chin-on-hand, staring vacantly out of the front windows. Leo looked as if he was daydreaming about being anywhere but there.

As Hugh approached the reception desk, Leo was joined by a doughy-faced young man with a limp ponytail and a nose ring. A name badge identified him as 'Tim'.

"Hey, Leo, what has ninety balls and screws old women?" Tim asked in a couldn't-care-less loud voice.

Leo shrugged uninterestedly.

"A bingo machine!" Tim announced before bursting into laughter.

Leo exhaled a bored breath. He slowly straightened up as Hugh arrived at the counter. Tim tugged at his nose ring, eyeing Hugh sullenly.

Pushing out a smile, Hugh motioned to the women. "What's that about?"

"Bingo," replied Leo. "It's on every afternoon."

"Every afternoon? You must get a lot of OAPs staying here."

"They're not staying here," said Tim. "They live here."

"What? You mean like the hotel doubles as a care home?"

Tim nodded. "Basically, yeah. Although not for much longer if things keep on the way they have been doing. The greyheads are dying off by the day. Two croaked last week."

Leo elbowed his colleague in the ribs. "Shut up, Tim. You'll get us in trouble."

Tim returned the favour. "So what? Who cares? We'll be out of a job soon enough anyway."

"Really? Why's that?" asked Hugh.

"Cos they're going to knock half of this dump down and renovate what's left into holiday apartments for rich southerners." A thick strain of bitterness permeated Tim's nasal northern voice.

"Knock it down," Hugh murmured, his eyes briefly drifting away from Tim to the room. "When?"

"Depends how long it takes for the all the greyheads to die."

"It would have been sold years ago but for them," said Leo.

Tim grinned at Hugh as if he was about to tell another joke. "Do you want to buy some bingo cards? They're a quid each."

A smile pulled at one corner of Hugh's lips. "I think I'll give the bingo a miss, thanks."

As the dining room doors swung shut behind the last of the bingo players, a trilling voice struck up from beyond them. "Mirror, mirror on the wall, who in this hotel is fairest of all?" it belted out, crackling with what sounded like feedback.

"Oh Jesus," groaned Tim. "Her majesty's on the mic again." He dodged aside laughing as Leo attempted to elbow him.

More of the high-pitched singing penetrated the doors. "Golden hair, flawless skin…"

Like a sailor lured by a siren song, Hugh approached the dining room.

"… she walks like a goddess, eyes all aglow."

The soprano voice vibrated in Hugh's ears as he opened the doors. The hotel's elderly inhabitants were seated at the circular tables or queueing at a sideboard laden with biscuits and bookended by big steel urns. A snake with a black underside and a red crest on its head stared down at them from amongst the foliage of the ceiling fresco as if seeking a victim to bite.

Hugh's eyes homed in on a figure occupying a small stage at the opposite side of the room. The slim, buxom woman was draped in a silky blue dress. Her long legs tottered back and forth on stiletto heels. Her bony fingers clutched a microphone wired to a speaker.

"Is she the most beautiful of them all?" The singer's voice rose an octave as she noticed Hugh looking at her. Her Goldilocks-curls swaying, she threw back her head and gave it everything she had. "Every head turns towards her. They all want to know."

Hugh weaved his way between the tables, passing a grand piano with a 'Do not use. Out of order' sign on its dusty black lid. Not breaking eye contact with him, the singer descended several steps to the parquet floor. Her movements graceful, if a touch unsteady, she approached him. He stopped at an empty table with a ripe red apple depicted on the ceiling above it. Likewise, his gaze never left the singer as he pulled out a chair and sat down.

As she drew near, the singer's long eyelashes fluttered like a butterfly's wings. Her watery, yet piercingly blue eyes gazed at Hugh like he was a long-lost love. The trio of cats emerged from under a neighbouring table and slunk around her ankles. Layer upon layer of makeup rendered her face oddly immobile. But no amount of foundation, eye shadow or blusher could entirely conceal the deep lines around her lips and at the corners of her eyes. A turkey-skin neck was visible through a sheer chiffon scarf. Voice falling to a honeyed murmur, she stooped towards Hugh. "He looked at me and my heart leapt up to the sky."

A powerful floral perfume swirled up his nostrils. As the singer moved ever closer, he had a sudden thought that she would try to steal a kiss. He resisted an impulse to pull away as she crooned, "A feeling so powerful, I thought I would die. The memory still haunts me, the pain won't fade. I thought I had his heart. I thought I had his–"

A strident voice cut into the song, "Dorothy!"

The singer gave a start, dropping the microphone onto Hugh's lap. In the blink of an eye, the cats vanished under nearby tables. As wide-eyed as a startled fawn, Dorothy straightened and retreated towards the stage.

Hugh turned to see a lanky figure striding towards him. Arthur Dankworth moved like a robot whose joints needed oiling. His pendulous hands swung at his sides as he goosestepped across the room.

Slurping tea from china cups, the old ladies watched proceedings as avidly as a theatre audience.

Hugh looked Arthur up and down. Although tall, the hotelier wasn't as towering as Hugh had expected. Had age shrunk Arthur or was it simply a matter of perception? Overlong tweed trousers and a baggy matching jacket appeared to point to the former possibility.

Arthur held out a hand to Hugh. Hugh eyed thick, knobbly fingers and dinner plate-sized palms that were grotesquely disproportionate to the thin wrists they were attached to. Arthur's hands certainly hadn't shrunk. If anything, they were even bigger than Hugh remembered.

Murderer's hands.

As his mother's voice reached out of the past, Hugh found himself visualising those huge hands locked on his throat. His unease was heightened by what appeared to be a flicker of hostility in Arthur's close-set eyes. Wondering if he'd done something to offend him, Hugh somewhat tentatively reached to shake his hand. Before he could do so, Arthur said brusquely, "The microphone."

"Oh right." Hugh passed him the microphone.

Arthur glowered down at him for a brief moment more, his pencil moustache almost visibly bristling. Without so much as a nod of thanks, he turned on his heel to approach the stage. His footsteps rapped on the floor as he marched towards his wife. Dorothy shrunk away from him, seemingly afraid he would lash out. He spoke to her in a voice too low to be heard.

Pouting like a scolded child, she flounced offstage.

Arthur approached a wire sphere half-full of what looked like ping-pong balls. The sphere rotated as he briskly wound a handle. He put a hand through a hole in its side and plucked out a ball. His dour voice rang out, "Two fat ladies, eighty-eight."

Markers at the ready, the old ladies pored over their bingo cards.

With the cats slinking after her, Dorothy stormed out of a door at the side of the stage. Hugh wracked his brain for what he could recall about the Dankworths. A vague memory prickled his scalp of Dorothy issuing commands and Arthur jumping to it. The balance of power in their marriage had obviously shifted.

The Dorothy of twenty-five years ago – the poised, elegant Dorothy that he'd thought was the most beautiful woman in the world – appeared to be a thing of the past. This Dorothy seemed like a cruel parody of her former self. Of all the things in the hotel that time had taken its toll on, she'd apparently suffered the most. He couldn't help but feel a twinge of sadness at the loss.

"Twenty-seven, gateway to Heaven," called out Arthur.

Hugh's gaze drifted away from the stage to what he judged to be the chair where his father had sat. He stared at the empty seat for a while before rising and heading for the double doors.

"Get up and run, thirty-one," Arthur shouted as if hurling an insult after him.

The spring-loaded doors closed behind Hugh, muffling Arthur's voice. Leo and Tim were chatting idly. They fell silent, eyeing Hugh as he passed by. He gave them a small smile. As he climbed the stairs, the pair of them burst into laughter.

"Bingo!" a voice cried out in the dining room.

Feeling the eyes of the portraits following him along the hallway, Hugh sang softly to himself, "The memory still haunt me. The pain won't fade…"

PART 2, CHAPTER 10

"5458… EDEH…" Hugh repeated like a mantra, staring blankly at the bed's silk canopy. What did it mean? He took out his phone and speed-dialled 'Louise'.

Her soothingly accentless voice came through the earpiece. "Hello there. I was wondering when you'd call. How's it going?"

"I think my dad might be here."

"Really?" Louise sounded more concerned than surprised. "What makes you think that?"

Hugh told her about the 'gobbledygook' that had come 'out of the ether'. "Surely it can't be a coincidence."

"You're probably right."

"So you think my dad's trying to…" Hugh sought for the right word, "*contact* me?"

Louise's silence hinted at an alternate explanation.

"Oh I get it." There was a slight needle in Hugh's tone. "You think Ava's playing me."

"I honestly don't know what to think, Hugh. Has Ava felt or found anything else?"

"No. None of us have." Hugh's gaze travelled from the frayed canopy to the damp-stained wallpaper. "Unless you count damp and dust."

"Sounds like the hotel's on its last legs."

"Yeah, almost literally. They're going to knock it down."

"Oh wow. When?"

Hugh frowned faintly. Did he detect a hopeful note in Louise's voice? "I don't know." He sighed into the phone, thinking once again but not saying out loud, *What am I doing here?*

"You sound fed up. Why don't you come home?"

Louise's urging tone tugged at Hugh's heartstrings. "I only just got here."

"So what?" The urging turned into pleading. "Come home, Hugh. Isabelle keeps asking where you are. I told her you're on a work trip, but I can tell she doesn't believe me."

Hugh smiled. "She's a hell of a lot more switched on than I was at her age."

"Do you want to speak to her?"

"No." Hugh fired the word at Louise as if she'd asked him whether he wanted a slap around the face. He added a touch apologetically, "What I mean is, I want to speak to her, but…"

"But what?"

If she asks me to come home, I'm not sure I'll be able to say no, Hugh answered in his mind, afraid that merely voicing the thought would weaken his resolve. He sat up at a knock on the door, relieved for an excuse to get off the phone. "Someone's at the door. I've got to go."

"Call me later, will you?"

"Mm-hmm. Bye."

"Love you," Louise said as Hugh hung-up.

He unlocked the deadlock and turned the handle. Even before he opened the door, an overpowering perfume told him who was on the other side of it. Dorothy's crimson lips curved into a smile at the sight of him, revealing faintly yellowed teeth. She'd changed into a flowing satin dress that matched her lipstick. A fresh coat of makeup had transformed her into a ghostly vision of white powder and thick mascara.

"I'm Dorothy Dankworth, the owner of this establishment," she informed him, batting her eyelashes. "I just wanted to check that the room is to your liking."

Hugh returned her smile. "It's fine, thanks."

"I'm glad to hear it." Dorothy's gaze glided up and down him, lingering on the gold band encircling his ring finger. "Where's Mrs Smith?"

Who? Hugh almost asked. He checked himself and answered, "She's at home with our daughter."

Dorothy peered past him as if making sure he was alone. "So you're here on what? Business? Pleasure?"

"Business."

Suddenly aware of his father's tobacco tin on the windowsill, Hugh sidestepped to block Dorothy's line of sight. His mind flashed back to her picking up the tin and sniffing it. Her sultry voice seemed to murmur in his ear, *It smells like autumn.*

Not for the first time, Hugh wondered whether his father had encountered Dorothy whilst retrieving the tin from the dining room. He stared at her as if trying to see into her mind.

Seemingly revelling in the intensity of his gaze, Dorothy took a breath that swelled her breasts against her dress. "I'll leave you to your business then, Mr Smith. If you need anything..." she paused suggestively before going on, "anything at all, don't hesitate to ask."

With that, she turned away and glided along the corridor, her skirt trailing like a bridal train. Even after she'd disappeared from view, Hugh remained where he was, as if her glacier-blue eyes had frozen him to the floor.

PART 2, CHAPTER 11

"You look like you've seen a ghost."

Hugh gave a slight start at Ava's wry remark. She and Graham were approaching from the opposite direction to Dorothy. Ava's bloodshot eyes made it look like she was suffering the consequences of a wild night out. Graham was focused on his phone, its backlight palely illuminating his round face.

"Dorothy Dankworth just paid me a visit," said Hugh.

"What did she want?"

"She wanted to know if everything was okay with my room."

Ava arched an eyebrow. "She hasn't knocked on my door."

"Mine neither," Graham said, without looking up from his phone.

A teasing chuckle slipped past Ava's lips. "Sounds like she's sweet on you. I'd watch out, if I were you, she looks like a proper maneater."

"You've seen her?" said Hugh.

"We've been exploring the hotel. She was up on the top floor. I didn't recognise her at first, what with all the wrinkles. Time really is a bitch. And so's Dorothy. She walked straight past us like we didn't exist. She smells of cats." Ava rubbed her eyes. "She set my allergy off something rotten."

Hugh ushered her and Graham into his room and shut the door. "Did you find anything else up there?"

"Cobwebs," said Ava. "Loads of them."

"And Tegenaria Domestica," added Graham, plonking himself down on the edge of the bed.

"Tegen-what?" asked Hugh.

"House spiders."

Ava made a C with her thumb and index finger. "The biggest, fattest ones I've ever seen."

She went into the bathroom and splashed water on her eyes. Hugh peered down at Graham's phone. Its screen displayed footage of a corridor lined with portraits and peeling wallpaper. A troupe of luminous green stick figures about three-foot tall appeared to be dancing maniacally along the righthand wall.

"What's that?" asked Hugh.

"It's footage from the top floor. It could be the spirits of children."

"Or dancing dwarves," chuckled Ava. She returned to the bedroom, dabbing her eyes with a towel.

Graham gave her an unamused glance. "Most likely, it's just the wallpaper patterns messing with the lasers." Looking at Hugh, he added, "The technology's glitchy. The 3D lasers are designed to home in on body joints – elbows, knees, etcetera. But they can be confused by patterns on surfaces, especially if the camera's being moved around. Then you get these little humanoids jumping around like madmen."

The bundles of gyrating sticks came to a stop at door inscribed with 'Salome'.

Holding the towel over the lower half of her face, Ava danced back and forth, swaying her non-existent hips.

Graham rolled his eyes. "What's that? The dance of the one towel?"

Ava swirled the towel around in front of him. "Haven't you heard of artistic licence?" She twirled to the chaise longue and flopped onto it. "So shall we find out if there's anyone around to have a chat with?"

Like an off switch had been flipped inside her, a sudden stillness descended over Ava. As her heavy eyelids drooped lower, Graham took out his handheld audio recorder and headphones. "Coldwell Hall, Day one, 7:06 PM, second attempt at contact."

Ava stroked the Saint Benedict Medal whilst taking belly breaths. "Close your eyes."

"Do you mean me?" asked Hugh.

"Uh-huh." As he did as Ava said, she whispered, "Take deep breaths. In through your nose. Out through your mouth. I want you to think of your dad. Picture his face. Can you see him?"

Hugh pictured his dad the only way he could – wet hair combed back, face tanned from a week of exploring St. Bees Head, pipe clasped in his teeth. "I see him."

"Hold on to that picture. Now think of something your dad used to say to you. Something that made you feel good. Can you hear his voice?"

Sleep tight, matey.

As his dad's voice came through faintly but clearly, Hugh felt a flutter of sadness. "Yes."

"Hold on to that memory. Hold on to his face. Hold on to his voice."

After an extended silence, a tremor ran through Ava's skinny frame. "I'm picking up some vibrations." She suddenly threw her arms wide and her voice boomed out, "Edmund Carver? Ed?"

Resisting an urge to open his eyes, Hugh focused as hard as

he could on his father's face and voice.

Sleep tight, matey, sleep tight...

Tears pricked his eyes. The sadness was intensifying, filling every part of him, pushing out everything else. The memory began to slip from his grasp.

Another moment of silence passed, then Ava said, "It's gone."

Hugh opened his eyes. Ava did likewise and sat up, yawning.

"Was he here?" Hugh asked, blinking back the tears.

"It's hard to say."

"You felt something, though."

Ava touched her solar plexus. "When you open yourself up to the other side, you almost always feel or hear something. But often it's just static. Like touching an old television or listening to an out of tune radio."

She glanced enquiringly at Graham. He shook his head. "I got nothing."

With a frustrated click of his tongue, Hugh approached a high-backed armchair and dropped heavily onto it. The frayed padding sent up a puff of dust. He rested his head against the backrest and stared off into space.

An audible grumble emanated from Graham's stomach. "I'm hungry."

"You're always hungry," said Ava. "What time is it?"

Graham glanced at his wristwatch. "It's almost half-seven."

Ava rose to her feet. "Come on then. Let's go see what kind of food they serve up in this place."

"From what I've seen, they probably serve up the same sort of slop as my mum's hospital ward," said Hugh.

As he stood up, something white caught his eye. Rising onto tiptoes, he plucked a small feather from a corner of the bed's canopy.

"Let me see that," said Ava. She ran a fingertip along the fluffy feather. "It looks like a goose feather."

"Could be a message," said Graham.

"A message?" echoed Hugh. "How do you mean?"

"Many spiritualists believe a white feather is a sign from a deceased loved one."

"When feathers appear, angels are near," said Ava. "That's what my grandma used to say whenever she found a white feather."

"So my dad *is* here?" Hugh's voice conveyed awe and unease in equal measure.

Graham pulled the pillowcase off one of the pillows. He plucked several identical feathers from the lumpy grey pillow. "Or maybe it just means the Dankworths need to invest in some new pillows."

"First my dad's name comes 'out of the ether'." Hugh held up the feather like a barrister showing evidence. "Now this. And you two still think it might be a coincidence?"

"Who said anything about your dad's name?" asked Ava.

"He's talking about the numbers – 5458," said Graham. "The corresponding letters in the alphabet are EDEH."

Ava pushed her lips out in thought. "What do the E and H stand for?"

"I don't know," said Hugh. His eyes travelled the room before returning to Ava. "But I'm sure it was my dad's presence you felt."

"Maybe it was, maybe it wasn't. Look, if you want, I can make up some rubbish about your dad watching over you from the other side. *Is* that what you want?"

Hugh was silent for a moment, seemingly considering the

offer, then he sighed and shook his head.

Ava patted her tummy. "All this talk is making me hungry too." She hooked an arm through Hugh's. "Let's go get some food inside us."

He resisted her pull. "I think I'll give dinner a miss."

With a motherly firmness, Ava said, "No you won't. Ghost hunting's a tiring business. You need to keep your strength up." She drew Hugh from the room, pronouncing cheerily, "Everything looks better on a full stomach. That's something else my grandma used to say."

PART 2, CHAPTER 12

Hugh watched with a mixture of amusement and amazement as Ava demolished a third helping of Cottage Pie. She washed down the gooey mashed potato and minced beef with a mouthful of lager, burped loudly and wiped her mouth with the back of her hand.

Hugh laughed. "I think you might be possessed by a Viking ghost."

"Ghosts don't possess people," Graham pointed out in his usual matter-of-fact way. "Demons do."

Ava's gaze swept over a sea of permed grey hair that shimmered in the soft glow of the chandeliers. Impeccably dressed old ladies were moving back and forth from the tables to the buffet trolley. To a soundtrack of silverware clinking against china, their seated companions worked their way through hearty helpings of Cottage Pie and overcooked vegetables.

"I bet I could make a fortune from this lot," said Ava. She beckoned to a pony-tailed figure slouching against a marble pillar. Tim dawdled over to the table, fiddling with his nose ring. Ava handed him her pint glass. "Fill that up, will you?"

He wordlessly turned to head for a door adorned with gold lettering that read 'BARROOM'. Ava eyed his bum speculatively. "Not bad."

Hugh laughed again. "You can do a lot better than him."

"Yeah well, beggars can't be choosers."

Graham prodded a biro at a paper serviette he'd been writing on for the past few minutes. "Heed. That's the only four letter word I can make out of EDEH."

"Heed," Hugh repeated, directing a pointed look at Ava. "Take notice."

Sweeping the air with her hands, she said dramatically, "Wherefore let him that thinketh he standeth, take heed lest he fall.

"What's that from?"

"The Bible. It means you need to be on guard not just against others, but against yourself."

As she was speaking, the double doors opened and Arthur entered the room.

"Evening, Mr Dankworth," chorused several of the elderly diners.

"Good evening, ladies," he replied as solemnly as if he were addressing mourners at a funeral.

Hugh watched Arthur stride towards the buffet trolley. Bending stiffly at the waist, the hotelier inspected what remained of the food. His bald head gleamed under the lights like a polished egg.

Ava chuckled. "Talk about punching above your weight."

Catching on to her meaning, Hugh said, "When I was ten, I thought Dorothy was the most beautiful woman I'd ever seen. What could a woman like that possibly see in a man like him?"

"Hmm, yes it's a mystery," Graham said dryly, glancing at the faded grandeur of their surroundings.

Ava let out a loud burst of laughter. "You're such a cynic, Graham. You'll never find love with an attitude like that."

"Okay, so she's a gold-digger," said Hugh. "But if that's all she is, why has she stayed with her husband even though his money appears to have run out?"

"Probably because by the time she'd sucked him dry, her looks were going the same way as this place," said Ava.

Graham let out a low *humph.* "Who's the cynic now?"

"I'm only telling it how it is."

Tim returned with a fresh pint of lager. Ava flashed him a grin and a wink. "Thanks, Tim."

Wrinkling one side of his nose, he slouched away. Upon catching sight of Arthur, he quickly straightened up and made a show of clearing used crockery from a table.

Ava turned her grin towards Graham. "I think I might be in there."

With a patient sigh, he resumed studying the numbers and letters on his serviette.

Hugh swallowed the last of his red wine, knowing he would need its help to get to sleep. "I'm going to I'll call it a night."

Ava looked at him as if he'd declared sex was overrated. "It's not even nine o'clock." She motioned to their fellow diners. "Are you seriously going to beat them to bed?"

"Looks like it."

As Hugh pushed back his chair, Ava flinched and whipped up the hem of the tablecloth. A pair of gleaming green eyes peered up at her from under the table. "Go away," she hissed at their sleek black owner.

With a derisive swish of its tail, the cat strolled over to a neighbouring table. Yowling plaintively, it pawed at the leg of a waxy-faced woman who'd barely touched her food. She held out a morsel of minced beef in her trembling palm. "There you go, Bel." Her voice was devoid of energy. The cat's little pink tongue darted out to lick off the gravy.

Ava's lips curled downwards in disgust. She downed her pint

like a thirsty workman. "Let's get a drink in the bar." She glanced at Hugh. "I'll put it on your room tab."

He watched her totter towards the barroom. As Graham rose to follow her, he asked Hugh, "What year was your dad born?"

"Nineteen sixty. Why?"

"It could be a date of birth. Fifth of the fourth of fifty eight."

Hugh did a quick mental calculation. "Sixty six. That's how old someone born in April of that year would be now. My mum's sixty."

Without moving his head, Graham slid Arthur a look. "I wonder how old he is?"

Hugh's voice dropped to a whisper. "Why would he have killed my dad?"

"Take heed and beware of covetousness." Graham's voice was portentously flat. "That's also from The Bible."

With that, he turned and lumbered towards the barroom.

PART 2, CHAPTER 13

Hugh climbed the central staircase to the top floor. A musty odour clung to the floral damask wallpaper of the hallways that branched out from the landing. The ever-watchful portraits gazed at him from their gilded frames.

He made his way along the dimly lit righthand corridor. Twisting his head from side to side, he read out the names on the doors, "Audry, Delilah…"

By the time he reached the side corridor, the gloom was deep enough to make him switch on his phone's torch. 'Salome' was etched on the first door past the corridor.

Hugh's gaze traversed the wall where the bundles of fluorescent sticks had danced wildly on Graham's footage. He placed a palm on the wallpaper. It had a cold, tacky feel. He pressed an ear to the door. The room beyond was as silent as a morgue. He tried the handle. Locked. He curled one hand into a fist. His knuckles hovered in front of the door for several seconds before he knocked on it. The noise seemed jarringly loud in the silence.

A few more seconds passed. No one came to the door.

He returned to the first floor. An air of tranquillity hung over the hotel. A feeling of being far away from the world. It wasn't hard to imagine why someone might want to spend their last few years here. Even with the creeping disrepair, it had to be better than withering away in some sterile care home. A wry smile flickered at the outer edges of his lips. Oh yes, it would be a wonderful place to see out your final years, just so long as you didn't mind sharing it with 'her majesty' and a murderous ghost.

Hugh shivered as he entered his bedroom. Was it strangely cold or was he just imagining things? His gaze lingered on the bed. He became aware that he'd taken the white feather out of his pocket. His thumb was stroking back and forth across its downy fronds.

Jerking his eyes away from the bed, he went into the bathroom. After brushing his teeth and undressing, he drew the curtains. He stared at the bed for another long moment before lying down on the side his mum had slept on. The sheets were cold enough to make goosebumps rise on his skin.

"Take heed and beware of covetousness," he murmured. But who had coveted who? Was Graham suggesting that Arthur had murdered his dad for coveting Dorothy?

Tell your mother it's true that she's the most beautiful woman in the world.

As the words played through Hugh's mind again, he shook his head. For sure, his dad must have found Dorothy attractive. But coveted her? No. He would never have betrayed his wife. Would he?

Hugh took out his phone and navigated his way to the Civil Registration index for UK births, marriages and deaths. He searched the births record for Arthur Dankworth. Three results came up. The first dated to 1895, the second to 1909. The third read 'Dankworth, Arthur Richard, Eskdale, December 1958'.

Right year. Wrong month.

He searched for Dorothy's birth record. Again, several results came back. He scrolled through them to 'Hodgson, Dorothy Elisabeth, Eskdale, April 1960.'

Surely that had to be the Dorothy he was looking for. "Right month, wrong year," he murmured. "Dorothy Elisabeth

Hodgson. D. E. H..."

His eyebrows scrunched together. 5458. EDEH. What did it mean? His voice emerged in an almost vanishing whisper. "What are you trying to tell me, Dad? Did Dorothy kill you?"

He looked at the empty air around him, willing it to respond. Silence throbbed in his ears. He released a heavy sigh. Was he seeing connections where none existed? Unless Dorothy could walk through walls, how on Earth had she got into the room?

He put down his phone, rubbing his aching eyes. God, what a day. It seemed like forever since he'd waved goodbye to Louise.

He switched off the bedside lamp. Darkness instantly pressed down on him like a suffocating weight. He turned the lamp back on. He lay reflecting on how, for years after his dad's death, he couldn't sleep with the light off. It was only after moving in with Louise that he'd finally been able to face the darkness again.

He reached for his phone and rang her. As if she'd been waiting for his call, she answered on the first ring and said, "I was just thinking about you."

"What were you thinking?"

"I was wondering what you're up to."

"Nothing much. I'm just lying in bed wondering how I'm ever going to sleep in this place."

"Do you want me to sing you a lullaby?"

Hugh smiled. "You might have to."

"So how was your evening, dare I ask?"

Hugh's amusement dissolved into a sigh. "Ava seems more interested in getting drunk than finding my dad's killer." His tone lightened as he changed the subject. "Where's Isabelle?"

"In bed. Fast asleep."

"She's a good girl."

"She's really missing you."

Hugh closed his eyes, Louise's words weighing heavily on his heart. "I'll call you in the morning."

"Call me whenever you want to. I'll be ready with a lullaby."

Hugh's smile flickered back to life. As he hung-up, though, his lips dropped into a straight line. He looked at his clothes, toying with the idea of joining Ava and Graham in the bar. He quickly shelved the notion. The last thing he needed was a hangover.

He retrieved the feather from his trouser pocket and stroked its delicate edge. It was the softest thing he'd ever felt, perhaps only rivalled by Isabelle's baby hair. The tension melted from his face, leaving behind nothing but weariness. Nevertheless, he didn't switch off the light.

PART 2, CHAPTER 14

S hluk!

The stomach-churning sound reverberated through Hugh's mind. It was like someone was slashing at a slab of raw meat.

His eyes sprang open. For a sickening second, he was ten-years-old again and his mum was clutching the paring knife above his dad's bloodied face. Then he blinked and the image was gone.

He sat up, hauling in a shuddery breath. Pale blue light was probing at the edges of the curtains. He glanced at his phone. It was 6:04 AM. He wondered what time he'd awoken on the day his father died. It must have been around now. The official time of death was 6:00 AM.

A message from Louise flashed up. 'Rock a bye baby on the tree top, when the wind blows the cradle will rock. When the bough breaks, the cradle will fall and down will come baby, cradle and all.'.

Smiling faintly, Hugh went into the bathroom. He stood under the steaming shower for a long time, kneading the tension from his shoulders. After shaving, he dressed in a short-sleeved shirt and trousers. He surveyed himself in the mirror. Were there a few extra flecks of grey in his hair? The bags under his eyes were certainly several shades darker.

He opened the curtains. A band of pink was splitting the sky above the hilltops. His gaze fell to the tobacco tin. According to the ghost hunting website where he'd read about how to catch ghosts, a drop in paranormal activity would indicate the trap was working. But obviously, in order for that to happen, there first had to be some sort of paranormal activity.

Pursing his lips in frustration, he turned towards the room. It felt like the silence was mocking him. He closed his eyes. "Dad, give me something. Anything."

You know I like a smoke first thing. It sets me up for the day.

His father's voice resonated in his head so clearly it was as if he was standing right beside him. Hugh's eyes snapped. He was alone.

He dug out his pipe, packed it with tobacco and lit it. The pipe bowl glowed as he drew smoke into his mouth and held it there, savouring its woody taste. He exhaled, letting his thoughts drift away with the smoke. He looked out of the window, watching the sun slowly rise into view. There wasn't a cloud to be seen. It was going to be a beautiful day.

The shabbily opulent room glowed pleasantly in the newborn sun. At that moment, it was difficult to believe anything bad had ever happened there.

A smile found its way onto Hugh's lips. He was starting to understand his dad's love for smoking a pipe.

After his smoke, Hugh followed the same routine he'd watched his dad go through countless times – let the pipe cool, empty out the ash, clean the bowl with a pipe cleaning brush.

Upon checking his reflection again, he was pleased to see his eyes were noticeably brighter. An image flashed through his mind of his father gazing into the same mirror moments before they'd gone downstairs to eat. Following his dad's example, he turned side-on and sucked in his stomach.

"Ready?" he asked himself, imitating his father's smoke-roughened voice. With a nod, he responded in his normal voice, "I'm ready."

Hugh slipped his feet into leather loafers and left the room. A faint waft of bacon enticed him along the corridor to the grand staircase. He came to a stop as pair of paramedics emerged from the opposite corridor, carrying a stretcher between them. The figure strapped into it was shrouded from head to toe in a blanket. As the paramedics descended the stairs, the blanket slid down, revealing a pink hairnet, closed eyes and a slack jaw.

With a little jolt of recognition, Hugh realised it was the waxy-faced woman who'd fed Bel minced beef at last night's dinner.

Several old ladies were looking on sombrely from the landing. "What happened?" asked Hugh.

"She had a bad heart," one of them informed him.

"Flo's been on borrowed time for years," added another.

Hugh followed the grim little procession downstairs, keeping a respectful distance. Tim was slouched against the reception counter, flicking at his nose ring. "Another one bites the dust," he commented as Hugh approached.

Hugh resisted an impulse to yank on the nose ring.

A breath of cool air entered the lobby as the paramedics made their way outside. Tim flipped up the countertop and trudged over to close the porch doors.

Leo appeared from the doorway behind the counter with a mug in each hand. "Do you want something?"

Hugh blinked. He'd been thinking about his mother's ashen cheeks and bloodless lips. How long did she have left? Weeks? Days? A sudden urgency came into his voice. "Is anyone staying in Salome?"

"You mean the room on the top floor?"

"Yes."

Leo checked the leather-bound reservations book. "It's unoccupied."

"Then I'd like to book it for a night."

Leo subjected Hugh to a quizzical look. "Why that room?"

"Does it matter?"

Leo stared at Hugh for a moment more, then turned to pluck a key labelled 'Salome' from a hook.

"What's going on?" Tim asked, returning to the counter. When Leo told him, Tim shook his head. "He can't have that room."

"Why not?" asked Hugh.

"Because the roof's knackered. Only some of the top floor rooms are usable. There are plenty of other rooms available."

"Thanks, but I'll leave it for now."

Tim and Leo exchanged a glance that seemed to suggest Hugh's reply chimed with some suspicion they had. Tim looked at Hugh intently. "I don't know why anyone would want to stay on the top floor. I don't go up there unless I have to."

"Me neither," said Leo. "It's seriously creepy up there, especially at night. I've heard some weird noises."

Hugh sensed he was being baited, but couldn't stop himself from asking, "Such as?"

"Such as floorboards creaking and doors banging in empty rooms."

"That's nothing," said Tim. "One time, I was taking some room service up there and I saw this drop-dead gorgeous woman out of the corner of my eye, but when I turned around she was gone."

"What did she look like?" asked Leo.

"I didn't get a good look at her face." Tim cupped his hands over his chest, simulating breasts. "But she had the biggest paranormal entities I've ever seen."

The two colleagues immediately fell about in fits of laughter.

"Ha, ha," Hugh mouthed flatly, but a genuine chuckle slipped out as he headed for the dining room. His mirth faded as he surveyed the elderly patrons quietly eating breakfast. Were they wondering when their time would come to be stretchered out of the hotel? His thoughts returned to his mum. He took out his phone and found the number for Rampton Hospital.

"I'm phoning about my mother," he informed the woman who answered his call. He lowered his voice. "Her name's Josie Carver."

The woman put him on hold while she called the ward. His blood beat in his ears as he waited for her to come back onto the line. After what felt like an excruciatingly long time, the woman informed him that his mother's condition was unchanged.

Hugh thanked her and hung up. He stood in frowning silence, trying to decipher his feelings. Was some small part of him disappointed that his mother hadn't deteriorated further? After all, if she died, he would never have to endure another visit to Rampton. What's more, he could walk away from Coldwell Hall and consign it to the darkest depths of his mind. Couldn't he?

He shook his head, knowing it wasn't an option. No matter what happened, he'd come too far to turn back now.

A waitress not much younger than the hotel's long-term guests approached and showed him to a table. "Tea? Coffee?" she asked.

"Tea," he answered.

The waitress pointed him in the direction of the breakfast buffet. He wandered across to it and perused an assortment of bacon, sausages and fried eggs swimming in grease. He poured himself a bowl of cereal and returned to the table.

Graham entered the dining room, looking pink-cheeked and

well-scrubbed. His wet hair hung like a dead squirrel against the back of his black t-shirt. Ava trailed in behind him, wearing sunglasses, flip-flops, outlandishly short shorts and a low-cut vest. She paused to cough into a tissue and blow her nose.

Graham headed straight for the buffet. Ava dropped onto the chair beside Hugh, removed her sunglasses and snatched up a serviette to dry her streaming eyes.

"I'm not hungover," she said defensively as if Hugh's eyes were judging her. "It's the sodding cats. Graham's going to take me to find a pharmacy after breakfast."

"It must be miles to the nearest pharmacy." Hugh's gaze strayed over Ava's shoulder as Arthur strode into the room. The hotelier's face seemed thinner than ever. His stilt-like legs barely bending at the knees, he marched towards the buffet.

"I don't care how far it is," said Ava. "I can't stay here any longer without antihistamines."

She poured herself a cup of tea from Hugh's pot and added a dash of brandy from her hipflask. She sipped the concoction with a sigh. Hugh watched Arthur examining the contents of the buffet.

Graham shambled across to the table and set down a plate laden with enough food to feed a small family. Ava puffed her cheeks, looking nauseated by the sight. She fortified herself with a gulp of tea.

"What time did you two get to bed?" asked Hugh.

"Late," Graham replied through a mouthful of sausage.

"We went on a ghost-hunting mission," said Ava.

Hugh lifted an eyebrow, intrigued. "And?"

Graham shrugged his rounded shoulders. "Same as before."

"Yup, all we found was another dancing dwarf," said Ava, stealing a slice of fried bread from Graham's plate and nibbling on it.

"Where?" asked Hugh.

"In the lobby," said Graham. "It seemed to be trying to get through the door behind reception. It was probably nothing. EMF readings didn't get above two."

"EMF?"

"Electromagnetic Field Radiation. I think the reader was just picking up emissions from light switches and old electrical wires."

"It's kind of surprising to find so little paranormal activity here," said Ava. She glanced at their fellow diners. "Especially when there are so many oldies here with one foot in this world and the next. Did you hear that one of them gave up the ghost last night?"

"Yes. I saw her being taken–" Hugh began, but was interrupted by Ava clapping her hands over her nose. She almost headbutted the table as a powerful sneeze rocked her. She whipped up the tablecloth, darting glances all around. "Where are you, you little sods?"

She looked up as the doors swung inwards. Dorothy glided into the room.

"Bloody hell, here comes the Angel of Death," said Ava, eyeing Dorothy's long-sleeved black dress. Overlapping waves of lace rolled down the narrow-waisted corset and flared skirt. The three cats followed close behind like courtly hangers-on.

Every pair of eyes in the room turned towards Dorothy as she swished forwards. Her face was a sombre mask of white powder. But there was something in her eyes – a certain glimmer – that suggested she was in her element.

Passing Hugh without a glance, Dorothy drifted from table-to-table, exchanging a few subdued words with their occupants, occasionally dabbing her eyes with a lace handkerchief.

"Christ, someone give her an Oscar," Ava said loudly enough to draw glances from the ladies at a neighbouring table.

As if she too had caught the mocking remark, Dorothy turned to approach the table. Her watery blue eyes looked at Hugh like no one else existed. "Good morning, Mr Smith."

"Good morning, Mrs Dankworth."

"I suppose you've heard our sad news. Florence Thornton, one of our best-loved residents, passed away last night."

"How did she die?" Ava asked, shying away from the ginger tom as he slunk past her legs.

Dorothy flicked her a perfunctory glance. "Necessaria Morte Mori," she sighed with a languid swirl of her handkerchief.

"I don't speak Latin."

"It means it was just her time to die," said Graham.

Dorothy afforded him an even briefer glance before her gaze returned to Hugh. "Yes, and they say the best luck is to die at the right time. Florence went quickly and peacefully in her sleep. None of us can ask for more than that."

Once again, Hugh was tormented by the image of his mother wasting away in a prison of steel bars and her own flesh. He blinked away from Dorothy's gaze, fearing she might read the pain in his eyes and somehow realise who he really was.

His lips lifted into a surprised smile as the flat-faced white cat peeked out from under the hem of Dorothy's skirt. "Who's this?"

"This is Yo-yo the Third," said Dorothy.

"The Third?"

"She's the third Yo-yo that's lived here." Dorothy pointed to the ginger tom, who was scrupulously licking his paws. "He's Sy the Second." Her long red fingernail moved to the black cat. "And she's Bel the First."

Yo-yo padded forwards to butt her head against Hugh's ankles. She nosed his fingers as he reached to stroke her luxuriously thick fur.

"You are privileged," said Dorothy. "Yo-yo's a shy girl. She doesn't let just anyone stroke her."

Hugh looked at Bel. A pair of inscrutable eyes stared back at him. Their oval pupils had a milky sheen as if filmed by cataracts. "How old is Bel?"

"She's twenty-eight." Dorothy's voice rang with pride. "She's one of the oldest cats in the world."

"Wow, amazing," Ava commented in a flat, sarcastic tone. She pressed a finger against her twitching nostrils to stifle another sneeze.

Her crimson lips moving like a cow chewing cud, Dorothy looked Ava up and down. Her gaze lingered on a tattoo on Ava's thigh of an androgynous figure wearing a flowery shirt and yellow tights. The figure had a white rose in one hand and a black staff with a small sack dangling from it in the other.

"The Fool," said Dorothy.

"You know Tarot?"

"I dabble with the cards." Dorothy closed her eyes. Reciting from memory, she began, "The Fool is young and carefree. The Fool sets off on a journey without knowing where they're going. The Fool symbolises beginnings and ends. Unlimited potential..." She opened her eyes and met Ava's gaze. "And unlimited stupidity."

The two women stared at each other for a brief moment. Then Ava erupted into laughter, prompting Yo-yo to dart back under Dorothy's skirt. The laughter degenerated into a hacking cough.

A flicker of concern crossing his usually impassive face, Graham asked, "Are you alright, Ava?"

She jerked to her feet and rushed towards the exit, scattering the other two cats. Shoving a rasher of bacon into his mouth, Graham stood up and hurried after her.

"Oh my poor babies," Dorothy said in a babyish drawl, reaching under her skirt to pick up Yo-yo. She kissed the cat's fluffy forehead. "Did the silly lady scare you?"

Seemingly having lost interest in Hugh, Dorothy carried Yo-yo to the buffet. She filled a bowl with milk and put it on the floor for the cat to lap up. A vague tingling between Hugh's eyebrows drew his attention to Arthur. The skull-faced hotelier was glowering at him with a dour intensity.

Hugh offered a bland smile. Arthur didn't return the gesture.

Shifting uneasily in his seat, Hugh resumed eating his cereal. The bowl was still half full when he pushed back his chair and headed for the lobby. Tim and Leo grinned at him from the reception counter like impish court jesters.

Hugh went to a front window. Graham's van was gone. *The Fool, is that who I am?* Hugh wondered. "Just a fool on a fool's errand," he murmured.

With that, he turned to go upstairs.

PART 2, CHAPTER 15

Hugh strode back and forth like a caged tiger. Every so often, he stopped and stared at the spot where his father had bled to death, then he resumed pacing.

His phone rang. 'Louise' appeared on the screen. He returned the phone to his pocket. He didn't want to talk. Years of bottled-up frustration were seething within him. He felt like he was about to explode. He needed to do something to release the pressure, even if it was only another fruitless attempt to contact the spirits of this place.

He glanced at his watch. The hour hand was tipping over into the afternoon. What was taking Ava and Graham so long?

The rumble of an engine drew his attention to the window. Graham's van pulled into the carpark.

Hugh hurried from the room. When he got to the landing, Ava and Graham were ascending the stairs. Ava's eyes were clearer and the surrounding skin was less puffy.

"You took your bloody time," Hugh snapped.

"The nearest pharmacy's twenty miles away," said Graham.

Ava rattled a packet of anti-allergy tablets. "Thank God for the miracle of modern drugs."

"I want–" Hugh began, but fell silent as Tim descended into view carrying a tray of dirty crockery. Hugh motioned for Ava and Graham to follow him.

"You want to have another go at contacting any resident

spirits," Ava said as they made their way past the omnipresent portraits.

"Did you use your powers to work that one out?" There was a sarcastic edge to Hugh's voice.

Ava chuckled. "Ooh someone's grumpy. Maybe your negative vibrations will make something happen this time." As she entered Hugh's room, her nostrils flared. "Those cats have been in here, haven't they?"

"No."

"Are you sure? Cats are sneaky little buggers."

Hugh made a show of peering under the bed. "No cats."

"Shall I get my SLS camera?" asked Graham.

"No," said Ava. "Let's just get on with it. This room's making my nose itch."

As she reclined on the chaise longue and reached for her Saint Benedict Medal, Graham set his phone to record. "Coldwell Hall, day two, 12:56 PM, third attempt at contact."

Ava inhaled slowly through her nostrils. Her nose twitched. She rubbed it, then refocused on her breathing. Hugh's hand slid into his trouser pocket, seeking out the feather.

A sneeze erupted from Ava, jerking her into a sitting position. "Sod this for a game of soldiers." She stalked into the bathroom, blew her nose and swilled down an antihistamine. "I don't think I can do this right now."

"I'll call reception for a maid to clean the room," said Hugh.

"It's not only the cat hair. I'm just not feeling it."

"Well is there anything I can do to help you *feel it*?"

Ava shook her head. "It's like sex. When you're not in the mood, you're not in the mood." She puckered her lips musingly. "I'm starting to wonder whether I'm ever going to feel anything here."

Hugh frowned. "What are you saying?"

"She's saying we might be on a hiding to nothing," chimed in Graham. "And I'm inclined to agree with her."

Hugh's gaze alternated incredulously between the two of them. "You can't seriously be thinking about giving up. We haven't even been here a full day."

"We've been here long enough for me to feel totally…" Ava sought for the right word, "blocked. Some places – and people – can do that to me. It's like spiritual constipation."

"Look, if this is about me having a go at you, I promise it won't happen again."

Ava swished a hand down the back of her head. "Water off a duck's back."

"Then what's the problem?" Anger abruptly took over Hugh's voice. "You think my mum's guilty, don't you? Go on, admit it. You never really believed me. You're only here for the money."

"Your promise didn't last long," pointed out Ava.

Hugh's expression flipped back to contrition. "Sorry, Ava. I don't know what's wrong with me today."

"There's no mystery to it. Your dad was murdered in this room. If I was you, I'd be freaking out too. And yes, I believe you. But whatever killed your dad isn't here now."

"Then where is it?"

Ava shrugged. "Spirits pass on. Demons go in search of other poor sods to torment."

Hugh shook his head. "You're wrong, Ava. The thing that killed my dad is still here. We just need to keep trying and it'll show itself."

She made a doubtful noise. "No matter how hard we try, if there's nothing to find, there's nothing to find."

"Listen, if you stay, I'll make it worth your while. I'll give you an extra hundred a day. Each."

"You're a nice bloke, Hugh. And yeah, I need money, but not badly enough to take you for a ride. I can do without that stain on my soul. It's dirty enough as it is."

"A hundred-and-fifty."

Ava ran her tongue over her lips at the tempting offer. Her crooked smile reappeared. "Okay, Hugh. I'll give it one more go." She turned to open the hallway door.

"Where are you going?"

"For a cig." Ava made a downwards motion with her palms. "Relax. Stressing won't help anything. Go for a walk. Take a nap."

Hugh released a slow breath and nodded.

Graham followed Ava from the room. Hugh resisted an impulse to sneak after them and make sure they really were staying. He perched on the windowsill, keeping an eye on Graham's van. His attention shifted to the open tobacco tin. Touching the soil as gently as if it were some rare and precious mineral, he murmured, "Where are you, Dad? Give me a sign. Send me another feather, if that was you. I just need something to let me know I'm on the right track."

PART 2, CHAPTER 16

Taking Ava's advice, Hugh lay down on the bed. His fingers sought out the feather. A sense of calm stole over him as he stroked it. His eyelids closed like theatre curtains at the end of an act. His phone rang again, but he'd already slipped too far into the realm of dreams to notice.

Dorothy glided through his mind. Not the Dorothy of now, but the Dorothy of twenty-five years ago – skin glowing, eyes sparkling, hair shining.

"Rock a bye baby on the tree top…" Her voice oozed out like honey. Hugh shuddered as if the words were caressing him.

Hitching up her lacy skirt, Dorothy got onto the bed. A musky, almost animalistic scent hit Hugh as she straddled his waist. He tried to lift his hands to push her away, but they seemed to be glued to the bed.

"When the wind blows, the cradle will rock…"

Her thighs clamped against his, trapping him in a scissor hold. Placing her palms on his chest, she pressed down with enough force to wind him. He grimaced as she dug nails as sharp as a cat's claws into his flesh. Pleasure mingled with pain as she rubbed her groin against his.

"When the bough breaks, the cradle will fall…"

Dorothy's voice was a husky whisper. Crow's feet came into sharp focus at the corners of her eyes as she bent forwards. Hugh's stomach twisted and churned. Her breath was as rank as rotten fish.

"And down will come baby, cradle and all."

All, all, all...

The word echoed through the dark recesses of Hugh's unconscious mind, each repetition amplifying the pressure on his chest. Dorothy pushed down with relentless force. Harder, harder, harder. His mouth gaped, but he couldn't get any air into his lungs. It felt like an elephant was sitting on him, suffocating him beneath its immense weight.

With a monumental effort, Hugh forced his eyelids apart. He found himself staring into a pair of oval pupils encircled by emerald irises.

Instinctively, he lashed out. Yo-yo sprang off him, landing nimbly on the carpet. The ball of white fluff streaked across the rug into the bathroom. Hugh sat up, gasping for air.

With a groggy shake of his head, he rose and staggered to the half-open bathroom door. His movements tinged with caution, he pushed the door inwards. He craned his neck, peering into the bath and behind the toilet. Yo-yo was nowhere to be seen. Wondering if she'd somehow managed to sneak past him, he turned to search the bedroom.

"Come out, come out, wherever you are," he said in a singsong voice, looking under the furniture, behind the curtains and even on top of the bed's canopy. No Yo-yo.

Where the hell was she? Had she vanished into thin air like a magician's assistant?

The confusion flickering across Hugh's features gave way to a goading grin. "What about you, you murdering coward?" he asked the seemingly empty room. "Do you like to play hide and seek too? Well come on then, let's play."

Without bothering to wait and see if the room accepted his challenge, he headed for the hallway.

PART 2, CHAPTER 17

Hugh knocked insistently on Ava's door. The instant she opened it, he exclaimed, "You were right! There was a cat in my room."

Graham poked his head out of the door across the hallway. "What's going on?"

As Hugh described his bizarre encounter with Yo-yo in the waking world and Dorothy in his dreams, Ava's eyes glimmered with fascination. "Maybe Yo-yo followed you from the dining room," she speculated.

"There's an easy way to find out how she got in the room," said Graham, tapping at his phone. He brought up the recent camera footage, scrolling through it to where Hugh lay down. "I thought you said Yo-yo ran into the bathroom."

"She did," said Hugh.

"Are you sure about that?" Graham pointed to the upper lefthand corner of the screen.

Hugh's eyes widened as he saw that the bathroom door was shut. A crease of doubt appeared on his brow, but he dispelled it with a firm shake of his head. "It *was* open when I woke up."

Tingling with curiosity, he watched Graham fast-forward through several minutes' worth of uneventful footage.

"Look!" Ava exclaimed. The bathroom doorhandle descended slowly, then snapped back up as if someone had lost their grip on it. The door swung inwards a few centimetres. A slender white shape slunk though the gap. Ava laughed in astonishment. "Clever kitty."

Her eyes shining like mercury, Yo-yo padded towards the bed. She briefly peered up at its occupant before jumping onto the mattress. Hugh stirred in his sleep as the cat climbed on top of him. She lay down with her front paws on his shoulders and her rear legs splayed across his hips. He let out a soft moan as she rubbed herself against him. After a minute or so, he jolted awake with an almighty gasp. Yo-yo leapt off the bed and bolted into the bathroom. He somewhat unsteadily stood up and pursued her. She didn't show her snub-nosed face again as he searched the bathroom and bedroom.

"Well that was the weirdest porno I've ever seen," Ava teased as Graham paused the recording.

Hugh turned towards the door to his room, deep lines etching themselves into his brow. "Could a cat have opened that door?"

"You mean on the night your dad died?" asked Graham.

"Yes. Do you think it's possible?"

"I've heard of cats opening drawers and cupboards, switching on lights, even turning on taps. But I don't see how even the cleverest cat could turn a key. Not without thumbs."

"Maybe one cat couldn't. But what about three cats working together?"

"So let me get this straight," said Ava. "You're suggesting Dorothy's cats let the killer into the room. And after the killer left, the cats double-locked the door."

"Why not? If you can speak to the dead, why can't Dorothy, or someone else around here, train cats to unlock and lock doors?"

Ava chuckled. "Fair point. But what about after the cats locked the door? How did they get out?"

Prompted by the question, Hugh strode forwards. Ava and

Graham followed him to his bathroom. His eyes scoured the room, coming to rest on the boxed-in pipework at the base of the sink and toilet. Squatting down, he examined the square gap where a pair of copper pipes curved up towards the hot and cold taps. He slid an arm into the opening, his fingers brushing across smooth metal and coarse wood. When he withdrew his arm, a mix of white, orange and black hairs clung to his skin.

"Well, well," said Ava. "There's a secret passageway after all."

Hugh's phone rang. He didn't take it out of his pocket. He knew it would be Louise calling. What was there to say to her? That he'd been sexually assaulted by a cat? Smiling grimly at the thought of how she'd react to that, he curled his fingers around the edge of the pipe boxing and pulled. The woodwork creaked but held fast.

"Let me try," said Graham.

Hugh moved aside. Graham's bearish shoulders curved forwards as he took hold of the boxing. His arms quivered. His face turned a shade of purplish-red. A cracking, tearing noise reverberated around the bathroom as the boxing suddenly came away from the wall.

Hugh's gaze traversed the exposed pipes to where they disappeared into a hole in the bath's side panel. Graham shone a keyring torch into the aperture. "There are a couple of floorboards missing back here."

"Let's check your rooms," said Hugh.

They went to Ava's room. As they trooped into the bathroom, a swan-necked woman wearing a tall, flat-topped crown looked down on them from a gilded frame. Graham tore off the pipe covering, dislodging several tiles in the process. His torch revealed more missing floorboards under the bath.

Hugh turned to head for Graham's room, but Ava laid a hand on his arm. "I don't think we need to destroy any more bathrooms. Okay, so we know the cats can get in and out of the rooms. But what does that actually mean?"

"Maybe it means we're not looking for something supernatural after all," said Hugh.

"Or maybe the cats aren't really cats," said Graham. "Maybe they're succubi."

"Succu-what?"

"Demons that drain the energy of their sleeping victims. In folklore, they often take the form of cats."

"Or maybe the cats are just creepy little pervs," Ava chimed in with a chuckle.

"Could Dorothy be a succubi?" asked Hugh.

"I very much doubt it."

"But what about my dream?"

"Freud believed dreams are the unconscious wish fulfilment of the dreamer," said Graham.

Hugh let out an incredulous laugh. "I don't want to have sex with Dorothy Dankworth."

"Well she's gagging to shag you," said Ava. "The way she was looking at you at breakfast, that woman definitely wants to jump your bones."

Hugh scrunched his face at the images the words conjured up. "So what now? How do we find out what the Dankworths and their cats really are?"

Ava pulled out a cigarette packet. "Let me have a think about it." She wrinkled one side of her nose at the white hairs on Hugh's shirt and the milky-looking stains on his trousers. "And while I'm having a think, do me a favour and change your clothes. You smell like a cat in heat."

PART 2, CHAPTER 18

As Hugh returned to his room, he envisioned Yo-yo, Bel and Sy under the floorboards, shadowing his every move. After making sure none of the cats were lurking around the room, he stuffed a pillow halfway into the hole in the side of the bath. He balanced the pipe boxing back in place, then rummaged through his suitcase for fresh clothes.

"Star-crossed hearts, undying flame. Bound by love, yet worlds apart…"

At the faint sound of singing, Hugh looked up from buttoning his shirt. He approached the door, the brittle soprano voice becoming louder with each step he took.

"With every beat, they curse their fate. A forbidden love they can't escape…"

He squinted through the spyhole. Dorothy swayed into view. She'd changed into yet another elaborate dress. A champagne-coloured bodice pushed her breasts up into a deep cleavage. The shiny material curved over her hips before widening into an expanse of rippled silk.

As Dorothy passed by, she threw a furtive glance at Hugh's door. Her voice rose an octave. "A love that blooms amidst the night, but forbidden love, oh what a plight!"

Hugh opened the door. Dorothy turned, wide-eyed, as if startled. "Oh, I'm sorry. I hope I didn't disturb you, Mr Smith."

Hugh found a smile for her. "No, you didn't. And please call me Hugh."

Dorothy's shimmering lipstick accentuated every wrinkle on her lips as she beamed back at him. "Hugh, Hugh..." she murmured as if familiarising herself with how it felt to say his name. Her nostrils flared slightly. "Is that cigar smoke I smell?"

Hugh was half-tempted to reply, *It's pipe smoke*, just to see her reaction, but instead he said, "Yes."

Tutting, Dorothy wagged a finger at him. "Naughty boy. Smoking isn't permitted in the bedrooms. But I think we can make an exception for you."

Hugh struggled to maintain eye contact as her sultry voice evoked a flash of his dream – her straddling him, grinding against him. He moved the conversation swiftly on. "What was that you were singing?"

Dorothy gave a languid waft of her hand. "Just a little ditty I made up. I sing every afternoon to let the old ladies know that bingo's about to start."

Old ladies. The way Dorothy said it made it clear she didn't put herself in the same bracket as them.

"My voice isn't what it used to be," said Dorothy.

Hugh hid his amusement at her blatant fishing for a compliment. "You have a lovely voice."

Dorothy batted her eyelids like a doll. "Thank you, Hugh." She reached out to touch his wrist. Her cold fingertips sent a slight shudder through him. Her smile broadened at his reaction. "I'd better be on my way. Bingo starts soon." She started to turn, but paused. "You know, there's something familiar about you." She gestured vaguely towards Hugh's face. "Something about your eyes. Are you sure you haven't been here before?"

"I'm positive. I'd definitely remember if I'd been somewhere as..." Hugh searched for the appropriate word, "*unique* as this before."

A girlish giggle escaped Dorothy. "Yes, I suppose you would." With that, she continued on her way, swaying as she sang, "In this tale of doomed bliss, their love exists eternal, aching for one last kiss."

Hugh watched her recede into the gloom of the hallway, an absurdly over-dressed figure, like something out of a romantic fairytale. He tried to imagine her plunging the knife into his dad. Could she have done it? The Dorothy of now barely looked capable of cutting into a tough steak. But what about the Dorothy of twenty-five years ago?

Another figure came into view, heading towards Hugh. He squinted as if doubting his eyes, then strode forwards, exclaiming, "What the hell are you doing here?"

PART 2, CHAPTER 19

"That's a nice way to greet your wife." Louise's words were laced with sarcasm.

Hugh peered worriedly over her shoulder. "Where's Isabelle?"

"My mum's looking after her."

Hugh caught hold of Louise's hand, drew her into his room and closed the door. She took everything in, her eyes wide with uneasy curiosity. "It's just as I pictured it."

Hugh's gaze darted around as if he was afraid the air might attack her. "You shouldn't be here."

"I was worried about you. Why didn't you answer my calls?"

Hugh's thoughts returned to his dream – Dorothy mounting him as if he were an unruly steed, pleasure blending with pain as she rubbed and clawed at him. Unable to bring himself to meet Louise's gaze, he looked out of the window. "I was taking a nap."

"All day?"

"I was tired. I didn't get much sleep last night."

"I can see that." Louise reached up to trace the outline of the dark smudges under Hugh's eyes.

He shied away from her touch. "You can't stay here."

"I don't think you should be alone."

"I'm not alone."

Catching his meaning, Louise asked, "Where are Ava and Graham?"

"They're taking a break."

"A break?" Louise tilted an eyebrow. "From what? What exactly have they done so far to justify emptying our bank account?"

"I'm not getting into this with you now." Hugh pointed towards the hallway door. "You need to leave."

Louise shook her head. "I'm staying. I should never have let you come here without me."

"I don't want to argue, Louise."

"Neither do I." Her tone was as firm as Hugh's. She crossed her arms.

Knowing from experience that Louise could be even more stubborn than him when she wanted to be, Hugh sank resignedly onto the bed. Her features softening, she sat down beside him. "You're pushing too hard, Hugh. You're going to make yourself ill like–" She broke off, seemingly realising it would be best not to speak her mind.

He slid her a knowing look. "Like my mum. That's what you were about to say, isn't it?"

Louise pushed out a sad smile. "I realise you don't want to hear this, Hugh, but like Ava said, you might have to accept that what happened here wasn't supernatural."

"I know."

Louise's eyebrows lifted high. "You know?" The surprise in her voice was tinged with a note of cautious hope.

Hugh motioned for her to follow him into the bathroom. As he showed her the cats' secret entrance, he told her about waking to find Yo-yo on top of him. He didn't mention the dream. She eyed him sceptically as he relayed his theory about the cats unlocking the door for the killer.

A little laugh slipped from her. "Sorry, Hugh, I'm just picturing a cat stood on its back legs with a key in its front paws."

"Well it either has something to do with the cats and their owners or we're back to ghosts and demons."

Frowning faintly, Louise returned to the bedroom. The creases between her eyebrows deepened as she looked at the tobacco tin. Her gaze moved back and forth between it and the hallway door, then drifted floorward as if she didn't know where to look or what to think.

Hugh approached her. His arms encircled her waist from behind. "I know you don't believe in ghosts, Louise, but believe me when I tell you this place is dangerous."

Her tone shifted from scepticism to exasperation. "Then why stay here?"

"You know why. It's going to take more than videos of cats opening doors to get my mum out of Rampton."

"Yes, but if you're right about the cats, then one or maybe even both of the Dankworths are murderers. I was only worried about your mental health before, but now I'm scared you might end up with a knife in you."

"I'm not going to let that happen." Hugh reached for the feather in his pocket. A curious blend of reassurance and sadness glimmered in his eyes. "Neither is my dad. He's here, you know. He's watching over me."

Louise scanned the room, appearing unsure whether to be comforted or disturbed by Hugh's words. She shook her head as if dispelling some momentary doubt. "You're right, Hugh, I don't believe in ghosts." She turned to look him in the eyes. "I vow to always stand by your side. Do you remember when I said that?"

Despite himself, Hugh smiled. "Of course I do. On our wedding day."

"Well that's precisely what I intend to do."

Hugh heaved a sigh. "I'm not going to be able to make you leave, am I?"

"Nope." Louise lifted her left hand, displaying a gold ring. "Till death do us part."

Hugh gently rested his forehead against hers, struggling with a mixture of concern and relief. The prospect of another night alone in this room made his stomach clench like a fist, but he would rather endure an eternity of Coldwell Hall than risk any harm coming to Louise. "Okay, but if you're staying, there are some rules. Firstly, I don't want you leaving my sight."

Louise chuckled, her breath tickling Hugh's face. "Don't worry. I'm a big girl. I can look after myself."

He drew back to eye her earnestly. "I'm serious, Louise."

"Okay. Fine. I promise not to leave your sight even for a minute."

As if to prove her words, Louise went into the bathroom, unbuckled her belt and started to pull down her jeans to sit on the toilet. At the last second, recalling that a camera was aimed at her, Hugh exclaimed, "Wait!" He pointed out the two mini-cameras. "Graham's got all our rooms under surveillance."

Louise frowned at the thought of Graham watching her every move. "Is it safe to go to the loo?"

"Yes, just leave the door open a crack and let me know if you hear anything from under the bath."

Louise closed the door, leaving a slight gap. "What are the other rules?"

"I don't know. I'll tell you when I think of them."

The moment Hugh heard the toilet flushing and the taps coming on, he opened the door fully.

Louise dried her hands, surveying the bathroom's symphony of gold taps and marble surfaces. "What a strange place. It reminds me of a theatre set."

A tingle of foreboding crawled up Hugh's spine as he thought about Dorothy and Arthur. "Rule number two – stay away from the Dankworths. Dorothy seems to think she's living in a melodrama. And Arthur... well, he just walks around like he hates the world."

A rise of realisation came into Louise's voice. "That was Dorothy I passed in the hallway, wasn't it?"

"Yes."

"I smiled at her, but she completely blanked me."

"I get the distinct impression she doesn't like other women. Especially not younger, beautiful ones like you."

The compliment brought a smile to Louise's face.

You're the most beautiful woman I've ever met.

As Hugh recalled his father's words to his mother and the sceptical, "*Ha!*" she'd shot back, he felt a sudden flush of love for Louise. With her, everything was so simple. There was no need for second-guessing. He knew she would accept what he said at face value. It made his head spin just thinking about the endless back-and-forth between his parents.

He wrapped his arms around Louise again, murmuring in her ear, "Thank you."

"For what?"

"For putting up with me."

"I love you, Hugh, even if you do drive me up the–"

Louise halted mid-sentence as a loud bang rattled the hallway door. Hugh quickly drew away from her and dashed to the spyhole. There was no one on the other side of the door.

"What was that?" Louise asked, coming up behind him.

"I don't–" Hugh fell silent as a luminous green blob about the size of a pound coin materialised on the opposite door. The dot darted around crazily, leaving shimmering trails in its wake. Thinking about the stick figures from Graham's footage, Hugh jerked open the door. Seemingly startled, the dot zipped along the wall. His heart pounding, he ran after the eerie light. It came to a stop on a door named 'Lola'.

He tried to touch the light. It disappeared and reappeared a short distance away. He reached for it again, slowly at first, then suddenly, as if trying to catch a fly. It evaded him, wavering and flickering like a mischievous spirit that had accepted his challenge to a game of hide-and-seek.

At a low guffaw from behind him, Hugh spun on his heel. He caught sight of two grinning faces. Leo and Tim were peeking out of a nearby doorway. One of them – Hugh couldn't tell which – was holding a laser pen that emitted a green beam.

As Hugh started towards them, they jerked backwards out of sight and slammed the door shut.

"Who are they?" asked Louise, stepping into the hallway.

"They're just a pair of idiots." Hugh hammered a fist against the door. "Open up, come on, open up!"

Muffled laughter and shushing came from inside the room.

"Open this door or I'm going to kick it in."

"If you do, I'll call the police," Leo replied in his dopey drawl.

"We were only having a laugh," added Tim.

With a gentle grip, Louise restrained Hugh's arm. "Like you said, they're just a pair of idiots. They don't know what this means to you."

Hugh drew in a slow breath. "Open up," he repeated calmly. "I just want to talk."

"Do you promise to be chill?" asked Leo.

"I promise."

A lock clicked and the door opened a few centimetres. Tim and Leo eyed Hugh warily through the gap.

"I wonder what your boss would think about you 'having a laugh' at a guest's expense?" asked Hugh.

"Go and ask him," retorted Tim. "I'll take you to him, if you want." When he didn't get a reply, he grinned like a poker player who'd successfully called an opponent's bluff. "You're lucky we haven't told Mr Dankworth why you and your weirdo mates are really here."

Hugh's heart skipped, but he kept his voice steady. "And why are we really here?"

Tim chuckled as if it was obvious. "You're ghost hunters."

Relief flowed through Hugh. For a moment, he'd feared they might have figured out his true identity. "What makes you think that?"

"I've seen that fat guy messing around with ghost hunting gear," put in Leo. "That stuff's a load of junk. You won't find anything with it."

"Not up here they won't," said Tim.

The cryptic remark piqued Hugh's curiosity. "What's that supposed to mean?"

"It means you're looking in the wrong place."

"Where's the right place?"

"I'll show you, but it'll cost you..." Tim ran his tongue contemplatively across the inside of his upper lip, "a hundred quid."

Hugh's dark eyes shifted between him and Leo. "This had better not be another joke."

"It's no joke," insisted Leo. "There's a door–"

"Shh," Tim cut him off sharply. He held out a hand, palm up.

"One hundred."

I'm starting to wonder whether I'm ever going to feel anything here.

As Ava's words replayed themselves to Hugh, he took out his wallet. At this point, anything had to be worth a shot. He counted out the cash. Tim handed off half to Leo.

"Now tell me about this door," said Hugh.

"It's in the basement," answered Leo.

A grin crawled up Tim's doughy face. "We call it The Door to Hell."

PART 2, CHAPTER 20

Hugh knocked on Ava and Graham's doors. Ava appeared with a glass of brandy in her hand and a cigarette drooping from her mouth. She broke into a broad grin at the sight of Louise.

"You don't seem surprised to see me," said Louise.

"Of course not," Ava replied with a wink. "I'm a clairvoyant."

"I knew it!" exclaimed Leo, nudging Tim.

A sandpapery laugh scraped from Ava's throat. "I knew you knew it."

Graham scratched his beard, eyeing Leo and Tim with an air of faint distaste. "So these guys know the deal, do they?"

"Yes, they know we're ghost hunters," Hugh replied, giving him a meaningful look.

Graham indicated he understood with a slight nod.

"They have something to show us," continued Hugh.

"Apparently it's The Door to Hell," Louise said, arching an eyebrow doubtfully.

Ava laughed again. "Ooh, sounds scary."

"It's no joke," Tim asserted with a touch of indignation.

"Yeah, this is for real," said Leo.

Ava sized the two of them up, her eyes narrowing to slits as she puffed on her cigarette. She downed her brandy, then tossed the glass carelessly onto her bed. "Okay, boys, lead the way."

Tim nodded as if acknowledging a challenge. He turned to head for the rear stairwell. The others followed along. Graham retrieved his camera baseball cap, then took up a position at the back of the little procession.

"Before the hotel, there was a brewery here," Leo informed them as they descended the stairs.

"We know." Graham's monotone voice echoed in the uncarpeted stairwell. "It closed down in 1950 and was demolished by Arthur's father, Gerald, to make way for–"

"Shh," Tim cut in as they reached the ground floor.

From beyond a door came the muffled sound of Arthur dourly calling bingo numbers. "Forty-five – halfway there… Number thirteen…"

"Unlucky for some," Ava said, waggling her eyebrows at her companions.

Tim continued down a short flight of stairs to a sturdy old door.

"Is this The Door to Hell?" asked Hugh.

With a grin on his lips and mischief in his eyes, Tim shook his head.

He took out a bunch of keys and inserted one into a black iron lock. As the door creaked open, the darkness beyond exhaled a dank breath. He flipped a switch. A lightbulb flickered into life, revealing steep stone steps, worn treacherously narrow by the passage of countless feet. Spiders scuttled across brick walls and disappeared into cracks in the crumbling mortar.

"Careful, it's slippy," Leo cautioned as they started down the steps.

Louise shivered as the damp air caressed her face. "It smells like… like mud and fish down here."

"It smells like a river," said Hugh. He glanced back at her. "Stay close."

A line of bare lightbulbs led them deeper and deeper into the bowels of the building. The walls changed from bricks to solid rock scarred by the crisscrossing marks of pickaxes. From somewhere came a steady *plink-plonk* of dripping.

"Is this a basement or a cave?" asked Ava.

Leo shrugged as if to say, *What's the difference?*

Plink-plonk, plink-plonk...

The unrelenting sound gradually grew louder, drawing them onwards to the bottom of the steps. A vast space bathed in intermittent pools of light stretched out before them. Beyond the last lightbulb, impenetrable darkness made it impossible to see how far back the basement went.

"Feel anything?" Hugh asked Ava.

She hugged her bare arms across her scrawny torso. "Yeah, bloody freezing."

His gaze moved to Graham. After perusing the footage on his phone, Graham gave a shake of his head.

Their footsteps echoed on flagstones as they made their way between piles of dusty old furniture. Graham stooped to avoid banging his head on the thick wooden beams that supported the rock ceiling.

Tim stopped at a couple of chairs with a padlocked wooden chest between them.

"What's this?" Hugh asked as Tim unlocked the padlock.

"It's my stash box," said Tim, flipping up the lid and taking out a cone-shaped spliff.

Hugh frowned. "We're not here to get stoned."

"Chill out. You stress too much."

"You're right, he does," agreed Louise.

Tim sparked up the spliff, exhaled a pungent plume of smoke, then passed it to Leo. After doing likewise, Leo offered it to Ava.

"I'll pass," she said.

"Why?" Tim asked with a sneery chuckle. "Does it mess with your powers?"

"No, but I've got precious few brain cells to spare as it is without smoking that stuff."

Hugh released an impatient breath. "Are you going to show us this famous Door to Hell or what?"

"Alright, keep your knickers on," said Tim, approaching a stack of chairs that was teetering against a big old bookcase. As he and Leo moved the chairs aside, cobwebs tore apart and dust filtered to the floor.

"Give us a hand here," said Leo.

The rusty paint tins cluttering the bookcase rattled as Graham and Hugh helped lift it away from the wall. Tucked away behind it, festooned in yet more layers of cobwebs, was a two-third height, handleless plank door. The door was padlocked at the top and bottom.

Tim shot Ava a *told you so* look. He pointed at the big brass padlocks. "Are they to keep people out or something else in?"

A solid-sounding *thunk* reverberated from the door as Leo gave it a kick. "The Dankworth family fortune might be hidden behind this."

"Nah." Tim spoke through a cloud of smoke. "It's definitely a portal to another dimension. Or something like that."

Ava stepped forwards and placed her palms against the door.

Tim jutted his grinning face towards her. "What do your powers tell you?"

"They tell me to tell you to shut up."

Nudging Tim aside, Graham zoomed his camera in on Ava's pinched little face. She moved her hands around on the rough wood like a doctor listening with a stethoscope.

Tim and Leo passed the spliff back and forth until it was almost burnt down to their fingers. Leo flicked it away into the gloom. "Is this going to take much longer? I have to get back to work."

"Yeah, me too," Tim said with a meaningful look at Hugh.

Catching his drift, Hugh pulled a couple more twenties from his wallet. "How long can you give us?"

"Fifteen or twenty-minutes tops," said Leo. "When the bingo's finished, old man Dankworth will notice we're gone."

"That's the deal," said Tim. "Take it or leave it."

Hugh handed over the cash. Tim and Leo grinned at each other, delighted with their negotiating skills.

Louise took hold of Hugh's hand and drew him aside. "Why would the evidence you need be down here?"

"It's probably not," Hugh conceded. "But at this point I'm willing to give anything a try." He smiled, trying to make light of the situation. "Who knows, maybe they're right about this being where the Dankworths keep their family fortune. Maybe they hide their family secrets down here too."

Ava removed her hands from the door and touched her Saint Benedict medal.

"You felt something, didn't you?" said Hugh, eyeing her intently.

She looked at him, her pupils shrunken to black pinpoints despite the dim lighting. "I'm...." Her voice was unusually toneless. "I'm not sure."

"What do you want to do?" asked Graham.

Her gaze sliding back to the door, Ava repeated, "I'm not

sure."

"What do you mean, you're not sure?" asked Hugh. He pointed at the padlocks. "We're going to break those off and see what's on the other side of this thing."

"*Is* that what you want to do?" Graham asked Ava.

Hugh's expression hovered between incredulity and irritation. "Why are we even talking about this? What am I'm paying you for if you won't–"

He broke off as Louise gave his arm a squeeze. The annoyance drained from his face as he looked into her hazel eyes. His gaze returned to Ava. "We'll do whatever you think's best."

Ava's thumb moved back and forth across the Saint Benedict medallion for a moment. The creases of uncertainty faded from her forehead. "Let's do it."

PART 2, CHAPTER 21

Leo stepped in front of the door. "If you break the padlocks, we'll get in trouble,"

"Old man Dankworth will never know," said Tim, his voice vibrating with anticipation at the prospect of finding out what was beyond the door. "No one comes down here but us."

Graham removed a zippered wallet from the back pocket of his jeans. "We shouldn't need to damage anything." He opened the wallet, revealing an array of lock-picking tools.

"Nice," said Leo, moving out of Graham's way. "I suppose you guys break-in to loads of creepy old places."

"Some." Graham's tone was one of dry understatement. He squatted down to examine the padlocks. "Give me some light, will you?"

Hugh directed his phone's torch at the heavy-duty padlocks. Graham chose a hooked and an L-shaped pick. He inserted the L-shaped pick, twisted it, then inserted the hooked pick. "It's a six-pin tumbler," he said, wiggling the hooked pick up and down. "You just need to lift all the pins above the cylinder and... Hey presto." The lock popped open. He turned his attention to the second padlock. Tongue poking between his ginger whiskers in concentration, he went through the same procedure. Moments later, both padlocks were dangling from one of his fingers. He rose and stepped aside. Ava moved away from the door too. They looked at Hugh as if to say, *Your turn.*

Leo and Tim giggled and jostled each other like over-excited schoolboys as Hugh stepped forwards. Hugh rested a palm against the door. The wood was cool. Splinters prickled his skin. He felt nothing out of the ordinary.

Plink-plonk, plink-plonk...

Hugh turned an ear towards the door. "I think the dripping is coming from here."

"It never stops," said Tim. "It annoys the crap out of me."

"I like the sound of it," said Louise. "There's something almost musical about it."

Grinning inanely, Leo swayed his arms about. "Yeah, you can dance to it." He winced as Tim elbowed him in the ribs.

"Pack it in," snapped Hugh.

"No, let them have fun," said Ava. "We need all the good vibrations we can get."

Stifled chuckles escaped Tim and Leo as Hugh returned his attention to the handleless door. He gave it a hard push. It didn't budge. Hooking a finger through each of the padlock staples, he pulled. The door scraped open a few centimetres, its hinges squealing as if they hadn't been used in eons.

Unhooking his aching fingers from the staples, Hugh put his face to the gap. For an instant, only darkness greeted his gaze. Then a pair of piercing emerald eyes and four fanglike teeth flashed into view. He reeled backwards as their owner spat a ferocious hiss at him.

"What was that?" gasped Louise.

"It was a black cat," answered Hugh, cautiously peering through the gap again.

"Was it Bel?" asked Leo.

"I think so." Hugh shone his phone through the doorway. It led to a circular room a fraction of the size of the main basement. Half-a-dozen wooden barrels about the same height as the door were clustered against the far wall. A large stone slab as thick as a bible occupied the centre of the floor. The cat was nowhere to be seen.

"How did she get in there?"

"God knows, but we'd better catch her," said Tim. "She's her majesty's favourite. Mr Dankworth will kill us if anything happens to Bel."

He and Leo curled their fingers around the edge of the door and dragged it fully open. Guided by the pale blue glow of their phones, they stooped under a wooden lintel into the room.

"Bel, Bel," Tim called out.

Taking hold of Louise's hand, Hugh followed them. Within the smaller room, the relentless plink-plonk of the drips seemed weirdly amplified, as if his brain was turning to water. His phone's torch highlighted lattices of tool marks etched into the rock walls like hieroglyphs.

Louise sucked in a sharp breath.

Hugh darted her a look. "What is it?"

"A drip went down the back of my neck." She feathered her fingers along the low, damp ceiling. "Isabelle would hate it here."

"Don't say her name in this place," Hugh rebuked. He immediately cast her an apologetic glance. "Sorry, Louise. It's just that…" He trailed off, unsure how to explain himself.

She offered him a small smile. "It's okay. I know where you're coming from." Her eyes roamed the gloom. "I get the strangest feeling that the walls are listening to us."

Graham's broad shoulders brushed against the doorframe as he entered the room. Slowly, almost timidly, Ava padded after him. She didn't have to stoop to avoid banging her head. "This doorway could have been made for me." There was a touch of forced jollity in her voice.

"It smells like a carpark stairwell," said Louise.

"It's the cats," Ava croaked like she was holding back a cough. "They must have sprayed all over this place."

"Maybe she can walk through walls," said Leo, sweeping his phone's light across the dark-grey walls.

"Maybe who can walk through walls?" asked Hugh.

"Bel. I don't see how else she could get in here."

"Bel, where are you, you stupid cat?" wondered Tim, peering into an iron-bound barrel.

Hugh approached the stone slab. He tapped the heel of his shoe against it, producing a hollow sound.

"It looks like the top of a church altar," said Louise.

"Altars are usually rectangular." Graham measured the slab up with his eyes. "I'd say this is about six-by-six foot."

"I wonder if there's anything under it?" said Hugh.

Graham picked up a rusty bucket tied to a coil of frayed hemp rope. "Could be a well."

"Nah," said Tim. "I told you, it's a portal to Hell. That's why it's sealed up. To keep the demons from escaping."

"What if–" Ava began, but a cough interrupted her. She cleared her throat. "What if you're right?"

Tim and Leo exchanged a glance. Tim twirled a finger beside his temple, provoking a snort of laughter from Leo.

Squatting down, Ava placed a palm on the slab as tentatively as if she were touching a hotplate. Lifting her hand, she examined some white specks on her fingers. She touched a fingertip to her tongue. "Salt."

"So what?" said Leo.

"In many cultures salt is used to keep out ghosts and demons," said Graham.

"Or trap them in," added Ava.

"Yeah and you also put it on your fish and chips," said Tim, prompting more laughter from Leo.

Hugh ran a fingertip along the slab. A fine scattering of salt covered its entire surface. "Who do you think put this here?"

"Do you mean the salt or the slab?" asked Ava.

"Both."

"Who cares?" said Leo. "We need to find Bel."

He and Tim set about searching the barrels. Ava lowered her palms back to the slab. Hugh wiped his own palms on his trousers. Even in that cold place, they were sweating. There was a look on Ava's face that he hadn't seen before. It wasn't simply intense concentration. Her small features were contracted into one big knot.

Ava suddenly snatched her hands away from the slab and clutched at her Saint Benedict medal.

"What is it?" Hugh asked eagerly. "What did you feel?"

"Nothing good."

"The camera's not picking anything up," said Graham, squinting at his phone.

Ava hunched her narrow shoulders so high it looked like she had no neck. "Well I am. And I don't like it. There's something not right here. This place is making me feel sick."

"I think the smell's coming from these barrels," said Louise, sniffing at the mould-speckled wood.

"It's not the physical smell, it's the psychic smell. It's..." Ava struggled to find the words. "I've never known anything like it before."

Hugh braced his palms against the edge of the slab and pushed. It didn't move. He gestured for Graham to give him a hand. In turn, Graham looked at Ava as if seeking her permission. At a nod from her, he squatted down.

"Why do you even want to know what's under there?" asked Louise. "What could possibly be there that will help us find out who—"

"*Louise,*" Hugh cut her off sharply. She clapped a hand to her mouth, realising how close she'd come to revealing the true purpose for their visit to Coldwell Hall.

Hugh returned his attention to the slab. "One, two, three, push!" He shoved with all his might, veins swelling on his neck.

As Graham added his strength to the effort, the sound of stone grinding against stone filled the room. Ava rose and retreated a step, rubbing the Saint Benedict medallion between her thumb and fingers.

The slab inched sideways, exposing a crescent of darkness. Hugh gagged as the pitch black orifice released a rotten-egg stench. At the same instant, Ava burst into a fit of coughing so violent it doubled her up. Graham sprang to his feet, arms outstretched to catch her lest she fell over. She wafted him away, pressing her other hand to her mouth. Her coughing subsided into wheezy breaths. She straightened up, gripping the medallion.

"Jesus, what a stink!" exclaimed Hugh, his voice thick with nausea.

Graham got back onto his knees. "Smells like sulphur."

He shone his keyring torch into the narrow gap, illuminating a vertical shaft. He pointed out some slimy red streaks that made it look as if the rock was bleeding. "Iron bacteria. It grows in water with a high iron content."

He reached his torch as far as possible into the aperture. On the edge of its light, maybe fifteen metres down, something glistened with an oily iridescence. The unrelenting symphony of drips echoed around the concave shaft.

"You were right, it is a well," said Leo, peering over Graham's shoulder.

"Duh, of course it's a well," scoffed Tim. "Why do you think the hotel's called Coldwell Hall?"

"They must have drawn water from here to brew beer," said Graham.

"I wouldn't drink that horrible smelling water," said Leo.

"Sulphur and iron bacteria aren't harmful, but I doubt they make for good beer." Graham sat up, absently stroking his beard in thought. "Perhaps that's why the brewery closed down. Something could have polluted the groundwater."

"Okay, so it's a smelly old well. Big deal," said Louise. She looked at Hugh. "Can we please go now?"

He started to rise to his feet, but froze in place as a distressed yowl came from below.

"Bel!" exclaimed Leo, dropping to his knees. As if in reply, another tormented yowl shot up the well.

"How did she get down there?" wondered Hugh.

"She must have fallen in."

"How could she fall in without us seeing?"

"I don't know, but we have to get her out of there."

Leo shoved at the slab. Tim, Hugh and Graham kneeled down beside him to help. The four of them grunted and quivered with strain.

Shivers ran up and down Ava's spine as a cacophony of yowls rang out. It sounded as if Bel was indeed being subjected to the torments of Hell.

"It's no good," gasped Hugh, drawing away from the slab. "The damn thing won't budge."

"Don't worry, Bel!" Leo shouted, his voice echoing back at him from the murky depths. "We're not going to leave you down there."

"It's a cat, you moron," said Tim. "It can't understand you."

"Yes she can. Bel's the cleverest cat I've ever known."

Cocking an eyebrow, Tim pointed into the well. "She was dumb enough to get stuck down there."

"Who says she's stuck?" said Hugh, thinking about the network of secret tunnels under the floorboards.

"Who says it's a cat?" Ava added cryptically.

"Oh, so what is it then, a ghost?" said Tim. His flat tone suggested that he was rapidly losing interest in the situation.

Leo put his face to the gap between the slab and the rim of the well. "Hey, maybe that's why we can't see her. What if she's died and turned into a ghost?"

Tim rolled his eyes. "Sometimes I wish you'd die and turn into a ghost."

Hugh pointed to the rope. "We could use that to lower a camera down the well."

Graham picked up the mouldy rope. The rotten fibres broke apart at the slightest pull. "I've got a rope in my van."

"Then let's go get it."

"There's no time for that," said Tim. "We've already been down here way too long."

"We can't leave Bel here all alone," said Leo.

"Fine, then you stay and keep her company."

Leo's dilated pupils travelled around the room. He shuddered as if imagining what it would be like to be there with only the piercing yowls for company. "Maybe we should tell the Dankworths where Bel is."

Tim snorted. "Maybe you should get your head checked." He pointed to the open door. "How are we going to explain that?"

Leo briefly scrunched his face in thought before conceding defeat with a sigh. "I suppose Bel will just have to stay stuck down the well."

"Listen, if that cat can get in and out of this room, I bet she can do the same with the well."

"Take it from me, he's probably right," said Hugh.

The yowls suddenly intensified, pulsing out of the well, ricocheting off the ceiling like some sort of sonic attack.

"I think you've annoyed it," rasped Ava, retreating from the shrill dirge. She clamped her lips together to suppress more coughing. The effort brought tears to her bloodshot eyes.

Louise reached for Hugh's hand. "Let's get out of here."

The tremor in her voice drew a wry sidelong glance from him. "What are you worried about? I thought ghosts and demons didn't exist?"

"They don't, but poisonous gases do. I'm starting to feel lightheaded."

As Louise finished speaking, Ava turned and scuttled towards the door, coughs racking her thin frame. She disappeared from view, the hacking and barking echoing around the basement.

Tim followed her, casting a glance over his shoulder. "Shift your arses. Mr Dankworth's going to notice the keys are gone."

"Poor Bel," said Leo, his eyes lingering on the well. "Poor old girl."

PART 2, CHAPTER 22

Once the last of them were out of the room, Tim thrust the 'Door to Hell' shut and clicked the padlocks back into place. They hastened through the jumble of furniture. The *plink-plonk* receded from hearing as they trooped up the steep stairway. Tim locked the basement door. They continued up to the ground floor. Ava was nowhere to be seen.

Leo listened at the stairwell door. "The bingo's finished."

"Not a word to anyone about this," Tim said to the others.

Hugh responded with a tilt of his head as if to say, *Surely that goes without saying?*

Tim and Leo slunk into the dining room. The others carried on up the stairs. Hugh knocked on Ava's bedroom door. Silence. "Ava, it's us." More silence. He turned to Graham. "Do you think she's okay?"

Graham sniffed the air. "She's having a cigarette."

Hugh raised his hand to knock again, but the door opened before he could do so. Ava's bleary eyes squinted at him through curls of smoke. In one hand, she held a cigarette. In the other, a tumbler of amber liquid. An empty brandy bottle lay on the bed alongside a little pile of cosmetics and clothes.

"Yes, I'm leaving," Ava wheezed, pre-empting the question on Hugh's lips.

He gawped at her as if he couldn't comprehend what he was hearing. "You can't be serious?"

"I've never been more serious. I'm getting out of here ASAP." Ava looked pointedly at Louise. "And so should you."

"But I've paid you to stay until tomorrow," said Hugh.

Ava put down her glass and dug a handful of crumpled banknotes out of her bag. "Here, have it back."

"I don't want it back. I want you to do what you're here to do." Hugh pointed to the floor. "There's something down that well. I want you to contact it."

An uncharacteristically little laugh rasped from Ava. "Uh-uh. No way."

Hugh threw his hands wide in exasperation. "What use is a clairvoyant who's scared to contact the dead?"

"What use is a dead clairvoyant?" Ava punctuated her retort with a drag of her cigarette. "No way in hell am I picking a fight with a demon."

"What makes you think it's a demon?"

"Because when looked into that well I only felt one thing – hunger. It was like the well wanted to swallow me whole. And now you've let that hunger out. Now it's everywhere." Ava's eyes darted around under their heavy lids. "Can't you feel it?"

Hugh held up a hand as if feeling for a breeze. "No."

"That's because your own hunger's out of control. You're so obsessed with finding out what or who killed your dad, that you can't see what's coming."

"And what's coming?"

Ava's bright eyes locked onto Hugh's, as if she were peering into the depths of his soul. "Death."

Death. The word sent a visible tremor through him.

"I've heard enough of this," said Louise, taking hold of his arm. He resisted as she tried to pull him away from the door.

"Whose death?" he asked Ava.

"I don't know," she replied. "And I'm not going to hang around to find out."

As if to illustrate the finality of her decision, she turned to stuff her belongings into her bag. Slinging the straps over her shoulder, she looked at Graham. "Are you coming?"

Before he could reply, Hugh said, "Stay and you can have Ava's pay."

"I'll stay, but not for the extra money," said Graham. "I can't just let that cat die down there."

"It's *not* a cat," said Ava.

"Then I need to know exactly what it is. You know the deal with me, Ava. There's nothing I hate more than unanswered questions."

She frowned up at Graham's steadfast face for a moment before breaking into a grin. She motioned to Hugh with her chin. "You're as bad as him." Taking off her Saint Benedict medallion, she beckoned Graham to lean down. As he did so, she looped the silver chain over his head. "Don't take that off until you're out of this place."

He nodded, indicating he would do as she instructed. "How are you going to get home?"

Ava shrugged. Her eyes twinkled with mischief. "Maybe Tim will give me a lift. He definitely fancies me." The glimmer faded as her gaze swept over her surroundings, taking in the gilt-framed paintings, cascading chandeliers, cobwebbed cornices and threadbare carpet. "To hell with this place."

With that, she threw back the last of her brandy and headed for the main corridor. From behind, bathed in the ethereal glow of the chandeliers, she looked like a little girl.

A spasm of anger distorting his face, Hugh shouted after her, "Go on then, run away. You were bloody useless anyway!"

Ava looked back at him, her eyelids drooping so low that only a sliver of white was visible. "He is a mighty king and terrible. He rideth on a pale horse with trumpets and other kinds of musical instruments playing before him."

Her voice was starkly matter-of-fact, devoid of emotion.

"What's that supposed to mean?" asked Hugh.

Without answering, Ava continued on her way. As she turned from view, Hugh's expression switched from anger to regret. He darted a look at Graham. "Do you think you can convince her to stay?"

"Even if I could, I wouldn't try to," replied Graham, unlocking his bedroom door.

"We don't need her," said Louise. "She can't get your mum out of Rampton."

"She said someone was going to die."

"No, she said death was coming. What does that even mean? I don't know and I don't think she does either." Louise gestured to the empty brandy bottle. "Did you see the way she downed that stuff? She's not thinking straight."

"What if it's the other way around? What if she's the only one of us thinking straight?"

Graham reappeared from his room with a bunch of keys dangling from one finger. "I'm going to get the rope."

As he started forwards, Hugh put a hand on his arm. "Stay here. I'll be back in a minute." He pointed at Louise. "And don't let her out of your sight."

With that, he ran after Ava.

PART 2, CHAPTER 23

Hugh came to an abrupt stop as he reached the main corridor. Ava was gone, but that wasn't what brought him to a halt. His ears had caught a whisper of sound. He looked over his shoulder as it came again – the softest murmur of a miaow. The hallway behind him was as empty as that in front. The gossamer thread of sound seemed to almost be weaving its way out of another dimension. He headed in its direction.

With every step, the miaowing became a fraction louder, gradually transforming into something between a whine and a yowl. He fancied he could detect a note of pained yearning in the eerie lullaby. He thought about Dorothy's warbling voice. Was she drifting along the corridors again, crooning to her elderly guests and whoever else might be listening?

A ceiling-to-floor red velvet curtain came into view at the end of the corridor. The shiny material swayed gently, although there was no hint of a draught.

"Mrs Dankworth?" said Hugh.

The hallway instantly became silent. The curtain stopped moving. Hugh reached out to draw it aside. A blur of movement filled his vision. He caught a flash of bristling ginger fur and blazing green eyes before the cat landed on him. He gasped as Sy's razor-sharp claws pierced his shirt and sank into his chest. For a few heartbeats, shock froze his limbs, then his hands shot up to try to yank loose the hissing feline. Sy's claws clung to him like fish hooks. With a wild fury, the cat clamped its teeth onto Hugh's uppermost hand.

A scream erupting from him, Hugh jerked his arm up so forcefully that the cat's claws were torn free. Blood speckled the curtain as Hugh flailed around with Sy dangling from his hand. Eyes popping out of its skull, the cat relentlessly sank its fangs in deeper.

"Let go, you little bastard!" yelled Hugh, slamming Sy into a wall. "Let go! Let go!"

Hugh pummelled Sy against the damask wallpaper over and over again. Each impact sent electric shocks of pain up his arm. There was a crunch of breaking bone. The pressure on his hand suddenly eased off. Sy's long, lithe body went limp, then dropped to the carpet with a soft thud.

Hugh's blood-dappled chest heaved with relief as he stared down at the cat. Its skull was caved in like a rotten jack-o'-lantern. He warily prodded a foot at the bundle of ginger fur. Sy showed no signs of life.

He looked at his hand. Blood was welling from a pair of puncture wounds on either side of it. His head snapped up as a chorus of plaintive mewls came from beyond the half-open curtain.

"Hugh!"

Darting a glance over his shoulder at Louise's exclamation, he saw her running towards him with Graham lumbering along behind.

Hugh raised his uninjured hand, palm out. "Don't come any closer."

"You're bleeding," gasped Louise, looking at his torn, bloodied shirt.

"It's nothing. Just scratches."

"How–" Louise broke off, her eyes becoming even wider as they fixed on the dead cat.

"Sy attacked me."

"Why?"

As Louise spoke, the mewling ratcheted up a notch. Hugh eyed the gloom on the other side of the curtain. Stacks of folded laundry occupied shelves built into the aperture. Tensed to spring backwards in case one of the other cats was waiting to pounce, he drew the curtain fully open. The mewling seemed to be coming from behind a couple of cardboard boxes below the bottom shelf.

Crouching down, Hugh peered between the boxes. He glimpsed a swatch of grey fur, a little pink nose and a pair of golden eyes. Another tiny form – this one jet black – jostled its way into view. As Hugh carefully moved aside a box, both kittens skittered to the furthest reaches of the cupboard. They were joined by a snub-nosed ginger kitten. All three dived behind a scrunched-up towel. The ginger kitten peeked over the towel, its eyes as round as pennies. Looking past Hugh at Sy, it let out a weirdly human cry.

Guilt twinging in his stomach, Hugh shifted sideways to block the kitten's line of sight. The kitten ducked down in alarm, leaving only the fluffy tips of its ears visible. "It's okay," Hugh said softly. "I'm not going to hurt you."

Louise stepped forwards, peering over his shoulder at the litter of kittens. "Sy was protecting his babies." As a furry black face popped into view, she continued, "Poor things. I wonder who their mother is?"

"I'd say it's Yo-yo," said Graham, photographing Sy's corpse from different angles like a crime-scene photographer. "They look like they've got some Persian in them."

"I wonder if anyone else knows about them?"

Hugh glanced at the dozens of little pebbles of poo dotting the floor. "I doubt it. Dorothy wouldn't leave them here like this."

"Neither can we."

Hugh pointed at Sy. "She'll chuck us out of the hotel for sure if she sees that."

"We'll hide him." Louise looked into the black kitten's heartachingly big eyes. "But we have to tell her about them."

"We will do, but first I need to deal with this." Hugh held up his injured hand.

Louise winced at the quartet of deep puncture wounds. "That looks nasty."

"You might need antibiotics," said Graham. "Cat saliva is full of pathogenic bacteria."

Despite his throbbing hand, Hugh smiled crookedly. "Is there anything you don't know?"

"Plenty. That's why I'm still here."

At the creak of a door opening, Hugh snatched up the dead cat and hid it behind his back.

A dumpling-shaped old lady waddled into the hallway. She smiled at them before heading in the direction of the grand staircase. Flesh-coloured hearing aids were hooked behind her ears.

Louise puffed her cheeks at the close-call.

"I've got a first-aid kit in my room," said Graham, turning to head back the way they'd come.

Hugh moved the cardboard box back into place and closed the curtain. Tucking the dead cat under an arm, he clutched his injured hand to staunch the bleeding.

As the tiniest of mewls tugged at her heartstrings, Louise said, "I don't like the thought of leaving the kittens alone."

"They'll be fine."

Somewhat reluctantly, Louise turned away from the cupboard and trailed after Hugh and Graham.

Hugh's gaze landed on the vase of dead flowers a few metres beyond the intersection of corridors. He sized up the urn-shaped vase with his eyes. "That looks just about big enough."

He removed the flowers and set about stuffing the ginger tom headfirst into the vase. Sy's floppy corpse threatened to become stuck in the fluted ceramic neck. Louise averted her gaze, swallowing queasily, as Hugh squished Sy into the vase's rounded body until only the tip of his tail was visible. He covered it with flowers, then stood back to survey his handiwork.

"Its bowels will release soon and stink this place out," said Graham.

"As soon as it gets dark, I'll sneak it out of the hotel," said Hugh.

They continued to Graham's room. Hugh unbuttoned his shirt and examined himself in the bathroom mirror. Blood was trickling from two sets of four scratches on his chest. Louise wetted a flannel. As she dabbed at the scratches, he washed his injured hand. Blood swirled down the plughole. Glimpses of white were visible within the bite marks.

"The little bugger's bitten me right down to the bone," said Hugh.

Graham came into the bathroom with surgical tape, antiseptic cream and a roll of bandage. Hugh flinched as Louise rubbed the cream into his wounds. "Jesus, that stings!"

"Don't be such a baby," she gently remonstrated. She set about bandaging his hand.

When she was done, he flexed his fingers experimentally. "That actually doesn't feel too bad. Thanks, nurse. Good job."

Louise didn't smile at the compliment. Her worried eyes stared into his. "Ava's right about one thing – this isn't going to end well."

Hugh shied away from her gaze. As if the burden of his thoughts was too heavy, he sank down onto the toilet lid and hung his head. Four crimson dots seeped through the bandage as he continued to flex his fingers.

Louise rested a hand on the back of his neck. At her gentle touch, he lifted his gaze to hers. A smile flickered on his lips. It vanished as a trilling voice called out from the corridor, "Bel! Sy!"

PART 2, CHAPTER 24

"It's Dorothy," said Hugh as the *rat-a-tat* of urgent knocking reverberated along the hallway.

"Bel! Sy!" The shrill shouts were getting louder.

"She's heading this way," said Louise, turning to Hugh. "What do we do?"

He drew in a deep breath, bracing himself for a confrontation. "We'd better go speak to her."

"I'll leave that to you," said Graham. "If it is Bel in the well, she'll die if I don't get to her soon." He tossed Hugh a faded black t-shirt. "Here, you can borrow that."

Hugh pulled the XXL t-shirt over his head. It hung on his shoulders like a shapeless sack.

Dorothy's voice jumped in volume as Graham opened the door. "Bel! Sy!"

All along the hallway, wrinkly faces were poking out of doorways to see what the ruckus was about. They didn't look concerned, merely curious. Doubtless, they were well acquainted with Dorothy's histrionics.

The woman herself swept into view, a sapphire-blue dress swirling around her as if possessed of a life of its own. Her Goldilocks curls swished from side-to-side as she hurried along, asking every guest in turn, "Have you seen Bel and Sy?"

"No," they replied, one after another.

As Dorothy drew near, Graham turned his back to her. "Don't

touch my gear," he told Hugh before heading for the stairs.

Concealing his bandaged hand in his trouser pocket, Hugh went into the corridor.

"Oh Mr Smith!" Dorothy flung her arms wide as if to embrace him. "These old women are useless, but perhaps you can help. I'm looking for–" She broke off, her powdered mask of a face crinkling as Louise stepped into view.

"This is my wife, Louise," said Hugh.

Dorothy looked Louise over slowly, like one cat studying another that had trespassed into its territory. "Pleased to meet you, Mrs Smith." The toneless greeting suggested she was anything but.

With a somewhat fixed smile, Louise replied, "Pleased to meet you too."

Dorothy eyed Louise's mousy hair and freckled features for a moment more before her gaze returned to Hugh. The breathless anxiety rushed back into her voice. "I can't find Bel and Sy anywhere. Have you seen them?"

"Bel and Sy?" echoed Hugh, feigning uncertainty. "Do you mean your cats?"

His apparent ignorance elicited a sharp retort from Dorothy. "Yes, of course I mean my cats."

"I'm sorry, I haven't seen them."

"But we do have something to tell you," Louise said as gently as a doctor preparing a patient for bad news.

One of Dorothy's eyes narrowed to an ice-blue glimmer. "What do *you* have to tell me?" Her tone made it clear that she doubted Louise had anything of worth to say.

"Actually, it would be better to just show you." Louise stepped past Dorothy. "It's this way."

Dorothy slitted her other eye like she was trying to work out whether she was being lured into a trap.

Hugh held out his arm for her to take. Her ruby lips lifting at the gentlemanly gesture, she hooked her arm through his. The elderly residents moved aside as he led her along the corridor. Chin held high, she matched his steps like a dance partner.

"Your wife's very beautiful," she said, observing Louise's graceful movements.

Hugh glanced at Dorothy. She was still smiling, but something in her tone sent a tingle of unease through him. "Thank you."

"How long have you been married?"

Hugh had to think for a second. "Almost eleven years."

"Do you have any children?"

"One. Isabelle. She's seven."

"Arthur and I have been married forty-six years. I was eighteen when we tied the knot. He was twenty-one. He was the ugliest man I'd ever met." Dorothy's voice was jauntily matter-of-fact. She tittered like a little girl confessing to being naughty. "I only married him because he'd inherited this place."

Hugh was momentarily silent, unsure how to respond to the brutally frank admission. "Do you have any children?"

Dorothy laughed like she'd never heard anything so absurd. She trailed a hand down her cleavage to her flat stomach. "Does this body look like it's carried a baby?" Without waiting for a reply, she declared with conversation ending finality, "I wouldn't ruin my figure for any man."

They walked on in silence to the laundry cupboard. Hugh eyed the wallpaper uneasily. The dark floral pattern camouflaged the blood-spatters where he'd crushed Sy's skull.

Raising a finger to her lips, Louise opened the curtain and carefully moved aside a cardboard box. For a moment, nothing except the crumpled towel was visible in the gloomy recess. Then three little heads popped into view, nestled together like fluffy clouds.

Dorothy gasped, her eyes huge with surprise and delight. Clasping her hands together as if in prayer, she sank to her knees. "Oh my darlings. My beautiful darlings."

She reached for the kittens. They mewled, but didn't try to avoid her hands, seeming to know instinctively that she posed no threat. She scooped up the grey kitten and cradled it against her chest.

The kitten nosed at Dorothy's cleavage, purring as she stroked its head. As if it didn't want to be left out, the midnight-black kitten ventured forth boldly and butted its forehead against Louise's hand. "Hello there," she said, running the backs of her fingers across its impossibly soft fur. Its big greenish-yellow eyes blinking up at her, it let out a low, yet somehow piercingly sad miaow, as if asking, *Are you going to look after me now?*

With a flash of something akin to jealousy in her eyes, Dorothy snatched up the black kitten. As it let out an alarmed squeak, Louise battled an impulse to grab it back. The kitten calmed down as Dorothy told it softly, "Hello, little one, I'm your grandma." She looked over her shoulder as a *miaooow* vibrated along the corridor. "And here, if I'm not mistaken, is your mother."

Yo-yo padded into view, stopping a few metres away from Dorothy.

"What have you been up to, you naughty girl?" Dorothy asked in a tone of playful rebuke.

Yo-yo's whiskers quivered as she responded with a series of short miaows.

Dorothy laughed like she understood what the cat was saying. "Yes, I know Sy's a handsome devil. I wouldn't have been able to resist either. But you should have told me you were expecting."

Mew, miaow, mew, mew, miaow.

A pained expression washed over Dorothy's face as if Yo-yo had levelled an unjust accusation against her. "How could you even think that? I would never let Arthur hurt your babies."

Louise gave Hugh an amused glance behind Dorothy's back.

Seemingly catching the look, Yo-yo flicked her snowy tail in annoyance. The grey kitten mewled as if something was bothering it.

"Are you hungry?" asked Dorothy. She returned the black kitten to the side of its ginger sibling, sliding Louise a look that said, *Keep your hands off*. She beckoned for Yo-yo to come closer. Yo-yo didn't move. The grey kitten's mewling grew more insistent. A note of command entered Dorothy's voice. "Yo-yo, come here and feed your baby."

With another contemptuous flick of her tail, Yo-yo turned and strutted back along the corridor.

"Yo-yo!" Dorothy called after her. Tossing her head haughtily, Yo-yo continued on her way. An exaggerated gasp issued from Dorothy. "Oh you disobedient Jezebel!"

She rose to stalk after the cat. Yo-yo quickened her pace, keeping just out of reach. Hugh and Louise followed along. They exchanged a glance as the vase came into view. Hugh's heart skipped a beat as Yo-yo peered up at Sy's temporary coffin. The cat rose lithely onto its hind-legs, balancing one paw against the lip of the alcove. It tapped its other paw against the vase, looked at Dorothy and emitted a mournful miaow.

"Yo-yo, be careful," she remonstrated, "That's valuable."

The vase rocked on its base as Yo-yo pushed harder.

"Stop that!" Dorothy hurried forwards to shoo Yo-yo away

and steady the vase.

Yo-yo scampered to a safe distance before turning to unleash a flurry of miaows at Dorothy.

Hugh almost fancied he could make out a word amongst the weirdly low-pitched sounds. *Look*, the cat seemed to be urging. *Look. Look.*

Her over-plucked eyebrows pinching into a wiggly line, Dorothy looked from Yo-yo to the vase. As if afraid of what she might find, she slowly stretched out a hand to remove the dead flowers. Like an obscene gesture, Sy's tail rose stiffly into view.

Dorothy's mouth dropped open. Hugh braced himself for the inevitable ear-splitting scream, but only silence flowed between her lips. With the grey kitten clutched to her bosom, she retreated until her back touched the opposite wall. Her skirt crumpled like a concertina as she slid to the carpet.

Yo-yo sprang forwards to snatch the kitten away in her mouth. With the ball of grey fur dangling by the scruff of its neck, she ran off towards the laundry cupboard.

Louise bent towards Dorothy. "Mrs Dankworth." She made the name sound like a concerned question. Dorothy stared through her as if she were made of glass.

The blank stare transported Hugh back to Rampton, to his mother's eyes that seemed to be adrift in a world far beyond this one. Shaking off the image, he reached for Louise's arm and drew her away from Dorothy.

Several grim-faced old ladies emerged from nearby rooms. "Is she breathing?" one asked with the pragmatism of someone accustomed to being around illness and death.

Hugh held a hand over Dorothy's mouth. A breath warmed his palm. "Yes. Mrs Dankworth, can you hear me?"

The softest of moans slid from Dorothy.

"Move aside!" a voice boomed from beyond the old ladies.

They parted before the tall, stiff figure of Arthur. He strode between them, displaying no surprise, as if finding his wife in a semi-catatonic state was a common occurrence. Eyeing Arthur's massive hands uneasily, Hugh stepped away from Dorothy. As Arthur stooped towards her, his skin stretched even tighter across his gaunt face, giving it the appearance of a living skull.

"Dorothy." His voice was firm, but his fingers were fearfully tender as he touched her cheeks.

She scrunched her face, twisting away from the gnarled digits as if revolted by them.

Arthur's deep-set eyes scrutinised the onlookers. "What happened?"

An old lady pointed at the ginger tail protruding from the vase. Arthur's shaggy grey eyebrows lifted a fraction, nothing more. His shovel-sized hands reached out to clasp the vase. He tipped it over, but Sy remained tightly entombed within.

"We found some kittens," said Louise.

Dismay seeped into Arthur's voice. "Kittens? How many?"

"Three. They're in the cupboard at the end of the corridor."

Arthur's beaky nose whistled as he sucked in a breath. His stern gaze returned to Dorothy. "How many times have I told you to get Yo-yo spayed?"

Ignoring him, she stared at Hugh with a fixed intensity that made him want to avert his gaze. In an effort not to appear guilty, he forced himself to maintain eye contact.

Arthur jabbed a finger at the vase. "What I want to know is, how did Sy get in there?"

"Maybe he got himself stuck," suggested one of the old ladies. "Cats get everywhere."

"But how did the flowers end up on top of him?" asked Dorothy.

Arthur locked his eyes on Hugh. "Well?"

Hugh blinked under the combined force of Arthur and Dorothy's stare. "How should I know?"

Arthur pointed at Hugh's bandaged hand. "What happened to your hand?"

"Oh it's nothing, just a cut."

Arthur kept his slate-grey eyes on Hugh as if trying to unnerve him into divulging additional details. When none were forthcoming, his gaze returned to Dorothy. He jerked big nose in the direction of the laundry cupboard. "We're not keeping those things."

"Yes we are."

"No, Dorothy, we're not."

"Yes we are, yes we are, yes we are!" she fired back like a spoiled brat that wouldn't take no for an answer.

Arthur pressed his lips together so firmly that they all but disappeared. His fingers curled into fists as big as lump hammers. Standing as bolt upright as he had done for the portrait in the lobby, he glowered at Dorothy. After mere seconds, though, his shoulders sagged and his lips drooped into an inverted smile. His voice resonated from deep within, seeming to carry the weight of a thousand such conversations. "You need your rest, my love."

She pouted up at him. "I want to see the kittens. Take me to them."

He lowered his head like someone resigned to their fate. "Yes dear." With a sort of robotic obedience, he bent to lift her to her feet. Supporting her by the elbow, he slow marched towards the laundry cupboard.

"Do you need any help with the kittens?" Louise called after them.

Dorothy shot a glare at her. "Not from you."

Louise glanced bemusedly at Hugh. "What did I do?"

An old lady offered her a benevolent smile. "I wouldn't worry about it, dear. She's always like that with younger women. She won't employ a maid under sixty. It's jealousy, plain and simple."

The lady's companions nodded sagely, murmuring, "Jealousy yes… Mmm, jealousy…"

PART 2, CHAPTER 25

Louise took hold of Hugh's uninjured hand and drew him back to Graham's room. Once the door was closed behind them, she said, "She suspects you killed her cat."

Hugh gave her a doubtful look. "She's too self-absorbed to see beyond the end of her nose.

"That woman's not what she seems. All the makeup and amateur dramatics are a…" Louise searched for the right word, "disguise."

Hugh thought about Dorothy's muted reaction to finding Sy. Was 'her majesty' a disguise? A character she was playing? "Then who's the real Dorothy Dankworth?"

"I don't know. I'll tell you one thing, Graham's not going to find the answer down that well. But we might be able to find it somewhere in this hotel. When you told me you were going to clear your mum's name, I thought it would be impossible, but now…" Louise eyed the shabby luxury of their surroundings. "Now I'm not so sure. I think there's a chance the evidence we need is here." She held up her hand as if she was gripping something. "Real evidence."

"Such as?"

Pursing her lips in thought, Louise looked at the portrait hanging over the bed. A regal looking woman with milky skin and strawberry blonde hair stared back at her. Louise's gaze moved to the hallway door. "Who are those men?"

"What men?"

"The ones in the portraits."

"I've no idea, but they're on every upstairs floor. There must be hundreds of them." The nape of Hugh's neck tingled at the mere thought of the portraits. "They make me feel watched wherever I go in this place."

"Maybe that's why they're on the walls. Maybe Dorothy likes to imagine them watching her, wanting her."

Hugh let out a scoffing little laugh. "Yes, she likes to pretend she's a queen and they're her admirers."

"Maybe they were once. But not anymore." A hint of sympathy crept into Louise's voice. "It must be hard for a woman like her. No children. A husband you can't stand touching you. What have you got when your looks are gone?"

"Cats."

Louise smiled at Hugh's dry reply. A faint frown chased her amusement away. "You don't think Arthur would hurt the kittens, do you?"

"I think he'll do as he's told."

From the deepening furrows on Louise's brow it was clear that she didn't share Hugh's certainty. "'He is a mighty king and terrible.'. That's what Ava said. What if she was talking about Arthur?"

"Arthur's no king. He's nothing but a meal ticket. Dorothy herself told me as much. Anyway, why do you care what Ava said? You think she's a fraud."

"I never said that. Just because I don't believe she has psychic powers, doesn't mean I don't take her seriously. She can read people like a book."

Hugh took out his phone. "How does the full quote go?"

"'He is a mighty king and terrible. He rideth on a pale horse with trumpets and other kinds of musical instruments playing before him.'"

Hugh typed the quote into the search bar. "It's from The Lesser Key of Solomon. A grimoire."

"A spell book?"

"It's basically a three-hundred-year old instruction manual for evoking demons. Listen to this." His voice becoming more uneasy with each word, Hugh read aloud, "'He is very furious at his first appearance, that is, while the exorcist layeth his courage; for to do this he must hold a hazel wand in his hand, striking it out towards the south and east quarters, make a triangle, without the circle, and then command him into it by the bonds and charges of spirits as hereafter followeth.'" He lifted his troubled eyes to Louise. "That's how to summon Beleth."

"Who's Beleth?"

Hugh typed the question into his phone. "'The demon Beleth, a king of Hell, is one of a trinity of catlike demons.'" He illustrated the words by turning his phone to show Louise a finely detailed drawing of a humanoid figure with a cat's head. Beleth was sat astride a white horse that was rearing up on its hind legs. His eyes glowed from within the hood of a long black cape. An almost equally long trumpet protruded from his whiskered mouth.

Louise read out the rest of the paragraph below the picture. "'Beleth is often joined by his fellow demons, Sitri and Yomyael.'"

"The names are strangely familiar, don't you think?"

"You mean Dorothy's cats? Are you trying to tell me you just killed a demon?"

Hugh didn't reply. He stared at his phone with the intense focus of someone attempting to solve a riddle. In an almost exultant tone, he read aloud, "'This Great King Beleth causeth all the love that may be, both of men and of women, until the master exorcist hath had his desire fulfilled.'"

When Louise greeted his words with a bemused expression, he continued, "Don't you see? Faust sold his soul in return for twenty-four-years of unlimited power." He swept a hand towards the hallway. "Dorothy sold hers in return for them. Her army of admirers."

"But they're just paintings. A lonely woman's fantasy." Louise stepped forwards, reaching for Hugh's hands and squeezing them imploringly. "The men in them aren't real. Beleth isn't real. Focus on what's real or your mum will die in Rampton."

He found himself averting his gaze from the stark reality in her eyes. "Say there is some 'real evidence' in the hotel. Where would we even begin to look for it?"

"What about the Dankworths' living quarters? Where do they sleep?"

"I don't know." Touching the feather in his pocket, Hugh asked in his head, *What should I do, Dad?*

Louise nibbled her upper lip in thought. "I should imagine they live on the ground floor. Somewhere close to Reception."

At her words, an image came to Hugh of a luminous stick figure gyrating its way towards a door. His voice took on a sudden decisiveness. "There's a room behind reception. We'll start there."

"Why there?"

"I..." Hugh faltered, not wanting to get into another argument about the existence – or non-existence – of supernatural entities.

Louise gave him a small smile, as if she'd read his mind and felt the same way. "I suppose that's as good a place as any to start. I bet Tim and what's-his-name would let us have a snoop around."

"For the right price, yes I'm sure they would." Hugh heaved a sigh at the thought of having to negotiate with the sniggering pair again.

"Shall we go speak to them?"

"We should wait for Graham to get back." Hugh glanced at a carriage clock on a shelf. "He's been gone for almost an hour. I shouldn't think he'll be much longer."

"Give him a call."

Hugh did as Louise suggested. His call went straight through to an answering service. "He must be in the basement."

A slight shudder ran through Louise. "I couldn't go down there on my own."

Hugh couldn't help but smile. "Why not? Are you scared Beleth might get you?"

Louise arched an eyebrow at the teasing remark. "Beleth, no. Arthur Dankworth, yes."

Her reply wiped the smile off Hugh's face. He, too, gave a little shudder as he pictured Arthur's 'murderer's hands' constricting around Louise's throat. "Do you think he's capable of murder?"

"That depends."

"On what?"

"On whether you're right about him doing whatever Dorothy tells him to do. Do *you* think he loves her enough to kill for her?"

"Yes." There was no trace of doubt in Hugh's voice. "Although I'm not sure I'd call it 'love'."

"Then what would you call it?"

Hugh answered with a word he understood only too well. "Obsession."

PART 2, CHAPTER 26

"Where the hell is he?" Hugh wondered as his call went through to Graham's answering service again. "He's been gone for hours."

"Perhaps he changed his mind and left with Ava," said Louise.

Hugh motioned to a bulging holdall. "All his gear's still here. There's no way he'd leave it behind." He glanced at the window. A velvety shroud of twilight was enveloping the garden. His gaze shifted to the hallway door. "Maybe I should go down to the basement and–"

"No," Louise cut him off, rising from the armchair to stand between him and the door.

"But what if Graham needs help? What if he's fallen down the well trying to rescue Bel?"

"There's no way he could fall down the well. I'm not sure even a cat could fit through that gap." Louise stepped forwards to take Hugh's hands. Her touch was as gentle as her eyes. "And I don't think anyone around here – not even Arthur – would be daft enough to take on Graham."

Her reassuring words brought a tender smile to Hugh's lips. "How do you always know what I need to hear?"

"Because I know you better than you know yourself."

They looked at each other silently for moment, their eyes speaking a language only they understood. Louise's unwavering gaze promised to be there for Hugh through thick and thin. In return, his eyes shone with adoration, letting her know she was his one true love, his rock.

Cupping his uninjured hand around the back of Louise's head, Hugh leaned in to kiss her. Her lips almost rivalled the softness of the feather. He inhaled her mellow, clean scent, using it to wash away the tension in his body and mind. He drew away from her at the sound of something being pushed under the door. An envelope slid into view. He quickly moved to squint through the spyhole. The shaggy-haired figure of Leo was slouching away with a stack of envelopes in his hands.

Hugh picked up the envelope and took out a sheet of paper. His gaze skimmed across a few sentences of spidery calligraphy. "You are cordially invited to the funeral of Sy the Second," he read out. "The memorial service will commence at 9pm in the garden. All attendees will receive a complimentary glass of Champagne."

"Perhaps we should go. I could do with a glass of bubbly."

A smile crawled up one side of Hugh's face at Louise's half-joking suggestion. "I wonder if her majesty's going to be providing the entertainment? She's one hell of a singer."

His sarcasm failed to elicit a matching smile from Louise. "I wonder if the staff will be attending."

Hugh's eyebrows lifted as he caught her meaning. "Of course they will be. What's the saying? Never let a good tragedy go to waste. Dorothy wouldn't allow them to miss out on a chance for her to be centre of attention."

"Which will give us a chance to search for evidence."

Hugh chuckled grimly. "At least Sy the Second didn't die for nothing."

Louise frowned. "Don't joke about that. It's not funny." At a clink of glass, she turned to the window.

On the patio below, Leo and a stooped old maid were setting

out Champagne flutes on a trestle table. Dozens of flickering candles illuminated their faces. Dorothy was tottering back and forth, appearing to do nothing except get in their way. A black rose fascinator was pinned to her hair. A birdcage veil encased the upper half of her face. Her movements were restricted by a figure-hugging black dress with a plunging neckline. Every so often, she theatrically dabbed her eyes with a frilly black handkerchief.

"Dorothy looks like she's getting ready for a virtuoso performance," commented Louise.

"Is she wearing a ring on the middle finger of her left hand?" Hugh asked.

Louise leaned forwards, squinting. "I can't tell. Why?"

"Because whoever summons Beleth has to wear a sliver ring on that finger."

"Oh, we're back to that nonsense, are we?" Louise heaved a sigh. "Who'd have thought a king of Hell would live in a hotel in the Lake District?"

Hugh flashed her a frown. "Give the sarcasm a rest, Louise. It isn't your style."

"I'm only trying to look out for you, Hugh. Remember why we're here. We're not after revenge. We're here to get your mother out of that awful place."

His irritation gave way to contrition. "You're right." He nodded as if trying to convince himself of his words.

A murmur of voices drew Louise's gaze back to the garden. Sombrely dressed figures were queueing at the table for their complimentary champagne. The mournful strains of a violin struck up from somewhere unseen. A figure in the middle of the lawn caught her eye. Tim was shovelling soil from a knee-deep hole. After every few spadefuls, he paused to glare at the champagne drinkers.

"Looks like just about everyone's outside," said Louise.

Dorothy's shrill voice rose above the violin, warbling, "Sy, my sweet Sy, it's time to say our last goodbye…"

"She sounds like she's in pain."

The smile that played at the edges of Hugh's lips suggested he hoped Louise was right. He peered out of the window. "I don't see Arthur."

"Me neither." Louise frowned uneasily at the thought that Arthur might be lurking somewhere inside the hotel. "What do you want to do?"

"We'll never get another chance like this." Hugh reached for her hand. It was even more clammy than his own. "Listen, why don't you go and wait in your car? What's the point of us both putting ourselves at risk?"

"Because two can search twice as fast as one." Louise gave an exaggerated wince as Dorothy belted out another verse of mournful lyrics. "Come on, let's get going. I don't think my eardrums can take much more of that."

PART 2, CHAPTER 27

Hugh poked his head out of the door as warily as a soldier embarking on a dangerous mission. The hallway was deserted. Hand in hand, he and Louise hurried from the room. He paused at the intersection of corridors to cast a glance from side-to-side. Only the portraits looked back at him. The vase with Sy's body crammed into it was gone. A scattering of wilted rose petals trailed away from the alcove towards the main staircase.

Under the watchful gazes of Dorothy's 'admirers', they hastened on their way. A deep hush hung over the corridor, as if the very walls around them were grieving for Sy. Their swift footsteps on the thin carpet seemed jarringly loud.

"God, does this hallway ever end?" said Louise.

Hugh echoed his dad's words. "It's an optical illusion."

"I'm starting to think everything around here's an illusion. I wouldn't be surprised if this place disappeared in a puff of smoke and we found ourselves back home."

When the landing came into view, Hugh raised a palm for Louise to stay put. He crept forwards to peer over the ornate bannister. The gleaming chandeliers had been dimmed to a soft golden glow. A fire crackled serenely in the hearth. Shadows performed an otherworldly waltz in its flickering light.

There was no sign of Arthur or anyone else.

Hugh motioned for Louise to follow him down the curved

staircase. They stole across the lobby to the reception counter. Hugh flipped up a hinged section of the countertop, lowered it behind Louise, then turned to the door and tried its handle. The door clicked open. He edged into an office somewhat chaotically crammed with filing cabinets, desks, telephones, and paperwork.

His gaze skimmed over the paperwork – printouts of guests' bills, inventories for groceries and toiletries. Louise looked in a desk's drawers. She pulled out a wad of red-lettered final demands. "Looks like the Dankworths are in trouble."

Hugh approached a door at the back of the office, turned the handle and slunk into a corridor starkly illuminated by a striplight. The bare white walls dragged his mind away from the lurid phantasmagoria of Dorothy and Arthur's little fantasy realm to the grim reality of Rampton. It was hard to believe two such places could coexist within the same world. And yet it struck him that, as different as they were, they served an eerily similar purpose. In their own way, both were refuges and cages.

As he tiptoed forwards, he got the sense that he was seeing behind the stage of a lavish theatre. The feeling intensified as the corridor opened up into a green-painted room with mismatched armchairs dotted around it seemingly at random. A cheap-looking modern coffee table cluttered with mugs and plates of half-eaten sandwiches occupied the centre of the room. Ornaments, mirrors and paintings were stacked against the walls like stage props.

Louise tapped Hugh on the shoulder and pointed to what looked like the vase he'd stuffed Sy's body into. A spatter of blood on its rim seemed to confirm that it was indeed the same vase.

Hugh suddenly found himself wondering if even Dorothy cared about the cats.

"It's all just a performance," Louise murmured as if in

answer. "A play put on for the guests."

Hugh gave a shake of her head. If this was a play, it was for her majesty's entertainment alone. Everyone else was just a bit-part player in her story.

They set about searching the room as quickly and quietly as possible. Apart from the occasional fat spider, all they found were more 'stage props'. Hugh glanced at his phone. It was almost half-past nine. "How long do you think the funeral will go on for?"

"I can't see it lasting more than an hour. The old ladies will be wanting their beds."

"Then we'd better get a move on."

Another short corridor led to a door with a square of cardboard sellotaped to its upper panel. A crudely drawn star enclosed a scrawl of writing that warned 'Dorothy's Room. Keep Out'. It reminded Hugh of a similar sign Isabelle had once stuck to her bedroom door.

"I suppose if that was the green room, this must be the star of the show's dressing room," whispered Louise.

Hugh suddenly put a finger to his lips. "*I heard something,*" he mouthed, turning his ear to the door, A plaintive mewl issued from beyond it.

"It's the kittens," said Louise.

Hugh ever so slowly twisted the doorhandle. The door creaked open a few centimetres. The reek of cat urine that escaped through the gap was enough to make his nostrils sting. A slant of light from the hallway fell across a clothes rack. The sagging metal rail was overloaded with a rainbow of frilly dresses.

Hugh gave a start as a pair of yellow eyes blinked at him like fairy-lights from amongst the folds of shiny material. A smooshed grey face emerged into view. The kitten was clinging to the ribbed bodice of a dress. As Hugh entered the room, it dropped nimbly to the floor and skittered from sight.

More dresses were overflowing from an open wardrobe. Tangles of lingerie dangled from half-open drawers. The floor was swamped with high-heeled shoes. Teetering stacks of hats, fascinators, handbags, belts, scarves and other accessories occupied numerous shelves and hooks. A floor-to-ceiling red velvet curtain covered most of one wall. In front of it was a big dressing table with an even bigger round mirror perched atop it. A couple of dozen bare lightbulbs fringed the mirror. Items of makeup, perfume bottles and jewellery cluttered the dressing table.

There was no sign of the kittens or any bedding, food or water for them.

Hugh flicked a light-switch. He squinted as the circle of lightbulbs came on. Several of the bulbs were out, but the rest sufficed to form a dazzling halo.

Their light shimmered on the framed photos that covered every spare centimetre of wall space. A few of the photos were black-and-white. The rest were in colour. All of them had Dorothy as their sole subject. They showcased her long limbs, slim waist and voluptuous breasts in a bewildering array of glamourous dresses. Her plump lips and beguilingly big eyes seemed to offer a promise of pleasure beyond comprehension.

The photos tracked Dorothy's journey from a fresh-faced young woman to early middle-age, telling tales of glitzy escapades. In one frame, she was posing against a backdrop of skyscrapers, in another a heaving ballroom. Hugh's gaze lingered on a photo in which she was perched atop a horse, like a heroine ready to ride off into the sunset. She looked to be about thirty and at the peak of her beauty. There was something almost profane about the perfect symmetry of her features and the flawlessness of her skin.

Look at me, her sapphire eyes seemed to command. *Look at me and fall to your knees!*

Hugh tiptoed into the windowless room, trying his best not to disturb the clutter. Something squidged against his shoe. Lifting his foot, he gave a little grimace of disgust. The sole of his shoe was smeared with faeces. Scanning the floor, he saw it was a minefield of cat turds, many of which looked as ossified as Dorothy's powdered face.

"She couldn't care less about the cats," said Louise.

Hugh wiped his shoe on the carpet. "That woman couldn't care less about anything except for herself."

Louise crouched down, holding out a hand. "Kittens," she called to them softly.

"What are you doing?"

"I just want to make sure they're okay."

"We don't have time for–" Hugh broke off as a faint scuffling drew his gaze to the curtain. He started forwards, but Louise caught hold of his bandaged hand. He winced as her fingers flexed nervously against the bitemark.

"What if it's *him?*" she hissed.

"Mr Dankworth, is that you?" Hugh ventured, unable to keep a slight tremor out of his voice.

Silence emanated from the curtain. Hugh ushered Louise back towards the door. He stared at the moth-eaten curtain for a moment more, his fingers curling and uncurling at his sides. Then he strode forwards, kicking aside stilettos and fossilised turds like they were fallen leaves. He swept the curtain to one side, revealing an alcove occupied by a small circular table. Tarot cards were scattered across the purple tablecloth, some face down and others face up.

Hugh's gaze was drawn to a card depicting a scythe-wielding skeleton riding a white horse. 'DEATH' was printed below the picture. He picked up the card and showed it to Louise.

"So Dorothy's in to Tarot," she said dismissively. "So what?"

A flicker of movement from under the table caught her eye. "Kittens," she cooed again, squatting down. She smiled as the black kitten poked its head into view. "Hello there, beautiful."

Its timidity disappearing at the sight of Louise, the kitten padded forwards, purring like a little motor.

"Where's your mummy?" Louise wondered as the kitten nosed her hand. She glanced around cautiously, not wanting to incur Yo-yo's wrath by handling her baby. "Yo-yo? Yo-yo?"

The name met with silence.

"I don't think your mum's interested in being a mum," Louise told the kitten. She curled her fingers under it and, cupping its hindquarters, gently lifted it into her arms. "Are you a boy or a girl? I don't know how to tell which you are."

Midnight was far more concerned with swatting playfully at Louise's long hair.

"Hey, you naughty little thing." With a light touch, she disentangled herself from a tiny paw.

Emitting a drawn out mewl, the kitten stretched its jaws wide open, like a chick waiting for food from its mother.

"You're starving, aren't you? Is there any food around here?" Louise's gaze travelled the room, coming full circle to Hugh. "There were some sandwiches in the green room. There might be some ham or cheese the kittens can eat."

Hugh echoed her earlier words. "Remember why we're here. Let's not get sidetracked."

Reluctantly accepting his words, Louise cuddled the kitten against her shoulder for a few seconds more before bending to put it down. Letting out a distressed miaow, it peered up at her with big round eyes.

"I'm sorry," she told it. "I'd take you home with me if I could. There's a little girl there who'd love you to bits."

Hugh looked at Louise as if questioning her sanity. "I'd drown that thing before I let it anywhere near Isabelle."

Louise treated him to a horrified stare of her own. "It's just a cat."

"I don't care what it is. Nothing from this place is coming home with us."

"I'd love to believe you really meant that."

Blinking away from Louise's probing gaze, Hugh made a sharp shooing motion at the kitten. It scuttled back under the table. "Come on, let's get this done."

He eyed the clutter, wondering where to begin, like a shopper paralysed by too much choice. Louise set about searching the dressing table. She opened a jewellery box. At the sight of several silver rings, Hugh's words rang in her mind – *Whoever summons Beleth has to wear a silver ring.* She clapped the lid shut before he could see the rings.

Hugh began rummaging through the wardrobe, pulling out jumbles of clothing.

"Don't make too much of a mess or they'll know someone's been in here," Louise cautioned.

Hugh glanced at the mounds of high heels, wilted flowers, empty champagne bottles and god only knew what else. He cocked a doubtful eyebrow at Louise. "This place already looks like it's been ransacked by–" He broke off as, from the corner of his eye, he caught a flash of ginger flying through the air. As something landed on his chest, he stumbled backwards, tripping over the debris littering the floor. Was it possible that Sy hadn't been dead after all, but merely unconscious? The thought shot through his mind as he landed on his backside. In the next heartbeat, he found himself staring into a small face with dark eyes and a twitching pink nose.

The ginger kitten sprang off him and dove under the table

"Jesus," he gasped, slightly winded. "I don't think these cats like me."

"Can you blame them?"

Louise leaned down to help Hugh up, but stopped midmovement. She did a double-take at something on the floor, a crease etching itself between her eyebrows. Carefully, as if she was excavating an archaeological site, she moved aside a dusty red high-heeled shoe and a pair of lacy knickers with blonde pubic hair crusted to the gusset.

A long-stemmed object emerged into full view, coated in what looked to be about a century's worth of dust. She picked it up, tracing a finger through the dust, revealing a lustrous black surface embossed with the golden initials 'E.C.'.

PART 2, CHAPTER 28

As carefully as if it was a priceless artifact, Hugh reached for his father's pipe. He blew the dust off the scorched bowl, put the stem to his lips and sucked. A stale taste of tobacco tingled on his tongue, conjuring up an image of his father so vivid he could almost reach out and touch it.

Tears welled up in Hugh's eyes. Louise ever so gently put a hand on his arm. "This is it, Hugh. This is the evidence we need."

A frown twitching across his forehead, Hugh took the pipe out of his mouth. "Is it? What does this prove?"

"It proves Dorothy withheld evidence. Which might be enough to get the police to take another look at the case." There was a soft edge of pleading in Louise's voice. "Let's get your stuff and get out of the hotel."

Hugh rose to his feet. He allowed himself to be pulled towards the door by Louise. A tremulous miaow drew his gaze back to the red curtain. Three pairs of gleaming eyes were staring at him from under its frayed hem. He stared back at them for a second, then closed the door.

Louise drew him swiftly back through the green room to the office. He cracked open the door to peek into the lobby. It was still deserted. He darted forwards to flip up the countertop. Once it was closed behind them, Louise puffed her cheeks and gave Hugh a wide-eyed look, as if she couldn't quite believe they'd actually accomplished their goal.

She started towards the staircase, but Hugh didn't move. "I don't want you going back up there."

"Why not?"

He gave her a look that that said, *Do you really need to ask?* "I want you to wait in your car while I fetch my things."

"Let's both leave right now. Who cares about some clothes?"

"It's not the clothes I'm bothered about."

"What then?" Louise's eyebrows lifted in realisation. "Your dad's tobacco tin."

Hugh nodded, although it wasn't so much the tin that he couldn't bring himself to leave behind as it was its contents. What if the ghost trap had worked, but in a different way to intended? What if it had drawn in his dad's spirit? He'd promised to free both his mum and dad. And he intended to keep that promise. Knowing how Louise would react to such a notion, he swiftly moved the conversation on. "And I need to talk to Graham."

"Try calling him again."

"I will, if he's not in his room." Hugh glanced around as an old lady dressed in black ambled into the lobby. His voice dropped to an urgent whisper. "The funeral must be over. The Dankworths will be here in a minute." He slid a look at the front doors, urging Louise with his eyes to do as he asked.

She thumbed her wedding ring. "I vowed to always stand by your side."

"And I vowed to protect you."

"You're just going to get your things, check on Graham, then come straight back to me?"

Hugh mustered up what he hoped was a reassuring smile. "Where else would I go?"

Loise eyed him undecidedly. "Promise me. Promise me on

your wedding ring."

Hugh held up his ring finger, displaying a gold band. "I promise. Now you promise me you won't come back inside this place."

Louise's eyes searched his for a moment more before she acquiesced. "I promise. Be careful."

With that, she turned to head for the porch. Hugh stood stock-still, his gaze fixed on the front doors as they swung shut behind her. For a few seconds, he seemed lost in thought, wrestling with some inner conflict. Then, with a decisive movement, he leaned over the counter and grabbed a key from a hook labelled 'Salome'.

Shoving it into his pocket, he ran up the staircase. He overtook the solemnly dressed old lady at the first floor landing. The portraits' faces blurred into one, like colours on a mixing pallete, as he sprinted along the hallway. His legs felt heavy, as if he'd been running for miles.

It wasn't me. It wasn't me.

His mum's voice echoed through his mind, spurring him on.

The corridor stretched on endlessly, echoing the countless hours he'd spent with his mum in the prison and his dad in the graveyard. When would it be over? When would they all finally be able to break free of Coldwell Hall's spell?

Upon suddenly finding himself at the intersection of corridors, he veered towards Graham's room. He entered without knocking. No Graham. Everything was just as it had been left. He dialled Graham. Yet again, the call went straight through to an answering service.

He looked floorward, frowning in thought. Surely Graham wasn't still trying to rescue Bel from the well.

A murmur of voices drew his attention to the window. The funeral was still in full swing. The mourners were gathered in the middle of the lawn, each taking turns to pick up a handful of soil and drop it into a rectangular hole. They filed past Dorothy, exchanging a few words with her before heading towards the hotel. Once again, Arthur was nowhere to be seen.

Hugh took out his dad's pipe and the key to 'Salome'. His gaze flitted back and forth between them before settling on the key. He returned the pipe to his pocket and ran from the room. Instead of turning towards his own room, he headed for the rear stairwell. Upon reaching it, he paused to look down the stairs. Uncertainty flickered his eyes. What if Graham had run into Arthur? What if the hotelier had imprisoned him in the well room?

It wasn't me. It wasn't me.

Hugh's uncertainty vanished as his mum's emotionless voice played through his head again. Graham would have to wait. Louise would have to wait. All the years his mum had spent rotting in Rampton, it ended now. Tonight.

He darted up the bare wooden stairs, his footsteps echoing around the stairwell. At the top floor, he eased the door open. He slunk into the gloomy hallway, gripping the key like a knife. At any second, he expected Arthur to march from a room and send him flying with a single swipe of a gargantuan hand.

As the gold lettering 'Salome' came into view, he slowed to a stop. His heart dancing as crazily as the troupe of luminous stick figures had done, he listened at door. The silence was loud enough to make his ears ring.

As quietly as possible, he slid the key into the lock and turned it. The door creaked open. A massive old wardrobe came into view, taking up almost the entirety of one wall.

He crept forwards, casting glances all around, tensed to fight or flee. There was no one in the room – or at least, no one he could see amidst the moonlight that streamed through the open curtains. He pushed the door to and flicked a switch. A cobweb-festooned chandelier flickered into life.

Hugh's gaze lingered on a gilt-framed painting at the head of the four-poster bed. A pale-faced blonde in a red dress was holding a silver platter, upon which the severed head of a bearded, black-haired man rested in a puddle of blood. John the Baptist's mouth hung open as if emitting a silent scream. Salome was looking off to one side, a barely-there enigmatic smile playing on her lips. Her sky blue eyes exuded a contradictory combination of innocence and desire. In contrast, John the Baptist's dark eyes looked more resigned than anguished, almost as if he was meditating on the tragedy of the human condition.

Hugh's gaze fell to the bed's crimson silk sheets. There was an imprint in their centre where someone appeared to have recently lain. He sniffed the air. A faint floral fragrance hinted at who that 'someone' might be. But why would Dorothy come all the way up here? Out of all the rooms what was so special about this one?

He turned to open the wardrobe. Empty. He checked a dresser's drawers. Empty. He peered behind an armchair and under the bed. Nothing. He went into the bathroom. No toiletries. No towels. Not even any toilet paper. Every surface was frosted with dust.

Was Graham right? Had the dancing dwarves merely been the wallpaper patterns messing with his camera's lasers?

Hugh returned to the bedroom and stared at the impression left on the bedding. Tentatively, as if something invisible might be lying there, he reached down to touch the indent. The sheet was cool and slightly damp, just like the air around him.

He frustratedly crumpled a handful of silk in his fingers. He'd been sure he would discover something significant here, the missing piece of the puzzle that would secure his mother's freedom and seal the fate of the Dankworths. As he straightened, his eyes paused on a section of wallpaper.

He traced the outline of a shallow dent with his fingers. It was surrounded by other identical dents – dozens of them – camouflaged at a glance by the busy floral pattern. It looked like someone had attacked the wall with a lump hammer.

Something else caught his eye – a row of vertical scratches on the wallpaper below the painting. The gilded frame was carved into roses whose thorny stems coiled around each other. He slid his fingers up under the frame, pulled it away from the wall and peered behind it. His eyes widened. He lifted the frame off its hook, exposing a cast-iron safe. He laid the painting on the bed, eagerly reached for a tarnished brass handle and tried to twist it. Unsurprisingly, it wouldn't move.

He turned his attention to a dial lock numbered one-to-a-hundred. Ava's gruff little voice sprang into his mind, chanting a stream of numbers. "Five four five eight," he repeated, rotating the dial to line up the corresponding numbers with a notch. His heart jumped at a soft click. He tried the handle again. This time, it turned and the heavy door groaned open as if awakening from a long sleep.

"Thank you, Dad," he murmured.

Eyes bulging with anticipation, he leaned closer, peering inside the safe. It didn't contain the Dankworth family fortune that Leo had alluded to. Instead, it was full of meticulously stacked photographs tied with red ribbons.

Hugh took out a bundle of a dozen or so photos and found himself looking at a thirty-something Dorothy with a middle-aged man. She was on her hands and knees on the bed, facing away from Salome and John the Baptist. The man's groin was pressed against her bare buttocks, his mouth agape, his eyes squeezed shut in a paroxysm of pleasure. Hugh undid the ribbon's bow. He looked through several more photos of Dorothy and the man having sex in various positions.

He dropped the photos onto the bed and reached for another bundle. In this set, a Dorothy that looked to be no more than twenty was with a man at least twice her age. Her stockinged legs were wrapped around his paunchy midriff. Her black dress was ruckled up above her waist. The man's head was arched back. His mouth gaped as if mimicking John the Baptist.

Hugh looked from the photos to the wardrobe. He swiftly approached the wardrobe, stepped inside it and closed the doors. A few centimetres above his eye level – at just the right height for Arthur – there was a gap big enough to point a camera lens through.

"Perverts," he murmured. Was that what the Dankworths were? A pair of common perverts?

A grim laugh escaped him at the possibility, but died in his throat as he recalled the red-lettered final demands Louise had found. What if the Dankworths weren't simply voyeurs, what if they were also blackmailers? Was that how they'd managed to avoid bankruptcy all these years, by blackmailing the men in the photos? A sickly sensation slithered through him. Had his dad been one of those men?

"Please tell me I'm wrong, Dad." Hugh's voice sounded eerily hollow in the enclosed space.

He opened the doors. Slowly, like someone approaching a sinister altar, he crossed the room. Questions hammered at his brain. What would it mean if his dad *was* one of those men? What if the Dankworths had tried to blackmail him? What if he'd refused to pay? What if they'd shown the evidence of his infidelity to his wife?

Despair sucked at Hugh's heart as he imagined his dad and Dorothy cavorting on the silk sheets. Every repulsive detail – the sweat beading his father's forehead, the curves of Dorothy's perfect breasts – sprang to life. He seemed to hear a faint moaning and gasping, the slap of flesh against flesh.

How would his mum have felt at seeing such a thing? Of course, she would have been devastated. Angry too. But just how angry? Had her rage rivalled the storm that forced them to seek refuge in Coldwell Hall? Had it driven her to plunge a knife into her husband?

Josie, you know there's no one more beautiful than you to me, Hugh heard his father crooning.

Had that been a lie?

He thought about waking to see his mum next to his father's corpse – the terror in her eyes contrasting with the emptiness of her voice as she said, *It wasn't me. It wasn't me.*

Had that been a lie too?

The questions wrenched a half-choked sob from Hugh. With a strange mixture of reluctance and eagerness, he resumed taking photos out of the safe and scanning through them. When he was done with each bundle, he flung it aside. Photos fluttered to the floor like confetti. They showed Dorothy's younger self *in flagrante delicto* with men of all ages, shapes and looks. Old, young, fat, thin, handsome, ugly – she appeared to have no preference. The only commonality was that all of them were deep in the throes of passion.

A sense of familiarity tugged at Hugh, a pull of something akin to recognition. It suddenly dawned on him where the feeling came from. He'd seen these men before. Their face lined the hotel's hallways, immortalised in oil paint, a memorial to Dorothy's monstrous vanity.

The realisation ignited a spark of hope. He hadn't seen his dad hanging on the walls.

With an almost manic urgency, he grabbed bundle after bundle from the safe. The roster of Dorothy's lovers seemed almost endless. How many men had she been with? A hundred? A thousand? He felt like he was drowning in a sea of obscenity.

Finally, there was only one bundle left. "Please don't let it be him," said Hugh, reaching for the photos slowly, then with a convulsive movement. Dorothy was straddling a non-descript man, the kind of man you'd walk past in the street without noticing.

"You said no to her!" The words burst forth in a rush of unadulterated relief. Hugh looked at the air around him. "I'm sorry for doubting you, Dad." Hate glimmered in his eyes as they swept across the scattered photos before settling on John the Baptist's severed head. "Now I understand why that bitch killed you. It must have driven her crazy to know she wasn't the most beautiful woman in the world to you." A sneer twisted his lips. "I wish I could have been there to see her face when you–"

He broke off with a start as the door swung open and a tall, suited figure stepped into the room. At the sight of Hugh, Arthur's face betrayed no emotion. But as he took in the photos, his bald head wrinkled like a pickled walnut. His grotesquely long, thick fingers curling and uncurling at his sides, he lifted his gaze to Hugh.

For several breathless seconds, both men remained rooted to the spot, their gazes locked. Tension hung between them like an over-tightened string, ready to snap at the slightest provocation.

Hugh moved, not much, but enough for his foot to disturb several photos. At the same instant, Arthur marched forwards. His beanpole legs swiftly ate up the distance between himself and Hugh. He lifted his arms, keeping them bolt straight, palms facing inward, fingers splayed.

Has he grown?

The thought flashed through Hugh's mind as Arthur loomed over him. He flung up his own arms. With a languid flick of a wrist, Arthur swatted them aside. Hugh gasped as the shockwave of the blow vibrated through him. He tried to retreat, but there was nowhere to go. Arthur clamped his hands onto Hugh's head, digging claw-like fingernails into his scalp. A scream tore from Hugh as a crushing pressure bore in upon him. It felt like two colossal boulders were pressing against his skull.

Willo-the-wisps of light bobbed in front of Hugh's eyes as, with the ease of a parent picking up a small child, Arthur hoisted him off the floor. Hugh's dangling feet flailed, hitting Arthur's shins. The hotelier's gaunt face registered no pain. His grey eyes smouldered with a dull intensity, like old coals. The wrinkles on his scalp deepened as he squeezed harder. Hugh screamed again, jerking around like marionette with tangled strings. He heard his skull creaking ominously, as if it were about to implode.

With a rigid swinging motion, Arthur hurled Hugh across the room. Hugh slammed into the wardrobe, cracking one of its doors. His legs twisted up awkwardly beneath him as he hit the floor. He struggled to get breath into his winded lungs, the room swimming in and out of focus.

Arthur scooped up a handful of photos. The images of Dorothy and her lovers ignited a wild light in his eyes. His other hand tightened into a fist, the knuckles so pale they seemed ready to burst through his skin.

Bang!

The whole room trembled as Arthur hammered his fist against a wall. The thunderous sound yanked Hugh's mind back through the years to the storm-racked night.

What's that noise? he heard himself asking in a frightened little voice.

Perhaps another tree was blown over, came his dad's reply.

It's coming from inside the hotel.

Bang! Bang!

Arthur smashed his fist into the wall twice more, then turned to Hugh. His lips like razors, his cheekbones sharp enough to cut the air, he strode across the room. Hugh desperately tried to move, but his limbs merely flopped about like dying fish.

Arthur reached down with his left hand. The last thing Hugh saw before the hand covered his face was a silver ring all but buried in the sinewy flesh of its middle finger.

PART 3, CHAPTER 1

A Conversation With The Devil

Hugh was surrounded by fish. Everywhere he looked, dead-eyed fish. Their bodies were slimy and bloated, their scales peeling away like old paint on decaying walls. He doubled over, clutching his stomach, choking and retching on their unspeakably rancid stench. The smell thickened to a suffocating density, wrapping itself around him like invisible tentacles.

You're dreaming, whispered a voice from somewhere deep within. *Wake up.*

Hugh strained against the tentacles. The pressure on his chest lessened. His eyes snapped open, but only darkness greeted him.

Waves of panic crashing over him, he instinctively tried to reach for his face, only to discover that his hands were tightly bound. His ankles too. A blindfold covered his eyes. A gag cut into his cheeks. He struggled desperately against his bonds, the coarse fibres scouring his skin. After a brief, futile struggle, he grew still, his breath whistling through his nostrils, his cheek resting against a cold, hard surface.

He flinched as fingers touched his face, pulling down the gag and lifting the blindfold. He found himself looking up into a fluffy white face. Yo-yo stared back from between a pair of ruby red stilettos, her almond-shaped eyes glowing like a summer sky at sunset. Stretching her mouth wide open, she exhaled a fishy purr in his face.

Hugh responded with an agonised groan. Between the nausea assaulting his stomach and the headache besieging his skull, his body felt like a battleground.

His gaze ascended slim ankles shrouded in fishnet tights, passing over knobbly knees to the frayed and faded hem of a dress. Hourglass hips curved into a flat stomach overhung by breasts tightly encased in black velvet. A silver medallion dangled against a thin, turkey-neck. Within the innermost of the medallion's two concentric circles, squiggly lines snaked around an upside down heart, meandering here and there like the doodles of a bored child, before terminating at a cross with flared tips.

A delicately defined jawline came into view, glossy lips, an arrow-straight nose, glistening blue eyes. All of it framed by golden curls that glittered like frosted cobwebs on a moonlit winter's night.

Her lips curling up like salted slugs, Dorothy performed a slow twirl on her high-heels. A scene unfolded in Hugh's mind of her gliding down the grand staircase to welcome him and his parents to Coldwell Hall. Was this the same ensemble she'd worn back then? If so, there could be no more doubt that she knew his true identity.

"Do you like my outfit?" she purred. "I wore it especially for you."

Her words seemed to confirm his suspicion. He became aware of a constant *drip, drip, drip* resonating in his ears like a heartbeat. An all-too-familiar eggy aroma tickled his nostrils. His eyes flitted around, taking in chiselled rock walls, thick roofbeams and iron-bound barrels. They landed on the well. Thirteen candles, alternating between black and green, formed a crescent around the slightly askew stone slab. Their flames painted wavering forms on the walls. Hugh's overwrought imagination morphed the shapes into humanoid figures that pranced about like gleeful spectators.

"Look at me." Dorothy spoke in a tone of soft command that sent a shudder through Hugh. It struck him that in putting on her outfit of twenty-five-years ago, she also seemed to have cast off her shrill, histrionic demeanour.

Refusing to give her the satisfaction of his obedience, Hugh kept his gaze averted from hers.

Bony fingers locked onto Hugh's jaw. Displaying a strength that belied her slender frame, Dorothy wrenched his face towards her. She planted a ferocious kiss on his lips. A fuzz of fine hairs above her upper lip prickled his skin. He tried to pull away, but she interlocked her fingers behind his head, forcing her tongue into his mouth, drinking his saliva, stealing his breath.

His head reeled as if he'd been punched. A deep heaviness dropped like a net over his already exhausted body, leaving him too drained to be scared or even disgusted.

Detaching her lips from his, Dorothy murmured, "Mmm, you smell just like your father."

Hugh's voice scraped out. "Is that what you did to him? Tried to force yourself on him?"

"I didn't need to do that to your father."

Despite his predicament, Hugh couldn't suppress a contemptuous smile. "If that's true, why isn't his portrait on the walls? Why aren't there any photos of him in your safe?" His smile contracted into a grimace. "And why did you kill him?"

Dorothy batted her eyelashes like a child trying to look innocent. "I didn't kill him. I loved him. Only for an hour, but it was one of the sweetest loves of both our lives."

"Liar." The word hissed through Hugh's teeth. "The only woman my father loved was my mother. He'd never have risked his marriage for you."

"You'd be surprised what men will risk for a woman like me." Dorothy's voice fell to a velvety whisper. "Or perhaps you wouldn't be surprised. Perhaps you've got a woman somewhere who you go to for the things your wife can't give you."

"I love my wife."

"Of course you do." There was no sarcasm in Dorothy's reply. It was simply an observation that one thing had nothing to do with the other. "I love my husband."

Hugh shook his head in grimly amused disbelief. "You call having sex with hundreds of other men 'love'?"

"You think there's only one kind of love?"

"No, but you said it yourself, you married him for his money."

Dorothy chuckled. "Well yes, of course I say that. Otherwise people would think I was mad."

"I've got news for you, you are mad."

A distinctly disappointed sigh slipped from Dorothy. "What a small man you are. It's difficult to believe you're the son of the man I knew."

"You didn't know my father."

"I got to know him better in the short time we were together than your mother did in their entire marriage."

"Oh really. Then who was he?" Hugh's words were steeped in derision, yet there was also an undercurrent of anticipation.

"He was far too good for your mother." Dorothy spoke as if stating a basic truth. "I asked him what he was doing with such a plain Jane. And do you know what he said? He said, I ask myself that same question every day."

As Hugh listened, tremors built in his body. God, he wanted

to hurt this hateful woman. He wanted it so badly he could taste it, a flavour as enticing as it was repulsive. "He wouldn't have said that."

"Oh you poor confused boy." Dorothy stroked Hugh's wavy hair like he was her pet. "You really don't know either of your parents, do you?"

"You're right about that. I never had the chance to get to know them properly. You stole that from me."

"Did I? Or did you steal it from yourself?"

Hugh's eyebrows bunched together. "What's that supposed to–"

He was interrupted by the scrape of the three-quarter-height door opening. Arthur stooped through the doorway, his bald head gleaming. He'd stripped down to his waist. The candlelight flickered on pale skin stretched over a little potbelly and jutting ribs. His scrawny, hairless chest was tattooed with the same strange symbol as Dorothy's medallion.

As he straightened, deep grooves carved themselves into his scalp. He pointed a long, thin stick at Hugh. "Why have you removed his blindfold and gag?"

"I wanted to talk to him," said Dorothy.

"Why? What is there for him to say?"

"Don't you want to know how he opened the safe?"

Arthur strode across the room, his hands dangling at his sides like wrecking balls. Hugh's heart palpitated as he thought about the almost inhuman pressure those hands had exerted on his skull.

Arthur towered above Hugh, his black tattoo rippling in the candlelight like a living thing. Hugh blinked as Arthur prodded the stick at his face. "Well, Mr Carver, out with it. How did you know the combination?"

"My dad told me," Hugh retorted with a defiant smile.

The wrinkles on Arthur's head grew even more pronounced. Confusion glimmered in his dour eyes.

"He's not going to let you get away with what you did," continued Hugh.

Arthur opened his mouth in a silent *ahh* of realisation. The tension melting from his scalp, he lifted his gaze to Dorothy. For the first time in Hugh's recollection, a semblance of a smile flickered on the hotelier's thin lips.

"The sweet boy thinks he has a guardian angel," said Dorothy, producing a small white feather from somewhere.

As she leaned down to tickle Hugh's nose with it, he glowered at her. "You're going to prison for the rest of your life."

"For what? For being so beautiful that no man could resist me?"

"That's a lie and you know it."

Dorothy glanced at Arthur. "Tell him."

Arthur locked his eyes onto Hugh, that same wild intensity flaring in them. "No man has ever been able to resist her." His voice was a strange brew of anguish and pride. "Not a single one."

"You're going to prison for blackmail and murder." Hugh strove to sound confident, but the tremor in his voice gave him away.

"Blackmail?" A laugh as soft as the feather slid between Dorothy's red lips. "He thinks this is about money."

Hugh thought about the expressions of almost feral ecstasy captured by the photos. "No, I know you get something else out of it." He turned a probing gaze towards Arthur. "But what about you? How could you watch your wife with those men? Are you so pathetic that you actually enjoy it?"

A telltale silence followed the question, then Dorothy answered for her husband, "There's nothing wrong with taking pleasure in watching someone do what they're best at." She lifted her chin high. "And there's no one better at this than me. Is there Arthur?"

"No, my love." Arthur's mixed emotions had given way to a flat, factual tone.

Hugh's eyes shifted to Dorothy, sparkling with cruel amusement. "That might have been true once, but not anymore. You're no Salome now. You're just an ugly old Jezebel."

Even as the words left Hugh's mouth, his brain yelled at him, *What are you doing? Are you suicidal?* But he couldn't stop himself. The need to not only hurt Dorothy, but to annihilate her pride, was all-consuming.

Ugly old Jezebel. The taunt seemed to linger in the air, as toxic as the sulphurous stench seeping from the well. Anger smouldered in Dorothy's eyes, poised to flare into a raging blaze. Her long fingernails twitched, seemingly eager to claw at Hugh. Her lips curving into a smile that teetered on the brink of a snarl, she held out an upturned palm to Arthur.

As if responding to a silent command, he placed the pipe and tobacco tin on her palm. High-heels clicking against the floor, Yo-yo slinking around her ankles, Dorothy approached the well. Holding the feather over the black aperture, she told Hugh, "There are no guardian angels here. There are only demons."

With that, she let go of the feather. As he watched it seesaw through the gap, a lifetime of grief swelled in his chest. Next she dropped the tobacco tin into the foul-smelling darkness. He bit down on his tongue, damming back the rising tide of anguish. Dorothy put the pipe bowl to her nose. Her bosom swelled as she inhaled deeply.

"Mmm, it smells of autumn."

Coppery-tasting saliva filled Hugh's mouth as his teeth sank into his tongue. Unshed tears stung his eyes.

With a casual flick of her wrist, Dorothy tossed the pipe into the well. As it disappeared from sight, Hugh's pain burst forth in a rush of bitter words. "Two of your little demons are dead because of me. I bashed Sy's brains out. And Bel's at the bottom of that well."

Dorothy's grin remained fixed in place. "Do you really expect me to believe you killed Sy? You haven't got it in you."

"Take the bandage off my hand. You'll find a bite mark."

Arthur flipped Hugh onto his front and tore off the bloodstained bandage. Hugh cried out as Arthur wrenched his arms up to display the scabbed-over puncture wounds to Dorothy.

Her smile faltering, Dorothy's gaze drifted down the well. The same blankness overtook her as when she'd seen Sy in the vase. For a moment, she was so utterly motionless that Hugh wondered whether she'd fallen into a state of catatonic shock. What sweet karma that would be. But then a strange sound began to build in her throat, something that somehow managed to be both a sob and a chuckle.

Yo-yo peered up at her, letting out a rolling *brrrrrrr*.

"Yes, you're right, my darling," said Dorothy, meeting the cat's golden eyes. "It's time to show him."

Hugh twisted his neck to look at Dorothy. "Show me what?"

Reverting to her usual theatrical self, she twirled towards him, warbling, "In the game of love, we dance and sway, our hearts beating fast, our souls at play. With every step, we risk and dare, for love's sweet prize, we'll courage bear."

"Show me what?" he repeated, his voice quivering somewhere between a demand and a plea.

Dorothy giggled as if that was obvious. "That I'm still the most beautiful girl of all."

PART 3, CHAPTER 2

Arthur retrieved a wicker hamper from just outside the door and approached the well. He took out a piece of chalk and a tape measure. Taking pains to make sure each side was of equal length, he chalked out a triangle large enough for someone to stand within. With even greater care, he set about replicating the symbol tattooed on his chest inside the triangle.

Dorothy looked on, cuddling Yo-yo to her shoulder, running her fingers through the cat's luxuriously thick hair. Swaying from side to side, she sang softly, "He loves me. He loves me truly. My Arthur loves me truly. Truly, truly, truly…"

As the little ditty went rhythmically round and round, it was accompanied by a series of *brrrrrrs* from Yo-yo.

It almost seemed like the Dankworths had forgotten Hugh was there, but he had a nagging feeling that he was being treated to a well-rehearsed piece of theatre. "So is this where you summon Beleth, Sitri and Yomyael?" he asked with a scathing little laugh.

Dorothy looked at him, her eyes glittering as if she saw straight through his bravado. "No. Only King Beleth."

"And will King Beleth come riding out of the well on his white horse?"

Arthur glanced up from his work to warn, "Keep our king's name out of your mouth or I'll cut off your tongue."

"Oh, we wouldn't want that," said Dorothy, pulling a face of faux concern. "It's such a lovely tongue."

She blew a kiss at Hugh. He shuddered at the memory of her tongue coiling around his like a hungry snake.

Once Arthur was done drawing the symbol, he returned to Dorothy's side. He poured salt on the floor around them, creating a circle. Crouching down, he examined his creation, scrupulously ensuring there were no gaps in the perimeter.

"Everything's perfect, my love," said Dorothy. "Oh wait, don't forget the wine."

As Arthur took a bottle of red wine out of the hamper, uncorked it and poured it into a silver goblet, Dorothy explained to Hugh, "King Beleth loves a good Burgundy." An impish smile played on her lips. "I seem to remember your father was rather partial to Burgundy."

Hugh mirrored her smile. "I went through every photo in that safe. There wasn't one in which you looked a day older than on the night you murdered my dad. Do you know what I think? I think being rejected by him destroyed your confidence. I bet you haven't tried it on with another man since then. I'm right, aren't I?"

The smile disappeared from Dorothy's eyes, but remained on her lips, making it seem more like a grimace. She stepped out of the salt circle and squatted down to rest a hand on Hugh's knee. "No, but it has been years since I was with a man." She glanced at Arthur. "A *real* man, that is."

Arthur's blank canvas of a face suggested that he'd long been desensitized to such taunts about his masculinity. Like a child putting out a treat for Santa, he placed the goblet of wine in the triangle.

Dorothy slid her fingers up Hugh's thigh. As they neared his groin, he bucked his hips. "Take your hand off me!"

Her smile broadened. "You pretend to be all proper, but really you like it rough, don't you? I can always tell what a man wants." She looked at Arthur. "It's one of my gifts, isn't it?"

"It isn't your gift, my love," he replied flatly. "It's King Beleth's gift to you."

For once, Dorothy didn't argue back. Her eyes returned to Hugh. As quick as a viper, she grasped his testicles through his trousers. Whilst he squirmed in agony, she spoke with a quiver of delight. "I had thought I was done with the game of love, but your visit has reawakened that need in me. I think I might play one last time. What do you think? Does an ugly old Jezebel like me stand a chance of finding love?"

"No," Hugh wheezed. "Nothing could make me love you."

Dorothy's laughter echoed around the basement. "And you call me vain. Sorry to hurt your ego, my sweet Hugh, but I'm not talking about you. I'll let you in on a secret. I'm bored with men. Just once before I get too old, I want to play the game with someone who knows better than any man where to touch me." Her voice dropped to a sultry murmur. "Someone like your wife."

Hugh glared at Dorothy as if attempting to burn holes in her with his eyes. "Stay away from my wife!"

"She's a mousey little thing, but there's something about her eyes. They're..." Dorothy struggled to find the words she wanted. She nuzzled her chin against Yo-yo as if seeking inspiration from her. "They're the softest eyes I've ever seen. A woman with eyes like that will take her time to give me what I need."

"A woman like that would never be interested in a disgusting hag like–"

Hugh broke off with a yelp as Dorothy twisted his testicles. "You don't know how wrong you are. By the end of tonight, your wife will be so in love with me she'll do anything I want. And not only that, you're going to help her fall in love with me."

Hugh gawped at Dorothy like he couldn't believe she actually existed. "You're insane. Totally and utterly insane. You're not even worth hating." His voice was suddenly so calm and certain that it took even him by surprise. "I feel sorry for you."

Dorothy snatched her hand away as if fearing she might catch something nasty from him. Her pretence of a smile evaporated. "I remember when you first came to the hotel. What happened to that brave, handsome little chap?" She shook her head sadly. "Your father's better off dead than seeing what you've grown up to become."

Hugh looked her in the eye, the conviction in his voice echoing the intensity of his stare. "My dad loves me."

Scrunching up her face like he was the most loathsome thing she'd ever seen, she rose and retreated into the circle of salt, "I was going to show you King Beleth's glory, but you're not worthy." She put down Yo-yo, then spread her arms, one palm facing up, the other down. Her voice rang out shrilly. "*Lirach tasa vefa wehl Beleth.*"

In response to the words, Arthur bent down. With a gentle motion that seemed more like coaxing than exertion, he pushed aside the thick stone slab. It scraped across the floor, revealing the round mouth of the well. Darkness beckoned from within the aperture, as deep and hungry as Dorothy's kiss.

Arthur retrieved the stick. He struck at the air above the chalk triangle, marking out its three points. Then he strode to Hugh and stood looking down at him, his eyes distant. Dissociated. With a rapid movement, he brought his palms together in a clap so loud it made Hugh's ears ring.

Arthur's deep voice joined with Dorothy's. "*Lirach tasa vefa wehl Beleth.*"

His palms crashed together several more times. Hugh's heart skipped as each thunderous impact sent shockwaves through him. In a burst of frantic energy, he fought against his bonds like a snared wild animal. Arthur pressed his palms against Hugh's chest, pinning him down. He kept them there, until Hugh subsided into quaking stillness. Then he pulled the gag and blindfold back into position.

Consigned to darkness once again, Hugh heard footsteps moving away from him. He flinched as Arthur resumed his rhythmic clapping.

"*Lirach tasa vefa wehl Beleth.*"

Dorothy and Arthur repeated the incantation in unison, their voices rippling through the air, washing over Hugh, engulfing him in fear.

The clapping quickened, vibrating outside and inside of Hugh. The chant circled the room ten, twenty, thirty times. Did it mean anything? Or was it just some nonsense Dorothy had made up?

"*Lirach tasa vefa wehl Beleth.*"

The Dankworths' clashing voices rose to a discordant crescendo. On and on, round and round, went the chant, until Hugh lost count of the repetitions.

"*Lirach tasa vefa wehl Beleth. Lirach tasa vefa wehl Beleth.*"

As suddenly as a candle being snuffed out, the chanting and clapping ceased. Silence briefly reigned over the room, then Arthur intoned, "Beleth! Beleth! O mighty king of Hell. O majestic lord of legions. We call unto thee. Come forth from your dominion."

"Great King Beleth, hear us now," piped up Dorothy, her voice uncharacteristically toneless. "It is you we call to, you and no one else. Only you are our patron in this world and the next. Only you have the wisdom and power we seek."

"Come forth, my king," beseeched Arthur. "Come forth into this triangle so that we may give you all the honour and praise you deserve."

With that, Dorothy struck up the chant again. "*Lirach tasa vefa wehl Beleth. Lirach tasa vefa wehl Beleth…*"

On the tenth repetition, a trumpet-like sound boomed out with such force that Hugh half-expected the roof to come crashing down. He writhed around as, for several excruciating seconds, the cacophony bombarded him. Then, just as abruptly, it stopped, leaving him in silence except for a high-pitched ringing in his ears.

PART 3, CHAPTER 3

A sound halfway between a soft purr and a revving engine began to build. *Brrrr... Brrrrr... Brrrrrr...*

Hugh's nostrils flared at a scent unlike anything he'd ever encountered before – an aroma as raw and jagged as his nerves.

"Welcome, mighty king!" exclaimed Arthur. "Forgive me, my master, for I must respectfully demand that you remain within the triangle until our business is concluded."

"Yes, forgive us," Dorothy joined in, her voice shorn of haughtiness. "We bow before your magnificence. Your perfection! Thank you for answering our call, your majesty. Thank you, thank you, thank you..."

As Hugh listened to Dorothy's ingratiating babble, it occurred to him that if this wasn't merely an act, the Dankworths would be unable to leave their protective circle.

There was one way to find out if Dorothy and Arthur were indeed true believers. Planting his feet on the floor, Hugh pushed in what he judged to be the direction of the door. The instant he moved, something landed lightly on his solar plexus. A familiar fishy breath brushed against his face. He flinched into stillness at the feeling of claws prickling his flesh.

"Why have you summoned us?" asked a voice like warm honey.

"King Beleth, as your loyal servants, we offer our souls and bodies to you," said Arthur.

"We already possess those things."

The seductively smooth voice flowed over Hugh, oozing into his ears, sliding down his cheeks.

"O most gracious king, we bring a sacrifice for your pleasure," said Dorothy. "His name is Hugh Carver. We give him to you, body and soul."

"His soul is not yours to give."

"Then accept his blood. You'll never taste sweeter."

"Remove his gag."

Dorothy's voice rose in response to the murmured instruction. "What for? He has nothing to say worth your attention."

"Dorothy," Arthur said in a cautioning tone.

Ignoring him, she entreated, "All I ask for is one night with this man's wife. Make her love me above all others. If this man's blood is not sufficient, then name your price."

"I'm sorry, O greatest and most magnificent of kings," spluttered Arthur. "My wife's desire makes her forget herself. We will obey you in all things, just as we obey Satan himself. Isn't that so, Dorothy?"

"Of course it is."

"Then do as our master says."

After a brief pause, Dorothy's voice rang out, "Yo-yo."

Hugh gave a start as something sharp grazed his face and snagged on the gag. Soft fur tickled his lips as the gag was pulled down. He gasped in a mouthful of air. It surged into his lungs, tasting of salt and sweat, like the residue of intercourse. He spat it back out as if he'd sucked venom from a snake bite.

"We've been waiting a long time to talk to you, Hugh."

He cringed away from the voice as if he was being touched by a gentle molester. A different voice, completely opposite in its gruff, direct tone, spoke up in his head. *Have you considered that the real target of the attack might not have been your dad?*

Was Ava right? Had the Dankworths, or whoever the velvety voice belonged to, expected him to return to Coldwell Hall? Had he played into the hands of his dad's killer?

"Who are you?" Hugh asked hoarsely.

"We have many names, but you may call us Beleth."

The voice soothed and scratched at Hugh, like a bundle of pins wrapped in silk. "What if I call you Arthur?"

"Arthur is not one of our names."

"O wisest and fairest of rulers, please don't waste your time on him," pleaded Dorothy,

"Time." The word sounded like a distant echo. "Time means nothing to us."

Hugh's scalp prickled as he recalled something else Ava had said. *Time means nothing to ghosts.* With the words, came an image of the paring knife endlessly plunging into his dad's eye. Hugh suddenly found himself voicing his own version of Dorothy's entreaty. "All I ask for is the truth. Who killed my father?"

"We will gladly give you that truth."

"No, please–" Dorothy cried out, but fell silent as abruptly as if Arthur had clapped a hand over her mouth.

"We will set you free," the voice continued. "We will set your mother free. We will bring peace to your father. And we will give you justice. But there will be a price to be paid."

"Name it," Hugh said in a barely-there croak.

"Blood. That is the price of your salvation."

Blood. Hugh saw the knife plunging in again, blood welling around the blade. So much blood. "Whose blood?"

"That will be made known to you upon the death of your mother."

Hugh's thoughts turned to his mum's empty eyes and sunken features. "When will she die?"

"That we do not know. We do know this – if you don't accept our help, your mother will die in prison, your father will never leave this place, your wife will be made to love another and you will die here."

Hugh pictured the knife once more, but this time it was in his own hand. Could he do it? Could he plunge it into someone? Could he watch their life drain away? How would he ever be able to look Louise and Isabelle – or, for that matter, himself – in the eye again?

"Freedom, justice, peace, all this we will give to you," promised the voice. "If you worship us, all will be yours."

Quietly, as if reasoning something through with himself, Hugh said, "If you're Arthur, you're going to kill me no matter what. So why should I humiliate myself? And if you're a demon, you don't want my worship, you want my soul. What good would it do me to have all those things you promise, if I don't have my soul?"

As Hugh fell silent, laughter rang out – a jubilant, triumphant cackle that was joined by a clapping as thunderous as a theatre audience applauding the grand finale.

"It's you, dear Hugh, that doesn't know what love is," Dorothy elatedly informed him. "True love isn't about gaining something, it's about losing something. Arthur was willing to pay any price to have me. You asked whether he enjoys watching me with other men. He hates it. The mere thought of it is worse than any physical pain. And yet he endures it for me. To make me happy. What are you willing to endure for your wife? What would you give to make her happy? *Nothing!*"

Dorothy spat the word at Hugh with such force that he winced.

She laughed at his reaction. "Louise deserves better than

you. Just like your dad deserved better than your mum."

Seizing hold of his fear and flinging it aside, Hugh let out a derisive snort. "Perhaps if my dad had agreed with you, he'd still be alive. But he didn't. And neither will Louise."

"We'll see about that." Dorothy spoke with what sounded like genuine gratitude. "Thank you, Hugh. Thank you for helping me to pick one last apple from the tree."

"O Lord of Lovers, O King of Lust," eulogised Arthur. "Tell us. What shall we do with this man, Hugh Carver?"

With the solemnity of a judge passing sentence, the whispering voice said, "Anyone who murders a parent shall not be punished by the usual forms of execution. They shall be sealed alive in a watertight sack along with venomous snakes and cast into the sea. Thus, they shall never again know peace in life or death."

As if all the oxygen had been sucked out of the room, an oppressive stillness took hold. Then, queasy with horror and seething with indignance, Hugh cried out, "I didn't kill my father!"

"Didn't you?" Dorothy practically squealed with glee. "Are you sure about that?"

At her question, images stuttered through Hugh's mind like a stop-motion film – the knife in his hand, the blade arcing towards his dad, himself whirling to run away, tripping over the rug, falling on his face. With a single word, he cast out the vile images. "Lies!"

"Maybe. I suppose you'll find out soon enough." In a quavering voice, Dorothy sang, "Will it be Heaven or Hell, when the curtain is drawn, and the truth starts to tell? Will it be The Lord of Lies or The King in the Skies?"

As she taunted Hugh, Arthur asked, "King Beleth, you spoke of snakes and the sea, but we have neither here."

"You have a well and a cat," came the reply.

In an instant, Dorothy's jeering delight turned into dismay. "But Yo-yo's the only one of my little darlings that I have left."

"We must all make sacrifices, my love," said Arthur, his dour voice betraying perhaps the faintest hint of pleasure. "And besides, you have three new 'little darlings' to look after."

Like that of an actor breaking character, Dorothy's voice became brutally raw. "Arthur Dankworth, you truly are the ugliest thing I've ever seen."

"And you, my wife, are the most beautiful thing I've ever seen." There was no trace of fawning flattery in Arthur's reply. It was simply a statement of fact.

A wet, sucking sound, reminiscent of someone trudging through mud, followed the bittersweet exchange. Hugh shuddered. Were the Dankworths kissing? He couldn't imagine anything more repulsive than the crimson slugs of Dorothy's lips pressing against Arthur's corpselike face.

"Say the words," murmured the voice.

"Thy will be done," said Arthur.

"On Earth as it is in Hell," added Dorothy.

Together they chanted, "King Beleth, we release you from this triangle."

"Return now to your infernal kingdom, so that we may bestow our gift upon you," said Arthur. "We thank you and praise and glorify you."

"And we praise and glorify almighty Satan on his throne of serpents," said Dorothy.

Again, they chanted in unison, "We release you, King Beleth. We release you, King Beleth."

The pungent smell of salt and sweat dissipated, only to be replaced by the eggy stench of the well. As if he too had been released, Hugh jolted into a sitting position. A startled miaow rang out as Yo-yo tumbled off him.

"Help!" Hugh yelled as loudly as his dry throat would allow. "Help! Help! Somebody help me!"

His cries were stifled as the gag was yanked up over his mouth. Something thudded into the side of his head. He toppled over like a bowling pin, bursts of light flashing behind his eyes.

"Congratulations, my brave little soldier," said Dorothy. "You get to keep your soul. I hope it's worth it."

PART 3, CHAPTER 4

"Oh Yo-yo, my beautiful Yo-yo." Dorothy's words were weighed down by sadness. "You're the only one left who truly accepts me for what I am. The only one who never judges me. What will I do without you? How will I go on?"

I'm sure you'll find a way, Hugh reflected dryly.

As if she'd heard his thought, a jolt of anger shook Dorothy's voice. "First this wretched little man murders your brother and sister. Now you have to die for him."

"To be fair, my love, she's going to die for you," Arthur pointed out.

"Oh shut up and get on with it, Arthur! I'm sick of the sight of this man."

Hugh's breath whistled through his teeth as something jabbed into his midriff. He curled into a ball, desperately trying to cling onto some semblance of calm. As he listened to Dorothy alternate between agonising over Yo-yo and berating Arthur, he wondered how long he'd been in the basement. It felt like hours. Louise must be frantic with worry. Had she ventured back into the hotel to look for him? The possibility left him torn between conflicting hopes. She might be his only chance for survival. But the thought of her being anywhere near the Dankworths terrified him almost as much as the prospect of being sealed up in a sack with Yo-yo and thrown down the well.

"This isn't going to work, Dorothy," grumbled Arthur. "The

sack has to be waterproof. If we put him in a duvet cover, he'll drown. He'll die fast. He's supposed to die slowly."

"What does it matter how he dies?" retorted Dorothy. "Just so long as he's dead."

"King Beleth was very specific. He must not be punished by some ordinary form of execution. He–"

"Yes, yes, I know what he said." There was a brief silence, then Dorothy's voice quickened at an idea. "What about those barrels? Could we use one of them?"

"They're old. They're probably leaky."

"So wrap a barrel in rubber bedding. Thanks to our clientele, we've got more waterproof sheets than we know what to do with."

"It could work."

"Of course it will work. Do it, Arthur. Do it quickly." A pained yearning emanated from Dorothy. "It's been so long since I last knew true pleasure. I need to feel *that* feeling again."

Hugh thrashed against his restraints as Dorothy's desperate desire conjured up images of her and Louise together, caressing, probing and tasting each other. The mere thought of it was more than he could bear.

An impossibly soft voice slithered into his mind. *Then say yes to us and it will be you, not Dorothy, who gets all you desire.*

Before he could respond, powerful hands clasped Hugh and lifted him off the floor. His flailing feet thudded into something that sounded as hollow as a coffin.

"Stay still," warned Arthur, flexing his fingers, giving another glimpse of their bone-crushing strength.

"Put him in upside down," Dorothy said with vindictive delight. "Like he put Sy in the vase."

A helpless sob wringed itself out of Hugh as Arthur turned

him upside down and shoved him headfirst into a tight, curved space. With jarring force, Hugh's head struck a hard surface. He gasped as his knees were jammed against his chin, leaving him scrunched into a foetal position. A pungent fragrance – a blend of old wood and rusted metal, with an underlying sour tang – filled his nostrils.

Resting a palm heavily on Hugh's feet, Arthur said, "Give me the cat."

"You're enjoying this, aren't you?" Dorothy snapped. "Go on, admit it."

"The cat."

Arthur's dispassionate tone only exacerbated Dorothy's anger. "Cruel! How cruel you are." Bitterness clawed at her voice, leaving it frayed and ragged. "Why did you have to make me love you? Why did you do this to me?"

"You did this to yourself, Dorothy. We all do."

The simple truth of Arthur's answer rendered her monetarily silent. Then, bereft of emotion, she said, "Goodbye, Yo-yo."

Hugh flinched as a warm, wriggling bundle was placed on his legs. Yo-yo's claws pricked the back of his thighs. Her fluffy tail swished against his face. A low, growling hiss resonated within the barrel's confines.

Hugh's heart palpitated wildly. He had to do something. Anything! With all his strength, he exploded upwards, kicking out. A downwards thrust brutally compressed his spine, ramming his knees into his face.

Finding herself wedged between Hugh's back and the barrel, Yo-yo writhed and wailed like a child in agony. He could do nothing but brace himself against her frantic biting and clawing. Searing pain ripped through him, like a whip was mercilessly shredding his back.

The faint light that had penetrated the blindfold disappeared. His eardrums pulsated at a series of loud clangs. He kicked out again, but the barrel was sealed tight.

As the clanging ceased, Yo-yo subsided into rigid, growling stillness. Not wanting to antagonise her, Hugh held himself as motionless as his quaking body would permit.

At the crinkle of something being wrapped around the barrel, Yo-yo erupted into another frenzy. Hugh choked on his screams as a flurry of claws and teeth tore into him. The next second, the barrel was being tipped onto its side. As its rusty iron bands crunched across the floor, its occupants tumbled over and over like clothes in a washing machine.

Drenched in darkness and pain, feeling as if his very sanity was being clawed to pieces, Hugh braced himself for the plunge into the well.

"Praise be to Beleth, giver of love," chorused the Dankworths. "Praise be to Satan, giver of life."

A sudden sensation of weightlessness enveloped Hugh. For a breathless instant, he hung in the air with Yo-yo attached to him like some sort of medieval torture device. Then, with a thunderous splash, the barrel hit the water.

The force of the impact knocked all the air out of Hugh. As she was crushed between him and the staves, Yo-yo's wails were extinguished like a match in the wind. For a long moment, he lay winded and dazed, barely registering where he was. Gradually, awareness seeped back in, and he almost wished it hadn't.

His mouth was full of warm, salty blood. He spat it out, only for it to be replenished by more trickling down the back of his throat. His nose felt strange – both numb and throbbing. Was it broken? His legs were tangled beneath him. A sharp pain raced along his spine as, gritting his teeth, he twisted onto his side. The barrel turned with him, flipping him facedown.

He repeated the manoeuvre, bracing his feet and knees against opposite sides of the barrel until the bobbing settled into a gentle sway.

Yo-yo lay motionless against his buttocks. Was she dead or merely unconscious? Warily, he felt at her with his tingling hands. He couldn't detect any flicker of life in her limp body. Her ribs gave way at a touch like broken bed slats.

Just in case Yo-yo's corpse decided to come back to life, he pushed it to the far end of the barrel and pinned it beneath his feet. He leaned his head back, the gag inflating with each rapid, wheezing breath. As his breathing slowed down, he became aware of the rhythmic *plop, plop* of drips drumming on barrel.

Another sound drowned out the dripping – the rasp of stone scraping against stone. Was Arthur pushing the slab back over the well? Hysteria gnawed at Hugh at the prospect of spending eternity entombed in this watery grave.

Calm down, he told himself. *Calm down or you're as good as dead.*

The barrel didn't seem to be taking on water. Arthur had done a good job of making it watertight. Did that mean it was airtight too? Hugh wondered how long would it take him to use up all the air. Minutes? Hours?

Carefully, methodically, he began to test his bonds. There was barely a millimetre of movement in the rope around his wrists. He shuffled his feet towards his hands. Rope had been wrapped around his ankles half a dozen times and tied off with a knot as hard as a rock.

Something that was both a scream and a sob forced its way out of him. It was hopeless. He could either suffocate slowly or try to kick the barrel open. He imagined the water rushing in and filling his lungs. A brief moment of agony, then it would be over. The thought of it seemed almost tempting compared to this sanity-destroying torment.

As if possessed by Yo-yo's spirit, he launched into a flurry of kicks. The barrel bobbed about, clunking into the walls of the well. After several minutes of frenzied, fruitless effort, he subsided into a gasping heap.

Isabelle's angelic face floated through his mind. He envisioned her looking on blankly as his coffin was lowered into the ground, just as he had done at his father's funeral. Only unlike his father's coffin, his own would be empty. She wouldn't even have the closure of knowing for certain that he was dead.

The last words he'd spoken to her rang in his ears – *I'll be back soon. I promise.* He felt like biting his tongue off for making such a liar of himself.

His thoughts turned to Louise. He pictured Dorothy approaching her. How would Louise react? With fear? With anger? With lust?

He ground his teeth as if trying to shatter them. How could he have allowed this to happen? Other than his mother, Isabelle and Louise were the only people in the world that he loved. How could he have failed them all so badly?

"I'm sorry," he sobbed against the gag. "I'm so sorry…"

His voice faltered. For some hazy period of time, he lay paralysed by despair. He came back to himself with a jolt, his lungs snatching at the air. He didn't seem to be able to expand them properly. A floaty, tingly sensation was seeping throughout his body. Part of him wanted to go with it, let it carry him away to… to where? Did it matter? Anywhere had to be better than here.

"No, you're not going to give in," he told himself, kicking an upper part of the barrel, thinking maybe he could make a hole big enough for air to seep in but small enough to keep the water out. Again and again, he thrust at the staves, struggling to get any leverage in the cramped space. Sweat trickled down his face, mingling with the blood that had accumulated there.

The staves held firm, as if was wrapped not just in plastic but in spells that made them unbreakable.

Knowing it was futile, yet not knowing what else to do, he scrabbled at the coarse wood with his fingers. Splinters stabbed under his nails. He felt his skin tearing and becoming slippery with blood. Simultaneously, he gnashed at the gag, striving to bite through the sodden material.

If you don't accept our help, your mother will die in prison, your father will never leave this place, your wife will be made to love another and you will die here...

Round and round, the monstrously soft voice swirled in his mind, driving him into an ever greater frenzy of kicking, clawing and gnashing. Suddenly, the gag fell away and began to scream, "Help! Help!"

His hoarse, cracking voice reverberated back at him, getting weaker with each repetition. His frantic exertions dwindled to sporadic convulsions. Louise's face flickered in his mind like a flame sputtering from lack of oxygen.

What are you willing to endure for your wife? he heard Dorothy jeering at him. *What would you give to make her happy? Nothing!*

"Everything," he clawed in enough air to gasp.

Prove it. Give us everything you have.

"Alright, I accept!" he bellowed, seemingly trying to shatter the barrel with his words. "I accept! I accept!"

PART 3, CHAPTER 5

Louise stared at the hotel's front doors. She glanced at the dashboard clock. Her gaze returned to the doors. Then the clock. Then the doors. Back and forth, back and forth…

Seconds seemed to morph into minutes. Where the hell was Hugh? She lowered the window, straining her ears for any clue to an answer. Silence flowed into the car, disturbed only by the occasional hoot of an owl or whisper of wind.

One by one, the lights in the hotel's front windows were extinguished. With each light that went out, the knot of worry in her stomach pulled tighter. Five more agonisingly long minute dragged by. Ten. Fifteen…

Another window went dark. Another and another, until only the lobby was lit up. Louise counted along the first floor windows to what she judged to be Hugh's room. The black glass returned her gaze, its meaning impossible to decipher.

"What are you doing, Hugh?" she murmured, reaching for her phone. Her call went straight through to voicemail, just as his calls to Graham had done. Was he with Graham? Were the two of them somewhere beyond the reach of phones?

Her mind raced with scenarios – Hugh confronting the Dankworths, Arthur attacking him, subduing him, dragging him down to some dark place. Her gaze slid to the fake well that the hotel's sign dangled from.

The knot in her stomach constricted painfully, too tight to

ignore. Silently apologising to Hugh for breaking her promise, she got out of the car. Anxiety propelling her like a phantom at her back, she hurried towards the front doors. Her footsteps slowed as she entered the lobby. Tim directed a disinterested glance at her from behind the reception counter.

"How did the funeral go?" she asked, striving to sound casual although her heart was drumming against her ribs.

Tim shrugged and resumed staring at his phone.

"Have you seen my husband?"

Without bothering to look up, Tim shook his head.

Louise's gaze roamed the lobby. A few empty champagne flutes were scattered around the tables. All was silent, except for the logs crackling in the hearth. The apparent calm only served to heighten her concern. She started towards the stairs, but pulled up abruptly as the dining room doors swung open.

With the poise of a model on a catwalk, Dorothy strode into view. Her face a vision of white and red, her eyes sparkling, she sashayed towards Louise. "There you are, Louise!" she exclaimed in a manner that seemed to suggest they were old friends. "I've been looking for you."

"H... have you?" stammered Louise. "Why?"

"I have a message for you from Hugh." Dorothy flashed Louise a smile. "Actually, it would be better to just show you."

At this echo of her own words to Dorothy, Louise found herself visualising Hugh stuck upside down in a giant vase. A strange cocktail of dread and laughter bubbled up inside her.

Beckoning for Louise to follow, Dorothy turned to go back into the dining room. Cautiously, casting glances all around, Louise poked her head into the expansive room. There was no one else to be seen besides Dorothy. The lights had been dimmed to a gentle golden glow. A slow tune was tinkling from the mechanical piano. Near the room's centre, candles were flickering atop a table. Dorothy glided towards the candlelit table, not bothering to see if Louise was following.

Louise looked over her shoulder at the front doors. Her instincts were tingling like crazy, urging her to flee. Glancing at Tim, she told herself, *If Dorothy tries anything, all I have to do is shout for help and he'll hear.*

Her gaze circled back to Dorothy. She stared at her uncertainly for a moment more before starting forwards. Her nostrils twitched. A musky scent permeated the air, tinged with a hint of mustiness, as if someone was using strong perfume to mask body odour.

Dorothy looked up from pouring Champagne into two glasses. She proffered a glass.

"No, thanks," said Louise.

With a *suit yourself* shrug, Dorothy sipped her drink and sat down.

"Where's Hugh?" asked Louise.

Dorothy didn't seem to hear. As she tilted her head back to swallow more Champagne, her gaze lingered on the ripe red apple dangling overhead. She lifted a hand, curling her fingers as if to pluck it from its branch. "It looks delicious, doesn't it?"

Louise kept her eyes fixed on Dorothy. "You said you had a message for me." Her voice vibrated with nerves.

Dorothy lowered her bright blue eyes to Louise, held her gaze for a moment, then looked floorward, exclaiming, "Here they are, my beautiful little darlings!"

Three pairs of fluorescent eyes peered up at Dorothy from beneath a nearby table. "Come here, my darlings," she cooed, holding out a hand.

The ginger tom and grey kitten retreated timidly from view. The black cat padded forwards boldly to nuzzle Dorothy's fingers. It miaowed as she scooped it up and kissed its nose.

"I think I'll call you Midnight." Dorothy looked at Louise. "What do you think?"

Louise shaped her lips into a neutral smile. She had the sense that Dorothy was toying with her, like a cat tormenting a mouse. *Just humour her,* she told herself. *Maybe she'll let slip what you want to know.* "It suits her."

Dorothy's glistening lips curved upwards. "You mean, it suits *him*." She lifted Midnight's tail. "You see how that looks like a semi-colon?" She pointed to two small pinkish holes spaced about a centimetre apart. "That means it's a boy."

"You seem to know a lot about cats."

"I know everything about them." A suggestive sparkle shimmered in Dorothy's eyes. "And they know everything about me."

"Such as?"

Her smile widening coyly, Dorothy motioned for Louise to sit down. Louise did so, positioning herself so that most of the table stood between her and Dorothy.

Dorothy leaned forwards, pointing a long fingernail at Louise's forehead. "Did you know that cats can control your mind? They can make you do things you'd never normally do." She chuckled. "You think I'm mad."

"No I–"

"Yes you do. I can see it in your eyes. But I'm not mad." Dorothy's finger moved to her own forehead. "I was just like you – a dull, dutiful little woman. My cats turned me into what you see now. Without them, I would never have followed my desires. I want to give that same gift to you."

Dorothy placed Midnight on the table, gently ushering him towards Louise. "He's yours."

Louise's eyebrows lifted in astonishment. The kitten made big round eyes, seemingly pleading with her to accept. She reached to stroke him, but drew her hand back before doing so. She was briefly silent, mustering the courage to speak her mind. "Maybe I am a dull, dutiful little woman, but I'm fine with that. All I want is for my family to be safe."

"*Safe*," Dorothy scoffed as if the word was worthy only of contempt.

"Yes, safe." There was a sudden steel in Louise's tone. "Where is my husband?"

Dorothy's smile remained fixed in place. "He's gone."

"Gone?" Louise parroted bemusedly. "Gone where?"

"I've no idea. He just said to tell you he was going for a walk."

"But… but it's dark."

"I'm sure he'll be back soon."

Dorothy's nonchalant demeanour seemed to suggest it was perfectly normal for someone to head out into the night without a word to their wife. Louise forced herself to maintain eye contact. *You're lying*, she wanted to say, but the thought of doing so made her throat cinch up like a noose. She started to rise. Her whole body stiffened as Dorothy reached out to catch hold of her hand.

"Where are you going?"

The question was asked with a soft intensity that sent a shudder through Louise. Resisting an impulse to yank her hand free and flee, she said with only a slight tremor, "I'm going to look for Hugh."

Dorothy flexed her long nails gently against Louise's flesh. "Sometimes men need to be alone."

"Hugh hates being alone in the dark."

Dorothy smiled as if tickled by the revelation. "Well don't wander too far. It's easy to get lost around here."

She uncurled her fingers from Louise's hand. As Louise

started to turn away, Dorothy said, "Aren't you going to take Midnight with you?"

Louise summoned up a small smile. "Thanks for the kind offer, but Hugh's not a cat person."

Dorothy arched a razor thin eyebrow. "Doesn't like cats. Doesn't like being alone in the dark. What *does* he like? Apart, of course, from dull, dutiful little women?" A husky laugh slid from her as if she'd told a joke.

Louise's smile disappeared. Part of her wanted to snatch up one of the glasses and chuck its contents in Dorothy's face. Another part suspected that in doing so she would be giving Dorothy exactly what she wanted. Drama. That was what Dorothy lived for. *We'll she's not going to get that from me,* Louise firmly told herself.

"Goodnight, Mrs Dankworth."

Louise's voice was as bland as her expression. It sucked all the amusement out of Dorothy's face. Taking care not to walk too fast or too slow, Louise headed for the doors. She felt Dorothy's eyes on her back every step of the way. Just what was Dorothy's game? Was she simply amusing herself? Or was there more to it?

Louise could still feel where Dorothy had touched her. There had been something needful, almost lustful in the way Dorothy had dug her nails in. The thought of it gave Louise a crawling feeling.

The instant she was out of the room, she quickened her step. By the time she reached the first floor landing, she was almost running. He feet thudded along the interminably long hallway. She kept flashing glances over her shoulder, half-expecting to see Dorothy in pursuit like some wild-eyed banshee.

She's an old woman. She can't hurt you, Louise told herself.

Her thoughts turned to Arthur. Cold sweat prickled her palms as she envisioned his long legs loping after her, his vast hands reaching for her. She froze at the sound of heavy footsteps up ahead. A gasp of relief escaped her as a broad, big-bellied figure emerged from the side corridor.

"Graham, where in god's name have–" she began, but he shushed her. He motioned with his eyes at the cardboard box in his arms. As if it contained a fragile antique, he carefully lifted its flaps.

Louise's brow twitched as if she wasn't sure what to think when she saw what the box contained. A sleek black shape was curled up like a shell amidst a towel. Bel's eyes were closed. The rise and fall of her chest was barely perceptible.

"She was on a ledge halfway down the well," Graham whispered. "It took hours, but I managed to lasso her and pull her up. She was soaked through. Almost hypothermic. I've given her a hot bath and she seems a lot better. I'm taking her to the Dankworths."

"Have you seen Hugh? He came looking for you."

"No."

"I tried to phone him, but all I get is voicemail. I thought maybe he was with you in the basement."

"I came up the backstairs about an hour ago. If he went down to the basement, it must have been after that or I'd have bumped into him."

Louise frowned in thought, then swiftly stepped past Graham to try the door handle to 'Helen'. The door swung inwards. She switched on the light. Her gaze swept over the room. Hugh's suitcase was where he'd left it on the floor. She peered into the bathroom. His toiletry bag was on the sink.

"All his things are still here," she said as Graham entered the room.

"No they're not." Graham pointed to the empty windowsill.

The creases between Louise's eyebrows deepened. "Why

would he take the tobacco tin but leave everything else behind?"

"Maybe he left in a hurry."

Louise thought about her bizarre encounter with Dorothy. "*He's gone*. That's what she told me."

"Who?"

"Dorothy. I spoke to her downstairs. She was even odder than usual. I almost got the feeling that…" A tremor of disgust took hold of Louise. "That she was flirting with me."

"Hmm, I wouldn't put it past her."

"What about murder? Would you put that past her?"

"She has all the traits of a narcissistic personality disorder. She's attention-seeking, grandiose, envious and entitled, but is she capable of murder?" Graham briefly mused the question over. "Again, I wouldn't put it past her, but I doubt she'd be the one to actually do the deed."

Spurred into motion by his words that echoed her own thoughts, Louise hurried from the room.

Graham followed her. He didn't need to ask where she was going. "Hang on a moment."

He retrieved the box and carried it to his bedroom. Ever so gently, he set it down by the radiator. Bel stirred but didn't open her eyes. "That's it, old girl," he whispered, "You just lay there and rest."

Louise smiled faintly at the display of tenderness that was at odds with Graham's usual demeanour. "I take it you don't think she's a demon."

Slinging a rucksack over his shoulder, he padded from the room. "She's just a cat. An unusually clever cat – she caught hold of the lasso and pulled it over herself – but still just a cat." As they made their way to the rear stairwell, he added, "And the well's just a well. I took every kind of reading – EMF, EVP, thermographic, night vision. All were normal."

"What about what Ava felt?"

"Ava's not been in a good place recently. She's drinking too much. It's affecting her ESP abilities." Disappointment creeping into his voice, Graham gestured vaguely at their surroundings. "I really thought this might be where I finally found the answers."

"What answers?"

"The answers to what's out there. *Is* there anything out there? I've been searching for years and I still don't know. Not for certain. And I need to be one hundred per cent certain."

"Why? What does it matter?"

"Because every question has an answer, just like every action has a consequence." The heaviness of Graham's tone made his words sound like a confession of failure.

"The answers you're looking for don't exist. And even if they do, they're not worth the price."

"Maybe they are, maybe they aren't. I can't know until I know, if you see what I mean." Graham frowned at his inability to express himself clearly. "The point is, I don't mind dying for the answers to my questions. But I don't want the bad karma of having someone else's death on my conscience – be it a cat or your husband."

As the ground floor door came into view, Louise put a finger to her lips. Her ears caught the faint tinkling of the piano. A voice trilled in time to the music, "Oh darling Dorothy. Your face reminds me of beautiful cats. Oh darling Dorothy. Roses are red. Skies are blue. I like cats. But not as much as I love you. Oh darling Dorothy, you're still the most beautiful girl of all…"

A quiver of revulsion ran through Louise as she listened to Dorothy's narcissistic ditty. She exchanged a glance with Graham, then they continued down the stairs. When they came to the basement door, he took out his lockpicking kit and set to work.

"I've changed my mind," he remarked, delicately feeling his way into the lock. "That woman would kill someone herself just for saying she wasn't the most beautiful girl of all."

"Yes and she'd probably say the cats made her do it."

There was a click. Graham straightened and opened the door. "How do you mean?"

As they descended into the dank gloom, Louise recounted what Dorothy had told her about cats being able to control minds.

"There might be something to that," Graham said. "Something scientific, not supernatural. There's a parasite. Its lifecycle begins in a mouse. But the mouse is only the intermediate host. The definitive host, the place where it really want to be, is a cat. The parasite affects the host's brain in such a way that it starts taking crazy risks. This makes the mouse more likely to be eaten by a cat. The cat can pass the parasite on to their owner via infected faeces."

"So Dorothy behaves the way she does because she's infected by this parasite?" There was more than a hint of scepticism in Louise's tone.

"Possibly. Or maybe she's just a psychopath." Graham's pace faltered as the 'Door to Hell' came into view, half-hidden behind the shelves. His voice dropped to a whisper. "Someone else has been down here. I made sure those shelves were all the way across the door."

Louise peered around, wide-eyed. There was nothing to be seen in the shadows except for cobwebby furniture and boxes. Graham pushed the shelves aside, picked the padlocks and dragged the three-quarter-height door open. He sniffed the air. "Beeswax. Someone's been burning candles."

He shone his torch at the slab. No sliver of the well was

visible. "Did you move it?" asked Louise.

Graham shook his head. "Stay behind me."

He ducked under the wooden lintel, sweeping his torch from side to side. Its beam passed over what looked to be a circle of salt, before landing on a chalk triangle. "Lirach tasa vefa wehl Beleth," he murmured at the sight of the squiggles and crosses the triangle enclosed.

"What does that mean?"

"It means someone's been summoning demons."

A corner of Louise's lips curled up as if she was grimly amused, but her eyes told a different story. She surveyed the room with an intensity that suggested she was striving to see beyond the visible spectrum. Her gaze halted on the barrels. "One, two, three, four, five… There were six barrels before. I'm certain of it."

Graham approached the barrels and crouched down. He ran a finger around the circumference of a dust-free circle on the floor. "You're right. One's missing." His torch traced along some parallel rust-coloured scratches that led towards the slab.

A look of sheer horror seized hold of Louise as the realisation finally hit her. "Oh my god, they've thrown him down the well."

Dropping to her knees, she shoved at the slab.

"Four of us only managed to move that a few centimetres," Graham reminded her.

"We've got to try! Hugh could be drowning down there."

"*If* he's down there."

"He is. I know it."

Louise looked up at Graham, her eyes filled with a frantic plea. Shaking his head at the futility of it, he took off his rucksack, sank down beside her and braced his palms against the slab.

They heaved and strained, muscles taut and trembling, feet scrabbling for purchase. Letting out a scream of frustration, Louise pitched forwards onto the slab. She pounded a fist against it, shouting, "Hugh! Hugh!"

"He won't be able to hear you." Graham glanced meaningfully towards the door. "But anyone up here will."

"We can't leave him down there."

"We're not going to. We need to go for help."

Tears trembling on her eyelashes, Louise gave a desperate shake of her head. "He'll be dead by the time we get back."

"Not if he's in a barrel. He'll be able to survive for hours."

Graham extended a hand to Louise. Reluctantly, she took it. As he helped her upright, her nostrils flared. "Do you smell that?"

Graham sniffed. "It smells like... like..." He trailed off, struggling to pin down a description.

"It smells like sweat."

Graham closed his eyes. "It reminds me of being at a concert, right in the middle of a mosh pit." His voice thickened. "Everyone's headbanging, jumping into each other. It's like a sauna. There's sweat everywhere."

With a shudder, he wrenched himself out of his daydream. He looked around, blinking, red faced, sweat beading his forehead, as if he had indeed just stepped out of a concert.

Louise filled her lungs with the smell. A fierce green glow igniting in her hazel eyes, she got back down on her knees.

"You're wasting time," Graham said as she thrust the heels of her hands against the edge of the slab.

Paying him no heed, Louise pushed with everything she had.

Squeezing her eyes shut, she groaned and gasped as if she was in the throes of labor. Rivulets of sweat streamed down her face. Every vein, every tendon in her slim neck stood out like cables strained to their maximum tension.

"You're just going to injure yoursel–" Graham's warning was cut short by a harsh, grinding sound from beneath the slab. He blinked rapidly, as if doubting his eyes. The square of stone was moving, scraping across the floor centimetre by centimetre.

"Careful!" Graham exclaimed as it suddenly shifted half-a-metre.

Louise's eyes snapped open as if she been jolted out of a deep sleep. Finding herself poised precariously over what appeared to be a bottomless void, she sidestepped her hands along the slab to safety. Lungs heaving like she'd sprinted up a mountain, she collapsed facedown.

Graham crouched to scrutinise the slab. Finding no hinges, tracks or other opening mechanisms, he regarded Louise with wide-eyed curiosity. "How did you do that?"

Her voice croaked out, "I don't know. I just found the strength from somewhere."

A nod from Graham suggested that she'd hit upon something. "It's like that urban legend about the mother lifting the car off her trapped child. It's called hysterical strength. It has something to do with motor neurons–"

"Shh!" Louise hissed as an eerily disembodied voice floated from the well.

"Help."

As she peered into the darkness, the haunting plea echoed from its foul-smelling depths again, sounding so remote it seemed to come from another dimension.

"Hugh!" she exclaimed, sobbing with relief. "Oh thank god. Thank god."

A rumble emanated from Graham's throat, as if he was pondering whether they had God or something else entirely to thank for Louise's feat of superhuman strength.

PART 3, CHAPTER 6

Hope laced with doubt coursed through Hugh. Was it really Louise? Or was it merely a figment of his imagination? A phantom conjured by desperation and despair? Fear took over as another possibility occurred to him – maybe it was Dorothy playing a cruel trick. He could just imagine her taking twisted pleasure from his cries for help.

"Hugh."

The voice penetrated the suffocating miasma of the barrel's interior again, dispelling his uncertainty. "Louise," he croaked, kicking weakly at the boundaries of his prison. "Help. Help."

"Hold on, Hugh. Graham's coming down."

Something thudded softly against the barrel. A rope?

"Descender. Check, Ascender. Check. Slings. Check…"

Although Graham's words were barely audible, their pedantic tone was enough to trigger a swell of laughter in Hugh. It erupted from his throat, a shrill cackle, utterly alien to his own ears. His chest heaving, he teetered on the brink of unconsciousness. But still the laughter kept on spewing forth, an unrelenting, insidious force, mocking him from within.

The barrel bobbed around as something splashed into the water. A crinkling, tearing sound penetrated the staves.

Bang! Bang! Bang!

Hugh's laughter died as a series of heavy blows shook the barrel. He squirmed away from the vibrations, huddling up against Yo-yo's corpse. Suddenly, light was seeping through the blindfold and cold air was stinging his lungs.

"Stay still or you'll flood the barrel," cautioned Graham.

Squinting as the blindfold was lifted from his eyes, Hugh rasped, "The Dankworths did this. They're insane."

"I'm aware."

Graham took out a penknife. "Come closer. I'll hold the barrel steady."

Hugh squirmed forwards, grimacing as the scratches crisscrossing his back rubbed against the barrel.

Graham sawed at the rope binding Hugh's wrists. "So the Dankworths tried to summon Beleth. Did they succeed?"

Uncertainty creased Hugh's brow. "I heard a voice."

"According to The Lesser Key of Soloman, Beleth 'speaketh with a very clear & subtle voice.'."

Hugh thought about the soft, precise voice of the demon the Dankworths had supposedly summoned. "It's all just a performance to them." He heaved a breath of relief as the rope fell away from his wrists. His fingers twitched as he flexed life back into them.

Graham shifted his attention to Hugh's ankles, his torch revealing a bloody mess of shredded material. Despite the gruesome sight, his voice remained flat. "Did they whip you?"

"No. Yo-yo did that."

Graham's eyes betrayed a flicker of surprise at the sight of the cat. With her mouth agape, Yo-yo looked ready to sink her fangs into someone, but the blood matting her fur and the lifeless glaze in her eyes told a different story. "Why did they put Yo-yo in here with you?"

Anyone who murders a parent shall not be punished by the usual forms of execution.

The whispered words rang out in Hugh's head, as if demanding to be spoken aloud. He remained silent.

Graham unwound the rope from Hugh's ankles. "Can you stand?"

Hugh wiggled his toes. "I think so."

Graham hooked his hands under Hugh's armpits and pulled him out of the barrel. Hugh gasped as glacially cold water enveloped him. His shoes touched what felt like a layer of sandy sediment. Ripples of oily-looking iridescent water bounced off the rock walls and lapped against his chest.

"I don't know about portal to Hell, unless Hell's freezing over," he said through chattering teeth.

Hugh's eyes widened as he spotted something floating in the water. Shudders wracking his body, he waded forwards. The water was so cold it paradoxically felt like hot needles were being stuck into every square millimetre of his flesh. The excruciating assault on his senses almost made him hanker for the womb-like warmth of the barrel.

He shakily reached out to pick up the tobacco tin. Clutching it to his chest as if he was afraid someone might try to steal it away, he turned in a full circle. The pipe and feather were nowhere to be seen. With his free hand, he explored beneath the water's surface.

"Put this on," said Graham, holding out a harness.

Reluctantly giving up his search, Hugh pocketed the tin. He struggled to slot his feet into the harness's leg loops. Numbness was spreading through his limbs, making his movements increasingly sluggish. By the time the harness was fully on, he felt like shackles were weighing him down.

Graham slotted a metal device with a hand grip onto the rope. He attached the device to Hugh using karabiners and a sling with multiple loops. Then he lifted one of Hugh's feet into the bottom loop. "Stand up on the loop." He pointed to the metal device. "Pull down on the ascender whist pulling the tail end of the rope upwards."

With his bandaged hand, Hugh took hold of the ascender. With the other, he gripped the rope and pulled. The rope slithered through his grip. "My fingers are too numb to hold on."

"Then you're going to die down here."

The brutally blunt statement sent a jolt of adrenaline through Hugh. He flexed and blew on his fingers. "Come on, you idiot." he berated himself, mustering up every ounce of energy and willpower he possessed.

Groaning with effort, he simultaneously stood up, yanked at the rope and pulled on the ascender. The belay device at his waist ascended the rope a few centimetres and locked in place. He repeated the process several more times, then slumped forwards in his harness, gasping as if he'd done a hundred chin-ups. Only his feet remained in the water.

"Keep going," urged Graham.

Fighting his body's traitorous desire to surrender to the cold, Hugh resumed the ascent. The rope bit into his flesh. His forearms felt like they were on fire. He welcomed the sensation. It was preferable to the numbness it replaced.

The higher he got, the narrower the well became, until his body was pressing against the reddish slime that seemed to bleed from the rock. He looked at his raw bleeding fingers, strings of saliva dangling from his agape mouth.

"I think I'm going to pass out," he wheezed, his vision sliding in and out of focus.

"No you're not," Louise called down to him. "You can do this, Hugh. Think about Isabelle."

"Don't say her name here." Hugh's voice was little more than a slurred whisper.

"Think about her waiting for you to come home," exhorted Louise.

Hugh pictured Isabelle's chocolate-button eyes. Fresh strength coursed through him at the thought of what it would do to those eyes if he didn't come home. He coiled his hand into the rope and dragged himself upwards. Again and again, he performed the arduous manoeuvre, thinking of nothing except getting back to Isabelle. His body slid across the rock, lubricated by slime. He gagged as the foul stuff found its way into his mouth. Vomit rained down on Graham's upturned face. Hugh didn't have the breath to apologise. A sob scraped up his throat as Louise came into view.

"That's it, Hugh, pull, pull!" she encouraged, leaning out precariously over the lip of the well.

His eyes blazing with resolve, he hauled himself towards her. She stretched out a hand. He resisted the temptation to take it, not wanting to risk pulling her into the well. One… two… three more times, he yanked at the ascender, then his head emerged from the well. Louise hooked her fingers under his armpits and heaved him over the rim. He slithered across the floor on his chest, leaving a snail-trail of rusty-red slime.

When his entire body was out of the well, he finally gave into exhaustion and collapsed onto his face. Louise pressed a hand to her mouth to stifle a sob as she surveyed the lattice of lacerations on his back. She gently rolled him over and propped his head on the rucksack.

"My god," she breathed at the sight of his crushed nose. "What have they done to you?"

Hugh lay winded and shivering as Louise set about carefully cleaning his face with her sleeves.

The rope creaked and grated against the rim of the well. Graham's sweaty red face soon appeared. His broad chest rising and falling rapidly, he hauled himself out of the well and unclipped his harness from the rope.

"They really did a number on you," he said, eyeing Hugh.

Hugh dredged up a faint smile. "I must look as if I've gone twelve rounds with King Kong."

"You're lucky to be alive," said Louise.

Graham's gaze shifted to the slab. "How did the Dankworths move that? Is there a mechanism?"

"No," said Hugh. "Arthur moved it. With one hand."

"I don't see how that's possible." Graham tugged at his beard. "There has to be a—"

"Does it matter how he moved it?" cut in Louise. She eyed the doorway uneasily. "We need to get out of here."

Hugh extended a hand towards her. She helped him up, revealing a patchwork of crimson smears on the floor beneath his back. Graham detached the rope from the roof beam it was anchored to. He methodically wound it around his hand and elbow before packing it away. Shouldering his rucksack, he cast a final glance around the room, his gaze passing over the slab, the salt circle and the chalk symbol.

He turned to survey Hugh's bruised and lacerated body, as if each injury were a piece to a puzzle he was determined to solve.

Averting his eyes from Graham's intense scrutiny, Hugh stared at the sigil – the inverted heart, the flared crosses, the seemingly random squiggles. It looked like a child's scribble, nothing but made up nonsense. With a sudden movement, he scuffed out the sigil. Then, hugging his arms around himself, he staggered towards the door.

PART 3, CHAPTER 7

Bouts of shivering attacked Hugh's limbs. His vision blurred intermittently, causing the steep stairway to twist and warp before him. Halfway up it, he sank to his knees.

Graham clasped Hugh's shoulders and lifted him to his feet. They resumed their ascent, Hugh half walking, half being carried. When they reached the ground floor, Louise put her ear to the door.

Silence.

She cracked open the door and peered into the dining room. The only light came from the candlelit table at the centre of the room. The candles cast a flickering orange circle, beyond which clustered deep shadows. There was no sign of Dorothy or anyone else.

Louise padded forwards, watching the shadows for any sign of movement. Their shoes squelching, Hugh and Graham followed.

Hugh's gaze was fixated on the candlelit table. "That's the table we ate at on the night my dad was murdered."

"Shh," cautioned Louise.

The black-and-red snake watched beadily from the ceiling as they weaved their way between the tables. All three of them froze as a sharp hiss vibrated through the air. Hugh darted a glance at the ceiling, half-expecting the snake to strike at him.

The hiss turned into words, soft and tremulous. "Mirror, mirror on the wall, who in this hotel is fairest of all?"

Dorothy emerged from the shadows, arms spread, chin high, like she was performing to a crowd. "Golden hair, flawless skin, she walks like a goddess, eyes all aglow. Is she the most beautiful of them all? Every head turns towards her. They all want to know."

As Dorothy glided forwards, Hugh caught hold of Louise's arm and drew her behind him.

Her breasts swelling against her dress, Dorothy raised her voice. "He looked at me and my heart leapt up to the sky. A feeling so powerful, I thought I would die. The memory still haunts me, the pain won't fade. I thought I had his heart. I thought I had his soul."

Graham lifted a hand, palm facing Dorothy. "Don't come any closer." His words were a flat warning.

Staring straight through him at Hugh, she warbled, "But my thoughts were wrong. Now desire turns to anger. Jealousy poisons my veins. Lost in a storm of rage and despair, I scream to the heavens, 'How do you *dare*?'"

On the last word, Dorothy's voice jumped to a scream. At the same instant, she snatched up a knife from a table.

Graham calmy picked up a chair and threw it at her. She screamed again as the chair hit her full on, knocking her flat on her back. Blood welled from a gash on her forehead. She touched a finger to the wound, then looked at Graham, her eyes shining with a dazed disbelief, seemingly struggling to understand how anyone could have the audacity to defend themself from her. Her ruby red lips parted. "Arthur!"

Hugh's eyes darted around the room, his heart palpitating in anticipation of the terrifyingly strong hotelier's arrival. He didn't have to wait long. The double doors flew open and Arthur appeared, his lanky frame silhouetted in a three-piece suit.

"Look what he did to me," wailed Dorothy.

Upon seeing her bloodied face, Arthur's grey eyes turned black. They slid towards Hugh, devoid of anything but rage.

Like a grotesque mannequin come to life, Arthur jolted stiffly into motion. He lifted his hands, fingers splayed. Hugh's legs gave way, as if the mere sight of the monstrous appendages was enough to cripple him.

Arthur's long strides swiftly covered the distance between himself and Hugh. Graham stepped between the two men.

"No, Graham!" cried Hugh. "Get away from him!"

Graham raised his thick arms, stepping one leg back, bracing himself to fend off Arthur. The men were about the same height, but Graham's much bigger build made him appear to loom over Arthur. The hotelier's pace didn't falter.

"I don't want to hurt–" began Graham. He broke off as Arthur caught hold of his foremost hand. With a seemingly effortless motion, Arthur bent back Graham's fingers. There was a cracking, snapping sound. Graham's eyes bulged as he watched his fingers being folded backwards onto his wrist. Broken bones tried to push their way through his skin. He dropped to one knee as if paying homage to Arthur.

The hotelier clamped his hands onto either side of Graham's head.

"Don't! Please don't!" Louise pleaded.

Her voice like velvet, Dorothy said, "Show them what true love is, Arthur."

Arthur's fingers flexed against Graham's skull. Graham futilely tried to prise them away, his eyeballs protruding further and further and further.

Hugh clutched at Louise, dragging himself halfway upright. "Run," he gasped. She didn't move, watching spellbound with horror as blood welled up around Arthur's fingertips.

Graham's face was a mute mask of agony. But there was

something else in his expression too – a dawning realisation. A wonderment.

"Run!" Hugh urged again, shoving at Louise. As she staggered backwards, he fell onto his face. She bumped into the candlelit table, knocking over the Champagne bottle. She snatched up the bottle and hurled it at Arthur. It bounced off his bald head with a dull clunk. He showed no sign of having felt it.

"He's not human," breathed Louise.

Graham pulled the Saint Benedict medallion out from under his t-shirt. As slowly as rusty gears grinding into motion, he began to stand up. Three words whistled from him, seeming to confirm Louise's suspicion that Arthur was merely masquerading as human. "Vade retro Satana."

Arthur's huge knotty knuckles whitened. His fingertips sank out of sight into Graham's scalp. Blood cascaded down the sides of Graham's face, dripping from his beard.

"Vade retro Satana," he repeated, battling his way upright. "Vade retro–" His voice faltered as a wet crunch like a snail being crushed came from between Arthur's hands. Almost luminously red blood squirted from Graham's nostrils. He staggered, but somehow managed to remain on his feet.

A half-scream, half-sob tearing from her, Louise grabbed a Champagne flute and flung it at Arthur. It skimmed past his head and shattered against a pillar, scattering glass over a table. A tiny black shape darted out from under the hem of the tablecloth. Midnight streaked across the floor into Dorothy's outstretched arms. She hugged the kitten, her eyes spitting blue fire at Louise.

"Vada retro Satana!" bellowed Graham, speckling Arthur's face with frothy red saliva. His hand dropped from the medallion to his pocket. He took out his penknife, raised it to his mouth and pulled the blade open with his teeth.

With a sickening squelch, Arthur's thumbs sank into Graham's temples up to the first knuckle. As Graham's eyes rolled back in their sockets, he thrust the knife into Arthur's throat.

A scream erupted from Dorothy.

Arthur's thin lips parted. Gurgling like a blocked drain, he pushed his thumbs all the way in. Graham's hand fell limply to his side, leaving the blade embedded in Arthur. Like a vice being unwound, Arthur's hands parted away from Graham's head. Clumps of scalp and hair clung to his fingers.

Graham crumpled to the floor. His limbs twitched several times, then he was still.

Arthur reached up to pull the blade from his throat and fling it aside. Blood spurted from a coin-slot sized wound.

"Oh my love, my love," cried Dorothy.

Arthur turned to her. For few heartbeats, his eyes saw her and nothing else. Then his gaze slid to Louise. Like a zombie, he staggered towards her. She stood motionless, mouth agape, appearing paralysed by the force of his glare.

Hugh flung his arms around Arthur's beanpole legs. Arthur bent to hammer Hugh's head with a fist. Hugh's whole body shook at the impact, but he clung on like a limpet. As Arthur lifted his fist to deliver another clubbing blow, blood sprayed from the knife wound onto Hugh. Arthur's arm hung in the air as if suspended on strings. A rattling wheeze issued from his gaping mouth.

"My love!" Dorothy exclaimed again.

This time, Arthur didn't appear to hear her. His eyes seemed to stare off into somewhere only he could see. Like a felled tree, he toppled sideways. His head slammed against a table before coming to rest on the floor. One final drawn-out gurgle trickled from him.

Hugh looked at Dorothy, glassy-eyed with concussion. She stared back, her eyes radiating hate. Clutching Midnight to her chest, she clambered to her feet. Not taking his eyes off her, Hugh grabbed a chair and pulled himself upright. They faced each other across the candlelit table.

Hugh heard his dad telling him to, *Say goodnight to Mrs Dankworth.*

"Goodnight, Mrs Dankworth."

His voice was flat, giving Dorothy nothing. She raised her chin, looking down her perfectly straight nose at him. She held his gaze for a moment, then turned her back on him. Her high heels played a slow tune on the parquet floor as, with the studied grace of an actress exiting the stage, she swayed towards the doors.

Hugh started to follow her, but Louise caught hold of his wrist. Her eyes shone with a light that was at once soft and resolute. "It's over. Let her go."

At the creak of the doors opening, his gaze returned to Dorothy. For a second, she stood framed in the light of the lobby, her blonde hair shimmering, her shoulders thrown back. Then doors swung shut behind her.

Hugh lowered his eyes to the chair where he'd sat eating tomato soup while the storm battered the hotel. Suddenly, he dropped onto it as if he'd fallen from a great height.

Keeping her eyes averted from Graham's mangled head, Louise knelt beside him and searched in vain for a pulse. She looked up at Hugh. "It *is* over, isn't it?"

He didn't reply.

"Isn't it?" she asked again.

Hugh closed his eyes, two words replaying relentlessly in his mind, *I accept, I accept, I accept…*

PART 4, CHAPTER 1

The Bill Comes Due

Isabelle skipped from her bedroom and down the stairs, humming happily to herself. She fell silent as she neared a door. As quietly as possible, she opened it and entered a gloomy room.

A pale shape lay amidst a tangle of plastic tubes on a trolley bed. The figure appeared to be little more than a skeleton. Isabelle tiptoed forwards, feathering a finger along one of the metal rails that enclosed the mattress. She turned to part some curtains and open a window just enough to allow in sunlight, fresh air and birdsong. Rising onto tiptoes, she sniffed at a big bouquet of flowers on a bedside cabinet. She nodded approvingly at their sweet scent.

"Morning Grandma," she said, leaning in to peer under the veil of tubes. Were her grandma's eyelids open a fraction of a centimetre? She couldn't tell. She stroked the back of a veiny claw of a hand. The skin was cold and dry. It reminded her of a snake she'd once held at a zoo.

Isabelle held up a drawing of a black cat peering from between the leaves of a bush. The cat's green eyes filled most of its face. "I did you a drawing of that cat I told you about. The one I saw in the front garden. It's the cutest thing ever."

At the sound of footsteps, Isabelle quickly slid the drawing under the bed. "Don't tell my dad," she whispered. "You know how much he hates cats."

"Hello there, sweetheart," Hugh said as he entered the room.

Isabelle responded with a *butter-wouldn't-melt* smile.

Hugh smiled back, crinkling the yellow bruises that flanked his crooked nose. "How's your grandma doing?"

"She's feeling much better."

"Is that your professional opinion?"

Isabelle's lips dropped into an unamused pout. "No. I can just tell."

Hugh's smile faded, too, as he looked at the waxy hollows of his mum's cheeks, the bruised-looking rings around her eyes, the bloodless outline of her lips. With an almost fearful tenderness, he brushed several strands of grey hair away from her eyes. "Morning, Mum."

He glanced at the proliferation of IV tubes that kept her alive. Alive but not living. He heaved a sigh. "What's the point?"

Shaking her head disapprovingly, Isabelle whispered, "I read about how people like Grandma can hear what's happening around them. So you should only say nice things."

Smiling, Hugh stroked Isabelle's hair that was as black as his mum's had once been. "You're right, sweetie. I'm sorry." A knocking drew his gaze to the hallway. "That'll be the nurse. Go let her in, will you?"

Isabelle bent to give Josie's hand a quick kiss. "Bye, Grandma." She skipped from the room, humming to herself again.

Hugh turned to gently lift one of his mum's hands, uncovering the dented old tobacco tin. A cool, earthy draught tickled the nape of his neck. "It smells like autumn," he murmured, glancing out of the window. Something black nestled amongst a pile of russet leaves caught his eye, but was gone in a blink. Frowning faintly, he scanned the garden. Whatever it had been was nowhere to be seen.

He turned as a woman in a blue tunic bustled into the room. "How's my favourite patient doing today?" asked the nurse.

"She's…" Hugh started to reply, but trailed off as his gaze came to rest once more on his mum's sallow, sunken face.

"She's doing amazing," Isabelle said, giving him a pointed look.

Hugh just about managed to find a grateful smile for her. His eyes quickly shifted to the nurse. "Cup of tea?"

"That would be lovely, thanks."

Even before the nurse finished replying, Hugh was on his way out of the room. He couldn't bear to witness yet again the daily ritual of her checking his mum's vitals, changing the IV bags, emptying the catheter and colostomy bags, cleaning her bedsores… On and on went the list of tasks. There was a brutal efficiency about the process that left him cold.

After filling the kettle, he went outside. He stood in the middle of the back garden, sucking in deep, cleansing breaths.

It smells like autumn, a voice seemed to murmur on the breeze.

He flinched at a touch on his shoulder.

"Are you alright?" Louise asked with a concerned little smile.

Hugh glanced towards his mum's bedroom. Music was tinkling through the open window – a show tune. One of his mum's favourites. "If I ever end up like that, promise me you won't keep me alive."

Louise reached for Hugh's hands. "What's wrong? There's something else bothering you besides your mum, isn't there?"

Hugh's gaze traversed the neatly kept flower beds, lingering on a dense rhododendron. He stared into the gloom between the dark green leaves. "I saw something out here."

"What?"

"I'm not sure. It might have been a crow." Unease creeping into his voice, Hugh added, "Or a cat."

With a sigh of understanding, Louise feathered her thumb back and forth across the smooth red indents that had formed over the bitemarks. "There are six cats that I know of living on this street. Three tabbies. Two ginger toms. And one black cat."

Hugh mustered up a smile. "I know I'm being silly."

"No you're not." Now it was Louise's turn to eye the bushes uneasily. "Why don't you call the police and find out if there have been any…" she searched for the appropriate word, "sightings?"

"They'd call me if they had anything to say." Hugh expelled a frustrated breath, "How does a crazy old woman just disappear like that?"

"I don't think they're going to find Dorothy now. I think she died weeks ago. She couldn't survive for long without Arthur."

Hugh made an uncertain noise in his throat.

Louise gave his hand a gentle squeeze. "Let's go inside and see your mum."

"I don't know if I can," Hugh murmured like a confession.

"Yes you can. She knows what you've done for her, Hugh."

His eyes shone with a desperate need to believe Louise was right. "Do you really think so?"

"Yes I do."

Hugh's brow furrowed as he wrestled with her words. As if trying to convince himself of their truth, he nodded slowly. A movement drew his eyes to the backdoor. Isabelle was looking at him from the doorway. He was struck more than ever by how much she looked like her grandma – the black hair, the dark eyes, the porcelain and rose complexion.

He waved at her. She didn't wave back. A tightness formed in his chest as he noticed how still she was. Isabelle was usually in constant motion, always fidgeting.

Abruptly pulling away from Louise, he started towards Isabelle. As he neared her, the tightness in his chest intensified to a sharp ache. Her eyes were full of tears.

"What is it?" he asked, knowing in his heart what the answer would be.

"It's grandma." Isabelle's voice was tiny, barely more than a whisper. "She opened her eyes and looked at me."

In an instant, Hugh's pain turned to a joy so profound he didn't know whether to laugh or cry.

"And then she died," continued Isabelle.

The feeling was snatched away like a wisp of smoke in the wind. It left behind a void. A hole as deep and dark as Coldwell Hall's well.

Bursting into tears, Isabelle flung her arms around Hugh. He cupped a hand against the back of her head, shushing her softly, a look of blank acceptance in his eyes.

PART 4, CHAPTER 2

One by one, the figures in black filed past the deep, rectangular hole. Among them were familiar faces – relatives and family friends Hugh hadn't seen in years. There were also a few unfamiliar faces. He wondered vaguely whether any of the latter were friends his mother had made during her earlier years in prison. Each mourner stooped to pick up a pinch of soil from a pile and drop it into the hole. The soil rattled against a gleaming wooden coffin.

"Only a dream, only a dream, of glory beyond the dark stream..." sang a small choir lined up a few metres from the graveside.

Staring blankly, fidgeting at something in his jacket pocket, Hugh appeared lost in thought

"How peaceful the slumber. How happy the waking. For death is only a dream..."

Dabbing her eyes with a tissue, Louise stepped forwards to take her turn. She looked at Hugh. He didn't move. She returned to his side, took his hand and gently drew him to the grave. He stared at the coffin, his forehead twitching as he struggled to make sense of his emotions. Or rather lack of them.

"She's in a better place," said a familiar gruff voice.

Hugh turned to the speaker. Heavy-lidded eyes peered up at him from under an ostentatiously wide-brimmed hat. A cigarette dangled from glossy pink lips, its smoke wreathing a thin, freckled face.

"Is she?" he asked.

Ava gave a little shrug. "So they say."

Hugh's gaze travelled down her inappropriately short black dress to the tattoo of a prancing figure on her thigh. "The Fool symbolises beginnings and ends, unlimited potential…"

"And unlimited stupidity," Ava finished for him.

Faint lines gathered between Hugh's eyebrows. "Five weeks, three days. That's how long my mum lived for after they let her out of Rampton. Was it even worth it?"

"I can try to ask her if you want."

A fleeting look of confusion passed over Hugh's face. His question wasn't about whether it was worth it for his mum. It was about everything he'd put Louise through. And it was about Graham's death. Above all, he'd been thinking about his ordeal in the barrel, the scars he'd been left with on his body and mind.

I accept. I accept.

As his desperate words echoed back to him, he quickly lowered his gaze from Ava to the coffin. "Leave her in peace."

"I'm so sorry about Graham," said Louise.

"Don't be." Ava spoke with a bluntness that seemed to suggest she was channelling Graham's spirit. "He got the answers he wanted. He died happy."

Louise shuddered, recalling the horrific sound of Graham's head being crushed between Arthur's hands. What answers had he got? That evil existed? That love could drive people mad? She'd seen no happiness in his eyes, only pain. She kept her thoughts to herself. This wasn't the time or place for such talk.

Fidgeting again with whatever was in his pocket, Hugh

reflected, "If death is only a dream and life is but a dream, then are we ever really awake?"

Ava chuckled. "I'm buggered if I know."

The sun emerged from behind a cloud. Its warmth on Hugh's back seemed to invite him to lie down beside his mum and close his eyes. "Through the storm, she always protects me. Staying by my side until her lullaby carries me away and we both get some much-needed sleep."

"Where's that from?" asked Louise.

"Mum sang it to me one night."

Louise smiled sadly, but said nothing more. It was obvious which night Hugh was referring to.

He took out the tobacco tin, removed its lid and tipped its contents into the grave. The soil played a soft tune on the coffin, then there was silence.

The mourners were drifting away. As Ava tottered after them, Louise said, "Thanks for coming."

Without looking back, Ava raised a hand in farewell. Hugh's gaze remained on the coffin. Louise stood silent by his side. Before long, a couple of gravediggers began shovelling soil into the grave. Spadeful after spadeful of it rained down, swiftly obscuring the coffin from view.

Hugh's spine went rigid as a shrill *BWHRRRRHHH* cut through the graveyard. For an instant, he was back inside the barrel with Yo-yo howling and clawing at him.

A bagpiper in full tartan garb and a feather bonnet marched between the graveyard's wrought-iron gates. A procession of black limousines was lined up on the road. At its front, a pair of white horses were pulling a white carriage. A top-hatted figure perched atop the carriage was geeing the horses along with leather reins.

BNRRRRR PHARRR. The mournful dirge filled the air like a

soul crying out in torment.

"He is a mighty king and terrible. He rideth on a pale horse with trumpets and other kinds of musical instruments playing before him," said Hugh, looking at the flower-festooned coffin within the carriage's glass walls.

"I don't call that melodious music." Louise hooked an arm through his. "And can we please, please not have any more talk about *that* kind of thing. That part of your life is over."

"It's not over until Dorothy Dankworth is–"

Hugh broke off as a small figure darted in front of the horses, causing one of them to jerk its head and stamp its hooves. He did a double take, then exclaimed, "Isabelle!"

Her long dark hair streaming behind her, Isabelle ran towards her grandma's grave.

Louise's eyes widened in concern and astonishment. Pulling Hugh along with her, she strode to meet Isabelle. "How did you get here?" She glanced past Isabelle. "Where's your Grandma Miriam?"

"She's at home," Isabelle answered breathlessly, her cheeks a bright, almost feverish shade of red. "She doesn't know I'm here."

"But how did you find your way here on your own?"

"I asked people."

"What have we told you about talking to strangers?" Hugh rebuked Isabelle.

She pushed her heart-shaped lips into a defiant pout. "And told you I wanted to come to the funeral."

"Funerals are no place for children."

"Why? Why can't I say goodbye to Grandma?"

"You can," said Louise. "You don't need to be here to do that."

Isabelle's eyes narrowed as if she suspected she was being

lied to. "Then why are you here?"

Defeated by her child's logic, Hugh and Louise exchanged a glance. Hugh reached for Isabelle's hand. "Come and say goodbye then."

He led her to the graveside. Her bottom lip quivered as she watched the gravediggers toss the last few spadefuls of soil into the hole.

Louise took out her phone and switched it on. "Mum's tried to call me five times. She must be worried sick. I'd better call her."

With a thudding finality, the gravediggers stamped the soil flat. Tears were suddenly flowing from Isabelle's eyes. "It's not fair."

Hugh put an arm around her shoulders. "I know, sweetheart, but..." His brain scrambled for something to say to console her. All he could think of was to echo Ava's words, "She's in a better place."

He regretted the empty platitude the instant it left his mouth. Isabelle subjected him to a look that made it clear she saw right through him. "That's a lie!"

She squirmed free from his embrace and sprinted away.

Louise lowered her phone from her ear. "What's the matter with her now?"

Shaking his head to say, *Don't ask*, Hugh ran after Isabelle. She raced between the gravestones towards a path. The bagpipes blared out as if urging her on.

"Isabelle, stop," Hugh shouted, gravel crunching underfoot as he chased her along the path.

Ignoring him, she veered out of sight behind the church. As Hugh rounded the corner, something darted from between two altar tombs. He stopped dead. Isabelle was nowhere to be seen. A small black cat was standing in the path, peering up at him with slitted eyes. As it prowled forwards to circle his ankles, Yo-yo's howls seemed to resonate from the darkest depths of his mind. The scratch marks that crisscrossed his back tingled at the memory of her claws tearing into him. His lungs strained for breath, as if he were once again trapped in the airless confines of the barrel.

Another creature emerged from between the tombs. Its hair was a wild tangle. A shroud of grime obscured its facial features. Its hands looked as if they'd clawed their way out of a grave. Long, horn-like toenails jutted out from beneath a tattered overcoat.

What was it? A man? A woman? Something else entirely? The questions stabbed at Hugh's trauma-stricken mind as the figure shuffled closer. A nauseating odour, reminiscent of a leaky colostomy bag, invaded his nostrils. Bloodshot blue eyes stared at him from between eyelids caked with some sort of crusty discharge.

Those eyes! He knew those eyes. He saw them in his nightmares almost every night.

"Dorothy." The name wrenched itself out of his throat. Panic gripped him even more tightly as his thoughts returned to Isabelle. He darted a look at the ivy-clogged gap between the tombs, No Isabelle. Anger vying with fear in his voice, he demanded to know, "What have you done with my daughter?"

In response, Dorothy put a hand into her coat pocket and pulled out a knife. Hugh made to grab it, but she opened her palm and proffered the handle.

Warily, alert to any possible trickery, he took the knife. It had a narrow, pointed blade. A blade very much like the one that had been thrust into his father.

Dorothy's ice blue eyes stared up at him expectantly.

"Where's my daughter?" Hugh's voice trembled on the edge of control. "If you've hurt her..." He left his words hanging ominously.

Dorothy raised a dirt-ingrained fingernail to her left eye. A single word scraped between her brown teeth. "Blood."

Blood. That is the price of your salvation.

As the repulsively soft voice whispered through his mind, Hugh shrank away from Dorothy. He tripped over Midnight, falling heavily onto his backside. Bending towards him, Dorothy repeated, "Blood."

Hugh gave a frantic shake of his head. "There was no demon. It was you. You're Beleth. You're the ghost."

Her voice rising to a harsh squawk, Dorothy yelled at him like an enraged parrot, "You're the ghost! You're the ghost!"

Midnight slunk around Hugh and her, yowling as if in agreement.

Dorothy thrust her face closer to Hugh. "You're the ghost!"

Her voice was like a razor cutting his brain. He raised the knife, pointing the blade at her face. God, he wanted to shut her up. He pictured the blade going in. The eyeball bursting like an overripe cherry. No one could blame him for doing it. One thrust and it would be over. She deserved as much and a thousand times more.

Dorothy presented the left side of her face to him. The tip of the blade quivered a centimetre away from her eyeball. Up close, clusters of curly grey hairs were visible on her chin. Her once slender, smooth nose had mutated into something as bulbous and bumpy as a cauliflower floret. Hugh found himself wondering if she was wearing a disguise. Or maybe her beauty had been the disguise. Maybe this was her real face.

"You're the ghost!" She was wailing now, practically pleading with him to take his revenge.

Freedom, justice, peace.

The words circled Hugh's memory. The first part of the

promise had been delivered. Now it was time for justice for his parents and peace for himself. What bliss it would be to fall asleep that night knowing Dorothy could never hurt him or his family again. All he had to do was push the blade through her eye into her brain.

Dorothy's blue iris twinkled at him, taunting, urging. Hugh's blood pounded with the desire to snuff out the last bit of light in her. His fingers tightened on the knife's handle.

A movement over Dorothy's shoulder caught his eye. Isabelle stepped onto the path, staring at him. *Is that my dad?* her big round eyes seemed to ask. *Could my dad really be about to kill someone?*

In a heartbeat, shame extinguished Hugh's murderous desire. Blinking away from Isabelle's gaze, he lowered the knife.

Dorothy fell silent. She stared at Hugh for a moment more, seemingly unsure what to do. Then, letting out the strange laugh-cry that Hugh had heard once before, she scooped up Midnight. The cat hooked a proprietorial paw around her neck, darting his little pink tongue out to lick her face. She stepped away from Hugh and turned to Isabelle. Hugh rose to his feet, poised to react should Dorothy make a move towards her. Part of him wanted Dorothy to do so. That would be all the excuse he needed to end this once and for all.

The laugh-cry still gurgling in her throat, Dorothy lurched into motion. Bereft of her former grace, she staggered towards a gate at the rear of the graveyard. Hugh's face twitched, caught between relief and disappointment.

Isabelle darted forwards and clutched his hand. "Who was that monster, Daddy?"

"That isn't a monster."

"Yes it is."

Hugh took a step after Dorothy, but Isabelle pulled him back.

Dorothy was almost at the gate. From a distance, she looked like a decrepit old tramp, someone to be pitied not feared.

"Oh good, you found her!"

Hugh glanced over his shoulder at Louise's relieved exclamation. Her brow furrowed at the turmoil in his eyes.

"*She* was here," he told her in a tone that left no doubt who he meant.

"The monster vanished," said Isabelle.

Hugh's gaze returned to the gate. Dorothy was gone.

"Vanished?" echoed Louise. "Where did she go?"

Isabelle answered with an enigmatic shrug.

As Louise tapped urgently at her phone, Hugh asked, "Who are you calling?"

"Who do you think?" She put the phone to her ear, her eyes darting all around as if she expected Dorothy to spring from behind a gravestone. "The police."

PART 4, CHAPTER 3

Hugh peered between the curtains at the darkening street. His eyes moved back and forth, delving into every bush, every shadow. A neighbour walking a Jack Russel passed by. The little dog suddenly barked and strained at its lead. Hugh craned his neck to try and see what the dog was pulling towards. Had it spotted a cat?

"Come and sit down, Hugh," Louise said from the sofa, where she was curled up in front of the TV with Isabelle. "She's not going to come here. And even if she does, the police are keeping an eye out for her."

Hugh's gaze lingered on the police car at the entrance to the cul-de-sac.

"Stop worrying, Daddy," said Isabelle. "The police won't let that monster hurt us."

"Dorothy's not a monster," Louise gently chided. "She just a very sick old woman."

"Sick like Grandma was?"

"Yes... Well, no, not exactly like Grandma was. It's difficult to explain."

With a biting intensity, Hugh said, "She *made* your grandma ill."

"Why?" asked Isabelle.

"Because you're right, she is a monster. A green-eyed monster."

Isabelle's soft little face twisted into a hard frown. "Then I wish she was dead. You should have killed her with that knife."

"Isabelle!" Louise exclaimed, giving her a shocked look. "You don't really mean that."

"Yes I do." Rising from the sofa, staring unblinkingly at her dad, Isabelle repeated in an accusing tone, "You should have killed her."

With that, she turned her back on him and strode from the room.

"Isabelle, come back here and–" Louise started to say.

"Leave her," interrupted Hugh, listening to Isabelle stomp up the stairs.

"She doesn't understand what she's saying," said Louise.

Hugh pursed his lips as if he wasn't so sure of that.

"I think she might be coming down with something," continued Louise. "She's all hot and sweaty."

"She's just tired out."

Hugh gave a start as another burst of barking reverberated around the street. Louise stood up, switched off the TV and put her arms around him from behind. "We're all tired out. Let's go to bed."

He heaved a sigh. "It doesn't matter how tired my body is, my mind won't allow me to sleep."

"Yes it will." Louise kissed the back of his neck. "I'll sing you a lullaby."

Howling winds tearing through the land, but Mum's love, like a shield, takes my hand...

As his mother's softly singing voice played through his mind, Hugh began to shake. Suddenly, as if a dam had given way inside him, tears flooded his eyes. Pressing his hands to his face, he sobbed, "I loved her so much."

"I know, I know," soothed Louise, tightening her embrace. She held onto him until his sobs eventually began to subside.

He turned towards her, his eyes full of tears and love. "I don't know what I'd do without you, Louise. Really I don't."

Smiling, she stroked his wet face. He didn't resist as she took his hand and led him from the room. She reached for a light switch, but he said, "Leave the light on."

Louise thought about it for a moment, then turned off the light. "I'm not afraid of Dorothy."

"You should be. She's a killer."

Louise tilted her head doubtfully. "Arthur was the killer. Without him, Dorothy's only a danger to herself. She'd probably be dead already if she had the courage to end it herself."

"And we wouldn't be worrying like this if I'd done what she wanted."

At Hugh's tone of self-reproach, Louise gave his hand a squeeze. "But then you wouldn't be my husband, because I couldn't be married to a killer."

You're the ghost! You're the ghost!

A queasy chill crept through Hugh as he thought about Dororthy parroting his words. Shivering as if the sensation was seeping into her, Louise headed for the stairs.

He withdrew his hand from hers. "I'm going to check everything's locked up."

Louise arched an eyebrow. Hugh had already checked the doors and windows multiple times that evening. "I'll look in on Isabelle."

As Louise ascended the stairs, Hugh approached the front door. After ensuring it was locked, he moved on to the backdoor and the downstairs windows. His last stop was the dining room that had been converted into his mother's bedroom. All the medical equipment was gone, except for the trolley bed. He rested a hand on the mattress. Had his mum known where she was? Had it meant something to her that she'd spent her final few weeks with her family?

A corner of paper poking out from under the bed caught his eye. He bent down to pick it up. His brow knitted into a frown as he looked at the drawing of a black cat peeking from a bush. "ISABELLE' was written in block letters above the cat.

He pivoted to hurry from the room. As he reached the landing, Louise emerged from Isabelle's room and whispered, "She's fast asleep."

Hugh showed her the drawing. "Dorothy's been here."

"Not necessarily. Don't you remember that drawing of a black cat Isabelle gave you before you went to..." Louise paused, reluctant to say the hotel's name, "*that* place? I bet this is the same cat."

Her words smoothed the creases from Hugh's forehead. He stared at the cat's round, smiling face for a moment more, then peered into Isabelle's room. She was laid on her side, head poking out from the duvet, apple red cheeks partially hidden by a fan of lustrous hair.

He couldn't imagine anything more perfect. "The most beautiful girl in the world," he murmured to himself, easing the door shut.

He padded after Louise to their bedroom. Feeling heavy all over, he undressed and got into bed without bothering to brush his teeth. He lay as rigid as a statue, acutely aware of every little sound – Louise moving around in the bathroom, the distant rumble of an engine. As Louise entered the bedroom and lay down, he rose to peer out of the window. The sky was fully dark. Lampposts cast their glow on neatly-trimmed hedges. All was as it should be. Silent. Still. Normal.

Louise said his name, patting the bed for him to lie back

down. He did so and she cuddled up to him. In a low, lilting voice, she began to sing, "Rockabye baby on the tree top–"

Hugh's mind flashed back to the dream of Dorothy straddling him, the image so vivid that he could almost feel her pressing against his groin. "Please, not that song. It reminds me of you know where."

"Close your eyes," whispered Louise. "Don't think about that place. Don't think about anything at all."

Hugh closed his eyes. Darkness immediately seized him, dragging him back to the howling, clawing hell of the barrel. His chest heaving, he started to open his eyes.

"Don't give in to it," urged Louise, holding him close.

Drawing in a slow breath, Hugh let his eyelids slide back down. He let the memories sweep over him. He let the insidious whisper gnaw at the edges of his sanity. *Worship us. Give us everything you have.*

"Don't give in," Louise repeated.

He focused on her voice. The memories slithered out of his mind. The whispers retreated into whatever dark pit they'd crawled from.

"Don't give in."

Louise's words were like a warm current, gently carrying Hugh away from the world. He didn't resist. God, he was so tired. All he wanted was to sleep… and sleep… and sleep… and…

PART 4, CHAPTER 4

Midnight slunk along the pavement, skirting a lamppost's circle of light. He hunkered down, eyes narrowing to shiny slits as a dog barked at him. He waited for it to move on, then prowled forwards. After darting across a driveway, he disappeared into a bush. Nestled in its hollow centre, he sat down on his hindquarters.

Light seeped through a nearby curtained window, casting a dull glow that dwindled before it reached the bush. The curtains parted a finger's width, revealing a glimpse of a face. Midnight's eyes narrowed again, like he was sizing up some prey. He sat perfectly still, indistinguishable from the surrounding darkness.

Before long, the dog returned. Its yapping reverberated through the night once more. Barely moving his head, Midnight gave it an indifferent glance that suggested it was unworthy of his attention. His eyes homed in on another twitch of the downstairs curtains. Moments later, the light went off. Soon afterwards, a light came on in an upstairs window.

Midnight lay down and set about methodically grooming himself, licking and nibbling at his plush fur. He became motionless as a white and grey tabby wandered into his line of sight. They locked eyes. The tabby froze in place for a few seconds. Then, its fur bristling and its ears flattened against its skull, it backed away from the bush.

The upstairs light went off. Midnight resumed cleaning

himself, effortlessly contorting his body to lick between his hind legs. When he was finished, he curled up, resting his chin on his paws, his gaze fixed on the house. A car passed by the cul-de-sac. The moon climbed into view above the houses.

As if at a silent signal, Midnight stood up and peered around. Crouching low, his belly grazing the grass, he stalked towards the house. Upon reaching the front door, he rose onto his hind legs and lifted the letterbox flap with one paw. Hooking his other paw through the slot, he pulled himself up. His rear claws scrabbling against the door, he arched his back and pushed his head into the letterbox. The rest of his body followed, flowing like melted rubber through the narrow opening.

The letterbox snapped shut as Midnight dropped to the doormat. He stood motionless for a moment, ears pricked for the slightest sound. The house was silent. As stealthy as a shadow, he climbed the stairs and advanced towards a door. Once again, he rose on his hind legs, draping a paw over a handle and gently pulling it down.

The door swung inwards just enough for him to slink through the gap. He paused in midmotion at a rustle of movement from a bed. Its occupant shifted slightly, then lay still.

Midnight approached the bed. In one smooth motion, he sprang onto it, landing lightly beside the sleeping figure.

Isabelle was on her back, arms at her sides, her hair spread across the pillow like a raven's wings. Her chest rose and fell steadily. A sheen of sweat coated her forehead.

With slow, infinitely patient movements, Midnight climbed onto her and tugged the duvet down, fully exposing her rosy, soft-featured face. He positioned his front paws on her shoulders, a low purr vibrating in his throat. His tongue flicked out, brushing against her lips, coaxing them apart.

Isabelle stirred again, moaning softly. Her eyes moved rapidly beneath their lids.

Midnight's purring intensified, his chest thrumming against hers. His tongue squirmed its way into her mouth, exploring its warm, moist interior. Saliva trickled along the delicate white spines that adorned the wormlike strip of flesh.

The gluey looking substance oozed onto Isabelle's tongue. Choking slightly, she turned her head to the side.

Midnight's tongue retracted into his mouth. His purring subsided. He rose, stepped off Isabelle and jumped to the floor, landing with the softest of thuds.

Isabelle's eyelids fluttered open. She sat up, licking her lips, surveying the room with a glassy stare. Her gaze passed over Midnight as if he was invisible. Moving as slowly and silently as the cat, she rose and left the room. He trailed after her as she made her way downstairs. She entered the kitchen, rising onto tiptoes to reach for a block of knives. She selected one with a long, slender blade.

Her eyes as fixed and unfocused as a sleepwalker's, she returned to the hallway. As she started back up the stairs, her bare feet skimmed past Midnight.

The cat shadowed her, its eyes tracking her every move, like a protective parent watching over their child's first wobbly steps.

At the top of the stairs, Isabelle turned towards a slightly ajar door. She nudged it wide open, stepped through the doorway and stood staring at the dark outlines of her parents. Her mum was snoring softly on her back, mouth agape. Her dad was curled up in a tight ball on his side, as if trying to squeeze himself into a small space.

Midnight stood sentinel by the door while Isabelle glided towards the bed. She lifted the knife, its blade angled directly downwards. Without a heartbeat's hesitation, she plunged it into her mum's left eye.

Shluk!

The blade sank in with a smooth, squishy sound, burying itself two-thirds of the way to the handle. Louise's limbs jerked as if electrified, her arms shooting out, striking Isabelle in the chest. Isabelle reeled backwards several steps before losing her balance and crashing to the floor.

Hugh woke up with a start. "Louise?" he whispered, reaching for her side of the bed. Something sharp sliced into one of his fingers. He snatched his hand back and switched on the lamp.

"Lou–"

His voice died at the sight of the blood. It was everywhere. On the mattress, the pillows, Louise's face, the knife's blade. Was it real? He closed his eyes, clinging to a wild hope that it was nothing but a figment of his imagination. A stress-induced hallucination. A waking dream.

His eyelids parted. The blood was still there, so red it hurt to look at.

At a flicker of movement on the periphery of his vision, another name found its way past his lips. "Dorothy."

Lurching from horror to rage, he grasped the knife's handle. Blood flicked from the blade as he yanked it free. He twisted towards the foot of the bed, his face warped into a mask of pure hate. This time, he would give Dorothy what she wanted. And he wouldn't stop there. He would keep on stabbing and stabbing until she was obliterated from existence.

He found himself staring into a pair of dark brown eyes.

"Dad?" Confusion quivered in Isabelle's voice. "What did you do to Mum?"

The knife dropped from Hugh's fingers. Words fell like dead things from his lips. "It wasn't me. It wasn't me."

Midnight looked on from the shadows. With a flick of his tail, he turned to patter down the stairs. He slipped through the letterbox and stole away into the night, flitting from darkness to darkness, as elusive as a wisp of smoke, as impossible to catch as a ghost.

THANK YOU!

Thank you for reading *How To Catch A Ghost*. I really, REALLY hope you enjoyed it. If you go on to read my other books, have an extra big thank you! I couldn't do this mysterious thing called writing without your support.

Can I ask a favour? If you have a spare moment, could you leave a short review or even simply a rating for this book? It would be hugely appreciated as reader reviews and ratings can make or break a book like mine that doesn't have the financial clout of big publishers behind it. If you do get chance to review my books then - deep breath - THANK YOU!!!

Oh and please feel free to get in touch. I'd genuinely love to know what you think about my books. You can find me on Facebook at @BenCheethamBooks

Best,

Ben

FREE BOOK

As an extra thank you for your support, you can enjoy one of my books for FREE simply by heading over to my website and joining my mailing list. To download your exclusive free eBook, go to bencheetham.com and hit the 'GET MY FREE BOOK' button.

I hope you enjoy the book!

BOOKS BY THIS AUTHOR

Don't Look Back
(Fenton House Book 1)

What really haunts Fenton House?

After the tragic death of their eleven-year-old son, Adam and Ella are fighting to keep their family from falling apart. Then comes an opportunity that seems too good to be true. They win a competition to live for free in a breathtakingly beautiful mansion on the Cornish Lizard Peninsula. There's just one catch – the house is supposedly haunted.

Mystery has always swirled around Fenton House. In 1920 the house's original owner, reclusive industrialist Walter Lewarne, hanged himself from its highest turret. In 1996, the then inhabitants, George Trehearne, his wife Sofia and their young daughter Heloise disappeared without a trace. Neither mystery was ever solved.

Adam is not the type to believe in ghosts. As far as he's concerned, ghosts are simply memories. Everywhere he looks in their cramped London home he sees his dead son. Despite misgivings, the chance to start afresh is too tempting to pass up. Adam, Ella and their surviving son Henry move into Fenton House. At first, the change of scenery gives them all a new lease of life. But as the house starts to reveal its secrets, they come to suspect that they may not be alone after all...

House Of Mirrors
(Fenton House Book 2)

What will you see?

Two years ago the Piper family fled Fenton House after their dream of a new life turned into an unspeakable nightmare. The house has stood empty ever since, given a wide berth by everyone except ghost hunters and occult fanatics.

Now something is trying to lure the Pipers back to Fenton House. But is that 'something' a malevolent supernatural entity? Or is there a more earthly explanation? Whatever the truth, Adam and Ella Piper are about to discover that their family's future is inextricably bound up with the last place they ever wanted to see again.

The Pipers aren't the only ones whose fate is tied to Fenton House. Three thieves seeking their fortune and a mysterious redheaded woman are also converging on the remote Cornish mansion.

Over the course of a single stormy night, each of them will be forced to confront their true self. How far are they willing to go in pursuit of their deepest, darkest desires? How much are they prepared to give in order to simply survive till dawn?

The Crow Tree

Deep in the forest is a cottage. A wicked witch once lived there, or so they say.

Now a new family is moving into the cottage. Hazel and her daughter, Lily, are trying to start over after a tragedy. The cottage appears to be the perfect place for them to rebuild their life. But appearances can be deceptive.

Old superstitions linger in the villages scattered throughout the forest. Tales abound of covens meeting beneath the moonlit trees. Locals hang sprigs of rowan in their windows to protect themselves from the Witch of Blackmoss Cottage.

Hazel and Lily have a dark history of their own that they're desperate to leave behind. But the past has a way of catching up with you and colliding with the present.

High on a hill above the cottage is a tree. A wicked witch was once burned to death there, or so they say.

Lily doesn't believe in magic. And yet, like the crows that flock to its gnarled branches, she's strangely drawn to the tree. Someone - or rather, something - is said to live in its hollow trunk. What if the tales are true?

The secrets of the tree might also hold the key to the secrets of Lily's own tragic past. But as she's about to find out, no good ever comes from meddling with forces you don't understand.

Mr Moonlight

Close your eyes. He's waiting for you.

There's a darkness lurking under the surface of Julian Harris. Every night in his dreams he becomes a different person, a monster capable of evil beyond comprehension. Sometimes he feels like something is trying to get inside him. Or maybe it's already in him, just waiting for the chance to escape into the waking world.

There's a darkness lurking under the surface of Julian's

picture-postcard hometown too. Fifteen years ago, five girls disappeared from the streets of Godthorne. Now it's happening again. A schoolgirl has gone missing, stirring up memories of that terrible time. But the man who abducted those other girls is long dead. Is there a copycat at work? Or is something much, much stranger going on?

Drawn by the same sinister force that haunts his dreams, Julian returns to Godthorne for the first time in years. Finding himself mixed up in the mystery of the missing girl, he realises that to unearth the truth about the present he must confront the ghosts of his past.

Somewhere amidst the sprawling tangle of trees that surrounds Godthorne are the answers he so desperately seeks. But the forest does not relinquish its secrets easily.

The Lost Ones

The truth can be more dangerous than lies.

July 1972

The Ingham household. Upstairs, sisters Rachel and Mary are sleeping peacefully. Downstairs, blood is pooling around the shattered skull of their mother, Joanna, and a figure is creeping up behind their father, Elijah. A hammer comes crashing down again and again...

July 2016

The Jackson household. This is going to be the day when Tom Jackson's hard work finally pays off. He kisses his wife Amanda and their children, Jake and Erin, goodbye and heads out dreaming of a better life for them all. But just hours later he finds himself plunged into a nightmare...

Erin is missing. She was hiking with her mum in Harwood Forest. Amanda turned her back for a moment. That was all it took for Erin to vanish. Has she simply wandered off? Or does the blood-stained rock found where she was last seen point to something sinister? The police and volunteers who set out to search the sprawling forest are determined to find out. Meanwhile, Jake launches an investigation of his own – one that will expose past secrets and present betrayals.

Is Erin's disappearance somehow connected to the unsolved murders of Elijah and Joanna Ingham? Does it have something to do with the ragtag army of eco-warriors besieging Tom's controversial quarry development? Or is it related to the fraught phone call that distracted Amanda at the time of Erin's disappearance?

So many questions. No one seems to have the answers and time is running out. Tom, Amanda and Jake must get to the truth to save Erin, though in doing so they may well end up destroying themselves.

Blood Guilt
(Steel City Thrillers Book 1)

Can you ever really atone for killing someone?

After the death of his son in a freak accident, Detective Harlan Miller's life is spiralling out of control. He's drinking too much. His marriage and career are on the rocks. But things are about to get even worse. A booze-soaked night out and a single wild punch leave a man dead and Harlan facing a manslaughter charge.

Fast-forward four years. Harlan's prison term is up, but life on the outside holds little promise. Divorced, alone, consumed by guilt, he thinks of nothing beyond atoning for the death he caused. But how do you make up for depriving a wife of her husband and two young boys of their father? Then something happens, something terrible, yet something that holds out a twisted kind of hope for Harlan – the dead man's youngest son is abducted.

From that moment Harlan's life has only one purpose – finding the boy. So begins a frantic race against time that leads him to a place darker than anything he experienced as a detective and a stark moral choice that compels him to question the law he once enforced.

Angel Of Death
(Steel City Thrillers Book 2)

They thought she was dead. They were wrong.

Fifteen-year-old Grace Kirby kisses her mum and heads off to school. It's a day like any other day, except that Grace will never return home.

Fifteen years have passed since Grace went missing. In that time, Stephen Baxley has made millions. And now he's lost millions. Suicide seems like the only option. But Stephen has no intention of leaving behind his wife, son and daughter. He wants them all to be together forever, in this world or the next.

Angel is on the brink of suicide too. Then she hears a name on the news that transports her back to a windowless basement. Something terrible happened in that basement. Something Angel has been running from most of her life. But the time for running is over. Now is the time to start fighting back.

At the scene of a fatal shooting, Detective Jim Monahan finds evidence of a sickening crime linked to a missing girl. Then more people start turning up dead. Who is the killer? Are the victims also linked to the girl? Who will be next to die? The answers will test to breaking-point Jim's faith in the law he's spent his life upholding.

Justice For The Damned
(Steel City Thrillers Book 3)

They said there was no serial killer. They lied.

Melinda has been missing for weeks. The police would normally be all over it, but Melinda is a prostitute. Women in that line of work change addresses like they change lipstick. She probably just moved on.

Staci is determined not to let Melinda become just another statistic added to the long list of girls who've gone missing over the years. Staci is also a prostitute – although not for much longer if Detective Reece Geary has anything to do with it. Reece will do anything to win Staci's love. If that means putting his job on the line by launching an unofficial investigation, then so be it.

Detective Jim Monahan is driven by his own dangerous obsession. He's on the trail of a psychopath hiding behind a facade of respectability. Jim's investigation has already taken him down a rabbit hole of corruption and depravity. He's about to discover that the hole goes deeper still. Much, much deeper...

Spider's Web
(Steel City Thrillers Book 4)

It's all connected.

A trip to the cinema turns into a nightmare for Anna and her little sister Jessica, when two men throw thirteen-year-old Jessica into the back of a van and speed away.

The years tick by... Tick, tick... The police fail to find Jessica and her name fades from the public consciousness... Tick, tick... But every time Anna closes her eyes she's back in that terrible moment, lurching towards Jessica, grabbing for her. So close. So agonisingly close... Tick, tick... Now in her thirties, Anna has no career, no relationship, no children. She's consumed by one purpose – finding Jessica, dead or alive.

Detective Jim Monahan has a little black book with forty-two names in it. Jim's determined to put every one of those names behind bars, but his investigation is going nowhere fast. Then a twenty-year-old clue brings Jim and Anna together in search of a shadowy figure known as Spider. Who is Spider? Where is Spider? Does Spider have the answers they want? The only thing Jim and Anna know is that the victims Spider entices into his web have a habit of ending up missing or dead.

Now She's Dead
(Jack Anderson Book 1)

What happens when the watcher becomes the watched?

Jack has it all – a beautiful wife and daughter, a home, a career. Then his wife, Rebecca, plunges to her death from the Sussex coast cliffs. Was it an accident or did she jump? He moves to Manchester with his daughter, Naomi, to start afresh, but things don't go as planned. He didn't think life could get any worse...

Jack sees a woman in a window who is the image of Rebecca.

Attraction turns into obsession as he returns to the window night after night. But he isn't the only one watching her...

Jack is about to be drawn into a deadly game. The woman lies dead. The latest victim in a series of savage murders. Someone is going to go down for the crimes. If Jack doesn't find out who the killer is, that 'someone' may well be him.

Who Is She?
(Jack Anderson Book 2)

A woman with no memory. A question no one seems able to answer.

After the death of his wife, Jack is starting to get his life back on track. But things are about to get complicated.

A woman lies in a hospital bed, clinging to life after being shot in the head. She remembers nothing, not even her own name. Who is she? That is the question Jack must answer. All he has to go on is a mysterious facial tattoo.

Damaged kindred spirits, Jack and the nameless woman quickly form a bond. But he can't afford to fall for someone who might put his family at risk. People are dying. Their deaths appear to be connected to the woman. What if she isn't really the victim? What if she's just as bad as the 'Unspeakable Monsters' who put her in hospital?

She Is Gone
(Jack Anderson Book 3)

First she lost her memory. Then she lost her family. Now she wants justice.

On a summer's day in 1998, a savage crime at an isolated Lakeland beauty spot leaves three dead. The case has gone unsolved ever since. The only witness is an amnesiac with a bullet lodged in her brain.

The bullet is a ticking time bomb that could kill Butterfly at any moment. Jack is afraid for her. But should he be afraid of her? She's been suffering from violent mood swings. Sometimes she acts like a completely different person.

Butterfly is obsessed with the case. But how can she hope to succeed where the police have failed? The answer might be locked within the darkest recesses of her damaged mind. Or maybe the driver of the car that's been following her holds the key to the mystery.

Either way, the truth may well cost Butterfly her family, her sanity and her life.

ABOUT THE AUTHOR

Ben Cheetham

Ben is an award-winning writer with a passion for horror and crime fiction. His novels have been widely published around the world. In 2011 he self-published Blood Guilt. The novel went on to reach no.2 in the national eBook download chart, selling well over 150000 copies. In 2012 it was picked up for publication by Head of Zeus. Since then, Head of Zeus has published three more of Ben's novels – Angel of Death, Justice for the Damned and Spider's Web. In 2016 his novel The Lost Ones was published by Thomas & Mercer.

Ben lives in Sheffield, England, where he spends most of his time shut away in his study racking his brain for the next paragraph, the next sentence, the next word...

If you'd like to learn more about Ben's books or get in touch, you can do so at bencheetham.com

Printed in Great Britain
by Amazon